MURDER AND AN IRISH CURSE

Hailed as "impressively original" by Midwest Book Review, the Book Magic Mysteries celebrate the magic in books. In this enchanting new story, Pippin Lane Hawthorne hopes her gift of bibliomancy will be enough to finally stop the curse that has plagued her family for two thousand years. But for every question Pippin answers about the past, a new one arises...

Armed with new information about her family's connection to Dagda and Morrighan, from the Tuatha dé Danann, bibliomancer Pippin Lane Hawthorne is more determined than ever to stop the 2000 year old Irish curse on her family.

When reporter Moira Quinn starts asking questions—and then ends up dead—Pippin discovers a personal connection that makes the quest for the truth even more personal.

With the help of her West Coast cousins, bookshop owner Jamie McAdams, and her twin brother, Grey, Pippin is determined to get to the truth once and for all. But the rumblings of the curse are close to home and the clock is ticking for more than one of the Lanes. Will Pippin be able to save her family or will she be too late?

MURDER AND AN IRISH CURSE

A PIPPIN LANE HAWTHORNE MYSTERY

MELISSA BOURBON

LAKE HOUSE PRESS

Published by Lake House Press

Print ISBN: 978-0-9978661-8-6

Cover Design by Mariah Sinclair | www.mariahsinclair.com

PIPPIN LANE HAWTHORNE (BOOK MAGIC) MYSTERIES

The Secret on Rum Runner's Lane, a prequel
Murder in Devil's Cove, book 1
Murder at Sea Captain's Inn, book 2
Murder Through an Open Door, book 3
Murder and an Irish Curse, book 4

Join my newsletter mailing list and receive a free exclusive copy of *The Bookish Kitchen*, a compilation of recipes from my different series.

For my parents, Marilyn and Bruce.
You are the absolute BEST and I love you forever and always.

And for Deborah Allen Holt.

You are the inspiration for Dabba, who has quickly become one of
my favorite characters. Thank you for your kindness and
generosity.

PRAISE FOR THE BOOK MAGIC MYSTERIES

#1 Amazon Bestseller!

"A combination of magic and mystery, "Murder In Devil's Cove" by Melissa Bourbon is a deftly crafted and impressively original novel by an author with a genuine flair for originality. While certain to be an unusual, immediate and enduringly popular addition to community library Mystery/Suspense collections, it should be noted for the personal reading lists of anyone who enjoys Women's Friendship Fiction, Cozy Animal Mysteries, or Supernatural Mysteries..."
—*Midwest Book Review*

"...Close reading as a super power[!] MURDER IN DEVIL'S COVE ha[s] all the makings of an original, unique story with a lovely tilt in advocacy towards literature fanatics. The heroine nature from Cassie's perspective was strong, and the female power got even better as Pippin grows up. Also, as a big fan of the Odyssey myself, I absolutely loved the role the epic played in guiding the narrative...Overall, I think this is a rewarding day read. The pages turn easily, and the characters are gripping enough for the reader to latch onto their motives and goals."
-29th Annual Writer's Digest Self-Published Book Awards

"The unraveling of the mystery involves Pippin's family

history (it goes all the way back to Roman times in Ireland), hidden clues, a long-lost keepsake, and a secret room. For mystery fans who enjoy amateur detectives who rely on mystical insights rather than Holmesian deductions, Murder in Devil's Cove will provide an entertaining read."

–Seattle Book Review

"A magical blend of books, mystery, and smart sleuthing. Melissa Bourbon's Murder in Devil's Cove offers mystery readers everything they crave and stands out in the crowded cozy genre. This captivating new series will leave readers spellbound."

~NYT and USA Today Bestselling Author, Ellery Adams

"This tightly woven mystery spins a web of intrigue where magic simmers, waiting for the perfect time to surface. I can't wait to read more about Pippin and what awaits her in the next Book Magic adventure."

~Dru Ann Love, Dru's Book Musings

Praise for Murder in Devil's Cove

This book had me at 'book magic' and wrapped me up in its unique plot from start to finish! . . . I really enjoyed the set-up, the plot, the characters and the setting; they all added intriguing layers to the story. . .

~Reading Is My SuperPower

I thought the author beautifully intertwined magic and mystery...Murder in Devil's Cove is an intriguing tale with forbidden books, a departed dad, family folklore, myste-rious magic, renovation revelations, and one bewildered bibliomancer.

This book totally sucked me in as the story tells the past as well as the present . . . a truly magical read for fans of cozies with a slight magical flair.

I totally loved it so I give it 5/5 stars.

~*Books a Plenty Book Reviews*

Filled with quirky characters and atmospheric descriptions of the quaint town of Devil's Cove, Bourbon hits all the right notes for a cozy: amateur sleuthing, several possible suspects, bookstores, and a touch of romance.

~*Elena Taylor, Author*

Blending a family curse and a hint of the paranormal with an intriguing mystery MURDER IN DEVIL'S COVE is a fantastic start to a new series.

~*Cozy Up With Kathy*

Praise for The Secret on Rum Runner's Lane

The Secret on Rum Runner's Lane by Melissa Bourbon is a fantastical book that I loved diving into. It was great from the first chapter to the ending.

~*Baroness' Book Trove*

This is the prequel to this new series and it had me hooked on the concept, the setting. and the characters.

~*Storeybook Reviews*

It may be a short story but it gives a thorough introduction of the characters as well as a picturesque view of Devil's

Cove. Sure to pique the interest of cozy lovers looking for a mini-mystery to draw them into a new series.

~*Books a Plenty Book Reviews*

. . . this was a quick read about characters that you immediately care about in a picturesque setting (two, actually).

~*I Read What You Write!*

THE SECRET ON RUM RUNNER'S LANE captures the uncertainty and underlying strength of women searching for their place in the world. It allows readers to get a glimpse of the past while seeing the glimmer of what's to come.

~*Cozy Up With Kathy*

The Secret on Rum Runner's Lane is a layered story with a well-developed backstory for a character whose decisions in that time period set the path for generations to come.

~*Reading Is My SuperPower*

The setting is enchanting with realistic characters you can root for. The mystery is perfectly solvable based on the clues hidden within the text. The paranormal aspect is an original idea.

~*Diane Reviews Books*

The author brings the story to life with her character development and vivid setting. I could feel Cassie's pain dealing with her family curse. I was totally transported into her world.

~*Socrates' Book Reviews...*

Praise for Murder at Sea Captain's Inn

power of bibliomancy became one of the best parts of the story . . . This is the first book I've read in the series and really loved it!"
~Books To The Ceiling

"Full of plenty of clues while still keeping you guessing until the end. The use of bibliomancy is a nice touch as well as the adorable deaf dog Sailor."
~Books a Plenty Book Reviews

"Ms. Bourbon writes in a way that makes the reader captivated and completely part of the story. I love this story and the characters."
~Baroness' Book Trove

Praise for Murder and an Irish Curse

*"I wholeheartedly recommend!...This book is rich with mythology and history with a bit of intriguing spell-casting and tarot, and the multi-generational characters add an exciting range of personalities from helpful to interfering, from sane to quirky, from open to secretive, from good to evil...**Top contender for my Best of 2022!**" ~Kings River Life Magazine*

*"**To say it's a page turner is not doing it justice.** The writing is so well done that the reader feels as though they are actually entrenched with the characters experiencing all the twists and turns that kept me enthralled throughout." ~Amazon Reader*

"I can honestly say that I could not stop reading this once I started..." ~Amazon Reader

"I do not know where to begin with a review of this book except to say that this series remains one of the best I have ever read." ~a BookBub Reader

"This series quickly became a favorite, and this book's a prime example of why. The book is well-written with well-rounded characters, and a well-thought-out, original plot. The various relationships are well-done. I was drawn into this enchanting story from the beginning and kept hooked throughout." ~a BookBub Reader

"The book's nail-biting conclusion and the events leading up to it will have readers holding their breath! ...The author puts the reader in a perfectly rendered Outer Banks setting. She brings myth and legend to life and her imaginary characters come alive on the page. Kudos for an outstanding cozy!" ~a Goodreads Reader

"No matter how much I tried to slow myself down while reading this book, I just wasn't successful. I flew through this book. I wanted to slow down because I could tell we were coming to an end and I wasn't ready." ~Amazon Reader

"The author expertly weaves a tale with enough twists and turns that will keep you guessing until the very end where the answer to the mystery is hiding in plain sight." ~Amazon Reader

Praise for Murder Through an Open Door

*"**Page turning Spellbinder**...Beyond the richness of this tale is the strong weaving of Pippin's inner experience and the tenacity it takes to let love in."* ~Amazon Reader

*"Without needing to think about it, 5/5 stars with **ease!**...Now I'm left chomping at the bits for the next book in this series!"* ~Amazon Reader

"I can hardly wait for the next book in this must-read Book Magic series." ~Amazon Reader

*"**Melissa Bourbon blockbuster fourth book in her Book Magic Mystery series is a must read** with a delightful writing style, complex ongoing mystery, wonderful characters, and a fascinating premise two-thousand years in the making..."* ~a BookBub Reader

*"**I love this series!** An intriguing mix of murder mystery, Irish*

myth, and family lore, with a touch of fantasy." ~Diane Kelly, mystery author

"I am happy to say that it was every bit as good as the first two, and has left me eagerly anticipating the next installment! " ~Cozy Mystery Review Crew

"Once I had finished the first chapter, I got chills up my spine and quickly set to work devouring this book. Pippin is such an interesting character, and I absolutely loved the bibliomancy magic that the author weaves into these pages...5 out of 5 stars." ~Bunny's Reviews

The Lane Family

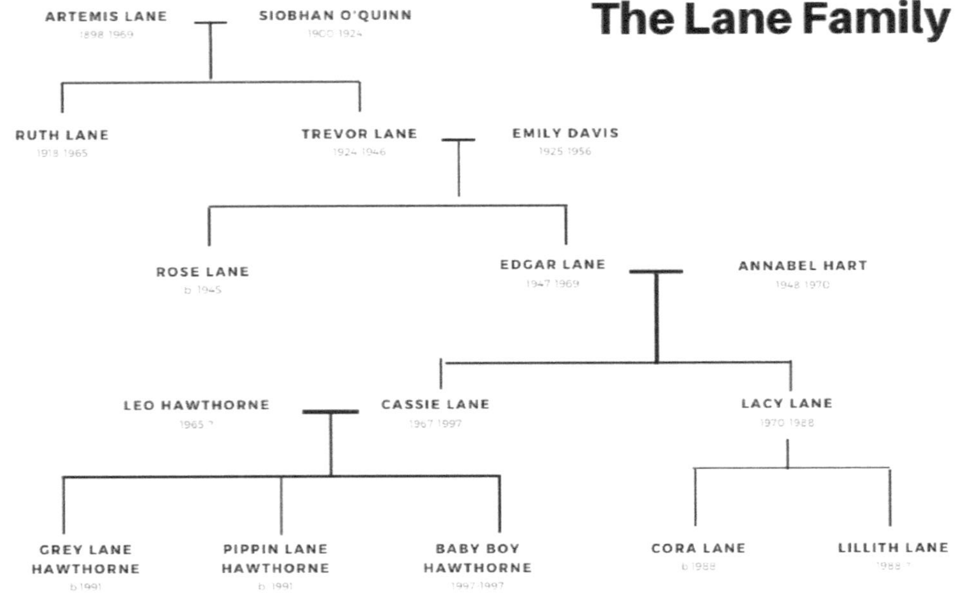

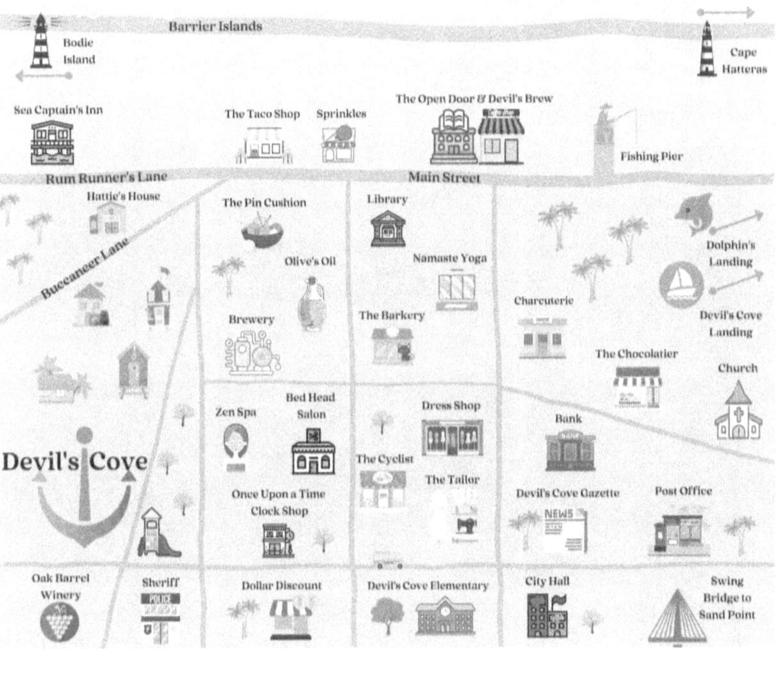

Barrier Islands
Bodie Island
Cape Hatteras
Sea Captain's Inn
The Taco Shop
Sprinkles
The Open Door & Devil's Brew
Fishing Pier
Rum Runner's Lane
Main Street
Hattie's House
The Pin Cushion
Library
Buccaneer Lane
Olive's Oil
Namaste Yoga
Charcuterie
Dolphin's Landing
Brewery
The Barkery
Devil's Cove Landing
The Chocolatier
Church
Devil's Cove
Zen Spa
Bed Head Salon
Dress Shop
Bank
The Cyclist
The Tailor
Devil's Cove Gazette
Post Office
Once Upon a Time Clock Shop
Oak Barrel Winery
Sheriff
POLICE
Dollar Discount
Devil's Cove Elementary
City Hall
Swing Bridge to Sand Point

MURDER AND AN IRISH CURSE

IRISH NAME PRONUNCIATION

Aodh - Ayd
Aisling - Ashling
Aoife - Eh-fa
Brú na Bóinne -Brū-na-boyn
Dubhshláine -Dŭb-hŭ-shlaine
O'Dulany - Dŭ-Lan-ē
Saoirse - Sere-sha
Seamus - Shay-mus
Siobhan - Shi-von

RETURN TO BRÚ NA BÓINNE

At the river they meet:
The Dagda.
The Morrighan.

The king and
the king maker.
The chief
and the phantom queen.
The bearded man
and the crow.

Forever more.

Until a broken promise.
The fearful Morrighan bringing
betrayal and
darkness.

The *coire ansic*
A stolen treasure.

Now forever empty,
of a man, his truest measure.

In the womb,
creations beget
of lies
and deception.

Her scars run
dark and deep
into the *River Boyn.*
Into the depths they seep.

From the ruins of a damaged heart
only the relics of a family will remain.
The schemes of a phantom goddess
destroying the future of his name.

The betrayed cursing the betrayer.

Hark! Rejoice!

For when the moon is full.
When the sea sighs at high tide.
When the stars blink bright
in the blanketed sky.
Listen for the crow.
For her cry in the night.

Turn once.
Turn twice.
Turn thrice.

Now, Battle Raven!
return to wence you came.

Now, Morrígu!
Back to your anointed king.

Now, Great Queen!
Lay with The Dagda
at *Brú na Bóinne,*

The king and
the king maker.
The chief
and the phantom queen.
The bearded man
and the crow.

Forever more.

PROLOGUE

"*I pray that the unpretended descendants of she who called herself Morgan Dubhshláine and Titus of Roma, within the dark side of Clann na Morrigna, return to Dagda what he so seeks and was taken from him. Only then will the curse that the truest god did place upon the children of the betrayers, and the unfortunate that came after, be broken.*"

~Seamus O'Dulany

5 Months Ago

Pippin Lane Hawthorne looked at the people sitting around Cyrus McAdams's living room. Jamie McAdams; her cousin, Lily; and her twin, Grey. The people who were going to stop the ancient curse that had plagued the Lane family for two millennia. Pippin's father, Leonardo Hawthorne, had tried—his efforts cut short by his untimely death. Now, they had to use the information and clues Leo had left to finish the job.

They just had to figure out how. No small feat since the Lanes had been trying for centuries.

Jamie adjusted his glasses and went into full professor mode. "Dagda was the chief of the Tuatha dé Danann."

"Like Zeus," Lily said. Her bangles jangled as she moved her hands, "The God of the gods."

Pippin had been learning about the Tuatha dé Danann, the ancient race of Irish deities. "Yes. He was the god of fertility. Agriculture. Magic. And wisdom."

"Exactly," Jamie said. "The druids. Time itself. Life and death. You name it, he probably had a hand it."

"And Morrighan?" Lily asked. "She was his wife?"

They all nodded. They understood the lore. What they didn't know was how to break the curse. Jamie continued, "Morrighan was the goddess of war. She was said to determine whether a soldier would walk off the battlefield or not. If you were a warrior, you did not want to see her, because that meant you were going to die."

"People also called her the Battle Raven," Pippin said. "She prophesied death."

Pippin thought about the divination the Lane women had. Along with the curse, which resulted in the Lane women dying in childbirth and the men perishing at sea, the women were also bibliomancers. They had the ability to foretell the future from the pages of an open book. They could reveal truths about the past. The books they used guided them. Her mother, Cassie, had seen it as an extension of the curse and hated it, but Aunt Rose viewed it as a blessing. She had taught Lily and Cora how to use it, but Pippin had only discovered her ability when she moved back to the Outer Banks Island of Devil's Cove.

"Some saw her as the mythic triple goddess, representing the maiden, mother, and crone cycle of life," Jamie said, "but that's pretty contested among scholars. Most see her as a deity who guides or protects a king. She was

Dagda's wife, so in some ways she was his protector since he was, essentially, the king."

"Morrighan," Pippin murmured. Then she said it louder. "Morrighan." She felt fire in her veins. She felt four sets of eyes on her. "Morrighan...Morgan," she said.

Lily fiddled with the bangles on her arm. "Okay, wait. What are you saying?"

"I'm wondering," Pippin said. "Could our Morgan Dubhshláine be connected to this goddess Morrighan? They sound the same, right?"

Lily stared. "As in maybe they're the same person?"

They sat in silence for a minute, considering the question. "Zeus and the Greek gods always disguised themselves as humans, right?" Grey questioned. "So, what if Morgan Dubhshláine was Morrighan the goddess's human 'disguise'?" He made air quotes around the word.

Jamie snapped his fingers and pointed at Grey. "Yes! That's exactly what she would have done if she was having a relationship with Titus."

Lily's eyes flashed. "Are you saying you think our ancestor is not Morgan Dubhshláine, but this Morrighan? That we're descended from mythological gods?"

Jamie sat back, one arm crossed over his chest and supporting the opposite elbow. He cupped one hand over his forehead. "If you would have asked me to believe that six months ago, I don't know what I would have said. Maybe hell no. But now? With your bibliomancy, Pippin, and with the curse in your family...now I say that, yeah, I think it's possible that your Morgan is actually *the* Morrighan."

Pippin shuffled this idea into the conglomeration of all the rest of the information she had surrounding the Lane family curse. "So, obviously, she bore a child by Titus."

"And what of the name Dubhshláine?" Cyrus asked, his voice circumspect.

"Titus died, so Morrighan gave the child a mortal name. The Dubhshláine name," Grey said.

Cyrus nodded thoughtfully. "Why that name? Why Dubhshláine?"

Jamie considered the question, filing through his mental Rolodex of information. "It's an Old Irish name, derived from either 'dubh', meaning 'dark' or 'black', or from 'slán', meaning defiance. My guess is she had the affair and the child in defiance of Dagda."

Lily leaned forward. "If Dagda is the god of everything, wouldn't he be totally pissed that his wife had an affair, and with a mortal dude, no less?"

"She betrayed him," Pippin said, then added, more slowly, as if giving the idea time to percolate, "What if it was never a pact between Morgan and Lir?"

Grey sat up and finished Pippin's thought. "What if Dagda, in anger over his wife's betrayal, cursed Morrighan and Titus's descendants."

"Not Lir," Pippin said.

"Not Lir," Grey repeated.

If this version of their history was true, it changed everything. They didn't need to make an offering to the sea god Lir or his son Manannán Mac Lir. They needed to make an offering to Dagda. Only he would be able to break the curse.

They all shifted their gazes to Seamus O'Dulany's book, *Dagda and the Curse of Morrighan,* sitting in the center of the coffee table. Grey moved to the edge of his seat. "We need to read that book."

Pippin didn't even try. She'd become a stronger reader since returning to Devil's Cove, but she still struggled. The thought of trying to read something written with a seventeenth century typeface, in addition to the odd phrasing and vocabulary of the time, was too daunting. With the added pressure of four people listening to her, she begged off. "I just want to listen and process," she said.

She sat back as the others took turns reading or summarizing the chapters of Seamus O'Dulany's book. It was just over a hundred pages and took the better part of two hours before they'd gone through the entire thing. Jamie read the last line of the last page. "Many will think this nothing but fanciful imaginings. Be assured, they are not. Dagda's curse of Morrighan is as real as Tuatha dé Danann. There is no falseness in the story. Bear it in mind. Both are true. I pray that the unpretended descendants of she who called herself Morgan Dubhshláine and Titus of Roma, within the dark side of Clann na Morrigna, return to Dagda what he so seeks and was taken from him. Only then will the curse that the truest god did place upon the children of the betrayers, and the unfortunate that came after, be broken.'"

"Read it again, please," Pippin requested, feeling that she was missing some nuance in the words. She closed her eyes as Jamie read the last lines again. When he finished, they sat in silence for a long minute. Finally, it hit her. She sat up suddenly. "Children. Seamus said children."

Grey spoke, "Children as in the descendants—"

Pippin cut him off. "But he mentioned the unpretended descendants. That means us. The real descendants, not the Ventatores or treasure hunters. That last line," she said, trying to articulate what she thought it meant. "Dagda put a curse on the children of the betrayers. The children of Morgan Dubhshláine and Titus. Not child," she said with emphasis. A chill swept through her. "Children."

"Twins," Grey said. "They must have been twins. If

Morgan...or Morrighan...was pregnant by Titus before he left Ireland, and then he died, she had to have had twins."

Lily drew in a sharp breath. "That's what this O'Dulany guy meant when he said that thing about strife from within and a resulting separation."

Earlier in the text, Seamus O'Dulany had used an old Celtic word when he'd written about discord that had been sown between two people named Aisling and Aoife. Pippin looked at Jamie. He seemed to read her mind. He carefully looked back through the pages until he found the passage in question. "Deirfiúr," he said. "He calls them sisters, and he says they're like Ceridwen's children."

"Who is that?" Lily asked.

"Ceridwen was a Welsh sorceress. She was a white witch in Celtic mythology. She used her power only to help others. She possessed poetic wisdom, inspiration, and the gift of prophecy. The source of her magic was her cauldron, which was a strong presence in Celtic mythology and with the Tuatha dé Danann."

"What's the point?" Grey asked when Jamie paused.

"The point is that there is a strong sense of good and bad in Celtic mythology. Kind of a yin/yang thing. Ceridwen had two children. Well, three, actually, but the third is a whole different story. The first two were Creirwy and Morfran."

He went back to the compendium Connell Foley—poor Connell Foley—had possessed about the Tuatha dé Danann, finding another passage and reading it aloud before tapping his finger on the page. "It's right here. He's saying that Dagda cursed the offspring of Morrighan and Titus before birth, and that curse damaged—or maybe divided—the sisters. He likens Aisling to Ceridwen's daughter, Creirwy, beautiful and pure. But Aoife was like her son, Morfran, who was slow-witted and disfigured."

Pippin plugged all this new information into place. With a jolt, she remembered the passage her bibliomancy had revealed to her from *The Secret Garden*.

"It is the child no one ever saw!" Exclaimed the man, turning to his companions. "She has actually been forgotten!...Poor little kid!" he said. "There is nobody left to come."

SHE HADN'T UNDERSTOOD it then, but now it took on new meaning. No one had realized there were two ancestors at the beginning of the Lane family tree. Aoife was the forgotten child. Not anymore, she thought. Aloud, she said, "So Seamus O'Dulany is saying that Aisling and Aoife were opposites just like Creirwy and Morfran were."

She completely mangled the Irish names, but it didn't matter, and Jamie didn't correct her. He tapped his finger on the page again for emphasis as he read. "'They split apart, two parts of a whole, separated forever. Morrighan and Titus begat Aisling, and the purist line called—" He looked at Pippin and Grey— "Dubhshláine." He read the next line to himself, then looked at them again. "It's just like Ceridwen's third child, Taliesin. Aoife was wrapped in a leather-skin bag and pushed out to sea."

"By her mother?" Lily asked, horror etched on her face. "What a bitch," she muttered, but Jamie shook his head.

"Not by Morrighan," he said. "By Dagda."

"But Aoife didn't die," Pippin said. An eerie dread spread like ink through her veins. "She didn't die, and she had children, and those children are cursed too."

Pippin remembered what Hugh had said...that he was a

descendant of Titus. That Titus had left a woman in Rome pregnant, and Hugh was from that ancestral lineage. But his knowledge of the Lane curse didn't make sense if he didn't have a connection to Morrighan. "He lied," she said, more to herself than to the others, but they all waited for her to continue. "Hugh...or whatever his name is. He said we had a shared ancestor. Titus. But he knows too much. He's cursed, too. Which means—"

"Which means," Grey said, "that we do share Titus as an ancestor—"

Pippin finished the thought, "—but we also share Morrighan. His line comes from Aoife." She thought about the bit of ancient parchment they'd found hidden away by Leo. In it, Morgan had told Titus that she'd wait for him. That their love transcended the obstacles they faced. "What if she really did love him? What if the biggest obstacle was that Morrighan was married to Dagda?" Pippin asked, thinking aloud.

Jamie spun around and paced. "There has to be more," he said. "Dagda cursed the descendants of Morrighan and Titus. But Titus was lost at sea. Coincidence?"

Pippin inhaled sharply. "Aunt Rose said the other part of the scroll fragment said something about Lir, the pact, descendants, and an offering or sacrifice. We've been thinking it was Morrighan who made a pact with Lir, but what if it was Dagda? What if he wanted Titus dead?" Her mind spun. "What if Lir took down Titus's ship because Dagda wanted him to?"

"Dagda wasn't known as a vengeful god," Jamie said, then more slowly, "but it's possible."

Cyrus cleared his throat. "Go back to the last passage of the book," he said, his voice deep and resonant.

Jamie opened to the last page and read aloud. "'I pray

that the unpretended descendants of she who called herself Morgan Dubhshláine and Titus of Roma, within the dark side of Clann na Morrigna, return to Dagda what he so seeks and was taken from him. Only then will the curse that the truest god did place upon the children of the betrayers, and the unfortunate that came after, be broken.'"

Jamie gave a sudden and incredulous laugh. "Oh my God."

All eyes turned to him. Pippin was the one to ask, "What?"

"If Dagda made a pact with Lir to take down Titus's ship, then Titus must have stolen from him. To Morrighan, their love might have been real, but Titus betrayed her if he stole from her husband. I can imagine Dagda being in a fury about that."

The scenario reminded Pippin of Jed and Lacy. Lacy, like Morrighan, had been in love, but just as Titus used the goddess, Jed used Lacy. Everything came back to treasure. Jed's treasure was the necklace, while Titus had been after something powerful. The hair on the back of Pippin's neck stood up. The books on Irish lore. Connell Foley had left a message about where he'd hidden Seamus O'Dulany's book, but the book he'd had on Irish history also told a tale. "Connell was trying to help us," she said. "He left clues for us to find this book, and he left the book on the Irish gods so we could connect the dots."

Jamie exhaled. He looked like a man who'd just discovered the meaning of life—shaken and low-key thrilled at the same time. "It's all connected." He paced the room again, like he was trying to realign the pieces in his mind.

"Tell us, my boy," Cyrus said.

Jamie held his hand up. "Wait. I'll be right back." He set Seamus O'Dulany's book on the coffee table and left, returning not two minutes later with a different book in his hands. Pippin recognized it immediately. It was the book about the history of Tuatha dé Danann found near Connell Foley's body. He flipped through the pages until he found what he was looking for, his chest rising and falling heavily with his breaths. "Okay, listen. Historically, there are four treasures of the Tuatha dé Danaan. Magical treasures. At first it was thought that they were brought by Tuatha dé Danann either from the Celtic Underworld or out of heaven. Later, it was said they were brought from the greatest cities of Tuatha." He tapped his finger on the open page. "The Stone of Destiny; the Invincible Spear; the Shining Sword; and the Cauldron of the Dagda."

"What do they do?" Lily asked.

"*Lia Fail*—the Stone of Destiny—is said to cry out in a thunderous voice, or roar with the power of the ocean when the rightful monarch stands upon it. It was brought to England in the thirteenth century," he said. "It's said to be the Coronation Stone in Westminster Abbey. Then there's the *Sword of Lugh*. The Invincible Spear. It's the sword of Lugh of the Long Arm. Lugh was the first king of the Tuatha. He was called the Long Arm because of the spear. Think of it like Zeus's lightening rod. It would grow so hot that it had to be kept in a vat of water so it wouldn't burn the earth."

Jamie's eyes skimmed over the next two pages, then continued. "Next is the *Sword of Nuada*, or the Shining Sword. The light of the sword is said to represent sacred knowledge and wisdom. And lastly, there's the *Cauldron of the Dagda*, a bottomless vessel which never runs dry. It provides a never-ending supply of whatever is needed. It's thought to have the ability of rebirth and regeneration. It belonged to Dagda, who was considered by most to be the greatest among the Irish gods."

"So the stone is in England. Supposedly. What about the rest—the spear, the sword, and the cauldron?" Pippin asked.

"Lost to history," Jamie said. He put down the book and picked up *Dagda and the Curse of Morrighan*. Once again, he turned to the last page and read: "'I pray that the unpretended descendants of she who called herself Morgan Dubhshláine and Titus of Roma, within the dark side of Clann na Morrigna, return to Dagda what he so seeks and was taken from him. Only then will the curse that the truest god did place upon the children of the betrayers, and the unfortunate that came after, be broken.'"

Lily frowned. "So we're supposed to find something that's lost to history?"

"Maybe it's some other object," Grey suggested.

They all fell silent for a moment. The idea of tracking down one of the four treasures of the Tuatha dé Danaan was daunting enough. If it was something else, they were doomed.

Pippin stared straight ahead, processing. "Would Dagda have considered something to be so valuable that he'd curse Morrighan's female descendants, so they'd all die in childbirth?"

Lily raised her brows and nodded. "It would certainly be a constant reminder to her of her betrayal," she said.

"What if he made a pact with Lir to swallow Titus?" Pippin said.

"Throwing in a curse on Morrighan's male descendants for good measure," Grey said dryly. "Lir gets to drown us all."

"Morrighan prophesied it, but couldn't stop it from happening," Jamie said.

Pippin felt the force of all the air leave her lungs, as if she'd fallen flat on her back, the wind knocked clear out of her. The lore of Tuatha dé Danann was real, and they were a living breathing part of it. She pressed her hands to her temples, trying to wrap her mind around what they had to do. "So, we have to figure out what Titus took, find it, and return it."

Grey muttered under his breath, clearly as shaken as Pippin was. "And just how in the hell are we supposed to do that?"

CHAPTER 1

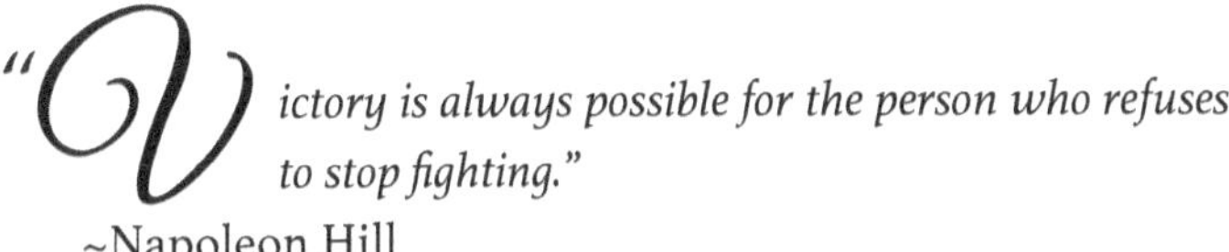

"Victory is always possible for the person who refuses to stop fighting."
~Napoleon Hill

Present Day

Pippin Lane Hawthorne read books, but not always in the same manner that others did.

Most people started at the beginning and read through to the end. They read the stories of fictional people leading their fictional lives. Pippin did that, too. Most people absorbed the setting and the characters and the plot. Those things didn't matter to Pippin. Her relationship with books went much deeper. They communicated with her on an entirely different level. The words, the lines, the passages all conveyed meaning separate from the story itself. It was as if she were taking in the soul of the book. The pages communicated something far more abstract. Less tangible in terms of comprehension. What the words actually said, and what they told her were two entirely different things.

Pippin's twin brother (older by just 73 seconds) had planted the seed in her mind that how she interpreted the words a book showed her was based on her own schema. Her own experiences—and lack thereof. Her understanding was one hundred percent subjective. She construed the meaning behind the words. She could never know with complete certainty that any of the insight she gleaned was correct.

Such was the life of a novice bibliomancer.

There were so many things about her divination she didn't know. In any given situation, would *any* book communicate something, or did it have to be a specific book? When it had come to solving her father's murder, a resurfaced memory had led her to *The Odyssey*. When she'd needed to gain a deeper understanding of the two-thousand-year-old curse that had been lain at the feet of the Lane family, she'd turned to *The Secret Garden*, which had been her mother's favorite book. In other instances, the books that had helped her felt purely coincidental. *Treasure Island. The Tale of Two Cities. Captain Blood.* She had no familial connection to any of these titles—that she knew of, anyway—but they had given her direction, none-theless.

She knew what she and Grey and Lily had to do. They needed to find the item Titus stole from Dagda and return it to him. It sounded so simple, but now she'd come to believe it was actually impossible. And that impossibility wore at Pippin's resolve, causing it to ebb and flow. After all, how does one find an unknown item that has been lost to history and return it to a deity that, until recently, she thought was purely mythical? Often, the challenges they faced seemed insurmountable. At other times she was bound and deter-mined to finish what her father had started, no matter the difficulties. She built up her hope because of the research Leo done and the discoveries he'd made.

The cousins wanted nothing more than to break the curse once and for all. But they had already tried. Leo had tried. Cassie had tried. Presumably most, if not all, the members of the Lane family had tried to break the curse at one time or another, to no avail. These failures were another thing that ate away at her resolve and determination. Right now, this moment was one of resignation. She'd done everything she could think of to break the curse on her family. The men were swallowed by the sea. The women died in childbirth. Nothing she had done had stopped anything. Of course, she wasn't sure how she'd actually know unless they tested the curse, putting themselves in danger. Sending Grey out to sea, or one of them getting pregnant, but still... None of them were *willing* to sacrifice themselves or the others to see if the curse was broken or still going strong.

They had no reason to believe anything had changed. Which left Pippin feeling dejected and lost. She didn't know what else to do.

THE INN WAS RUNNING SMOOTHLY. She'd taken only a few guests leading up to the holidays and at the moment, the last three were tucked into their rooms for the night. Hazel Hood, a traveling innkeeper who had been like her personal Mary Poppins—appearing just when Pippin needed her most—had jumped headlong into a whirlwind relationship with the curmudgeonly Doctor James Wilkenson. She hadn't originally intended to stay on Devil's Cove indefinitely, but the good doctor had changed her plans. Hazel had moved from the little room just off the kitchen at the inn to a small apartment above the Doc's practice. She worked five days a week at the inn, had helped Pippin get procedures in place, and now, more than six months later, the inn ran like a well-oiled machine. At this point, Pippin didn't think she could manage without Hazel.

Breakfast for the next morning was prepped, everything was locked up tight, and Pippin and Sailor, her honey-colored Vizsla, had walked on the beach—well, Pippin had walked while Sailor had chased the gulls. Now, with Sailor by her side, Pippin retreated to her bedroom. It had been Leo's study when she was little. She had taken it over to free up more rooms for guests.

She walked straight to the built-in bookshelf and found the hidden lever that only a select few knew about. She pressed it and a section opened with a quiet click. "Let's go," she said. Sailor couldn't hear her, but Pippin spoke anyway, patting the side of her leg as a visual cue. Sailor's tail whipped back and forth. She followed Pippin into the secret passageway, waiting by her side while Pippin closed the door, trotting up the stairs after her.

The stairs led to a small room...her father's secret hideaway. This was where he'd kept his research and the books most meaningful to him. Clues about the curse and how to break it. If she had any hope of success, she felt sure it was through something her father had left behind.

Sailor went straight to her bed, turned around until she positioned herself just so, and settled into sleep. Pippin was far from ready for bed. She started for the bookshelves that lined part of the back wall but stopped short when she spotted a book on the floor. She looked around, as if someone had put it there and was now hiding, but of course that was impossible. The small study had a desk, two chairs, the built-in shelves, and a little occasional table. There was no place to hide.

The book, though, hadn't been there the last time she was up here. On the cover was the profile of a rabbit, the sky in the distance like a painting streaked brown, gold, and amber. *Watership Down*, by Richard Adams. Pippin vaguely remembered a cartoon movie version of the story, but if she'd seen it as a child, she didn't remember. She crouched to pick it up, the question of how it had ended up on the floor circling in her mind. Books didn't just magically fly off the shelves. Usually.

She turned the well-worn paperback over in her hands. There had to be a reason it was just lying there for her to find. She could figure out how it got there later...if there was even an explanation. For now, though, she went with her gut, which told her it was important. She sat at the desk and placed the spine on the blotter. "What do you have to tell me?" she asked quietly, as if the book itself had ears and could hear and respond to her question. She didn't know how her bibliomancy worked. She just knew that it did.

She let go of the front and back covers, letting them fall open. Pages fluttered briefly, and then they settled. Instantly, the words of a single paragraph darkened. Undulated. Lifted and seemed to hover just above the page. She blinked, as if her eyes were playing tricks on her, but no, the words were still there, waiting for her to read them.

*"Bigwig was right when he said he wasn't like a rabbit at all,"
said Holly. "He was a fighting animal—fierce as a rat or a dog.
He fought because he actually felt safer fighting than running.
He was brave, all right. But it wasn't natural; and that's why it
was bound to finish him in the end. He was trying to do some-*

thing that Frith never meant any rabbit to do. I believe he'd have hunted like the elil if he could."

PIPPIN READ THE PASSAGE OVER. And then again. Grey, in a moment of skepticism, had told her that any message was impossible to interpret because she was the one who assigned meaning to it, and that meaning came from her experiences and her knowledge. He was right, but at the same time, he was wrong. She—and whoever was with her when she used her divination—did interpret the messages from the books. But sometimes they were perfectly clear and didn't need analysis or mystical deciphering.

Like now.

She was like this character Bigwig. She was an animal, fighting for the safety of her family. She fought because it was safer than not fighting. Safer than running. Because Cassie had already proved that running didn't work. Pippin's mother had left Cape Misery on the Oregon coast, ending up on the Outer Banks of North Carolina. She'd traded one ocean for another, but she hadn't been able to hide from the curse. It had still taken her.

And, of course, there were all the Lanes who had come before. Artemis, who they thought had changed his name from O'Dulany to Lane on the passage over from Ireland. The curse had taken his wife—Pippin's great-great-grand-mother, Siobhan—during the crossing. The Pacific Ocean had taken Artemis. The fact of the matter was that the curse could not be outrun.

She went back to the lines from the book. Like the Bigwig character, Pippin was brave. And as Holly said about Bigwig in the paragraph, Pippin's battle also wasn't natural.

She was at war with Tuatha dé Danann. They were Ireland's race of mythological deities…only they were *real*. They were real and because of them, the entire Lane family was forever doomed. No, not forever.

God, her head ached. She woke Sailor and they left the Burrow. In the bedroom, they both settled in their beds. Sailor stretched and made a mewling sound. She envied her dog. Sailor had nothing to worry about. She was fed, walked, played with, and loved. It was an easy existence. Or at least it was now. When the dog had been on her own, scrounging for food and trying just to survive, life hadn't been so carefree. Once Pippin got the dog to trust her, things had changed. They had each other. And Pippin had Grey, Daisy and Ruby, Lily, Hattie Juniper Pickle, Cyrus McAdams, and Jamie. She had a community of people around her now. Even with all her support, would the battle to break the curse finish her, as Bigwig's unnatural fight was bound to finish him?

"I guess that remains to be seen," Pippin muttered. Eventually, she drifted off to sleep.

CHAPTER 2

"*And even honorable men keep secrets for the safety of those they love.*"
~Micheline Ryckman, *The Maiden Ship*

PIPPIN DIDN'T THINK manifestation really worked, but right now she was out of ideas. She wanted to talk to Hugh...what was he to her, a distant cousin? Whatever—or whoever—he was, she wanted to manifest him into her presence.

Now would be good.

She stood at the corner of Buccaneer and Rum Runner's Lane, her arms by her sides, her hands fisted. Sailor watched her with big eyes, as she said Hugh's Gaelic name over and over. Manifesting. So far it wasn't working. The man she had spent the last several weeks searching for was not on this island.

She remembered a conversation she recently had with a woman who'd recognized Hugh. She'd called him a ghost. With Pippin's recent discoveries about her ancestry, it suddenly didn't seem so farfetched to believe that he might actually have some supernatural power. Maybe *he* had taken Dagda's cauldron two thousand years ago, disguised as a Roman soldier.

It was possible, though her hypothesis that he was a Venatore—one of the treasure hunters searching for the ancient coins locked safely away in a bank deposit box—seemed more likely.

The scene of Dagda cursing Morrighan's descents played like a movie in her mind's eye. Titus sailing away from the Emerald Isle in a wooden vessel. Morrighan standing on the shore in her mortal form of Morgan Dubhshláine, watching the billowing sails, unaware that she carried Titus's children in her womb. Dagda finding out about Morrighan's betrayal. Wrapping one of the babies in a leather-skin bag and pushing the infant out to sea.

"I still can't believe it," Pippin said, her words evaporating into the air. It was so...inhumane.

Sailor looked up at her, her tongue hanging from her mouth. It was in the forties today, but the dog panted anyway. Pippin scratched the Vizsla's honey-colored fur and then she crouched down until she was nose to nose with her. She held either side of the dog's face. "It's okay, girl," she said. Sailor's deafness didn't matter. Pippin talked to her all the same, and Sailor's tail wagged as if she could hear the tenor of Pippin's voice. "It's okay. I'm going to figure this out."

Or, like Bigwig from *Watership Down,* she'd die trying.

She turned in a slow circle, taking one last look around. There was no sign of Hugh. So much for manifestation. Her cell phone buzzed. She pulled the device from her pocket, glancing at the screen before swiping to unlock. "Hey Greevie," she said, a playful note in her tone as she called her brother by the nickname she had for him.

"Hey Peevie," Grey said, using hers. "I just dropped off a custom order off-island. Thought I'd stop by." Her brother stopping by at odd times had become almost a habit. She knew he was checking up on her to make sure the elusive Hugh hadn't materialized and abducted her...or worse, killed her...in an effort to get his hands on one of the valuables he and the Venatores, were after.

Of course, he didn't know she was *trying to* get Hugh to show up. At this very moment, in fact. "You don't have to worry about him stealing anything," she'd told Grey, more than once. The two Roman gold coins, which dated back to the first century, as well as the copy of *Dagda and the Curse of Morrighan*, the seventeenth century book written by another Morrighan and Titus ancestor, Seamus O'Dulany, were safe at the bank. Only she, Grey, and Lily had access to the box.

"Sure."

"Good. I'll be there in a few," he said, but something in the undertone gave her pause.

"Is everything okay?"

That pause again, but he cleared his throat and said, "Yeah. I got you a Christmas tree."

"Oh! Really?" She perked up. It hadn't felt like Christmas inside the inn without a tree, and she hadn't had a chance to get one yet. She and Grey each had a small box of ornaments from their childhood with their grandparents. A few even dated back to their time on Devil's Cove before their parents died. She'd yet to unwrap them, but with a tree in the house, she'd take the time to revisit the past through the memories that were sure to be triggered by the ornaments.

"Really," Grey said. "See you soon."

Pippin smiled to herself as she tucked her phone back into her back pocket. She shifted her immediate priorities. She knew she needed to find Hugh. To ask him some questions. To find out more about what he wanted. Why he was here. But since he was a ghost and she had no idea how to locate him, she let the idea of a Christmas tree flood her senses. It gave her a sense of levity and joy she hadn't felt in weeks. After all, Grey had promised to stay away from the Sounds and the Atlantic, and she wasn't pregnant, so neither of them were in imminent danger.

She scratched the top of Sailor's head to get her attention. "Let's go home," she said, and they started up the street, heading back to the inn.

By the time Grey pulled up in his white work truck a short while later, Pippin was ready. She'd dug an old Christmas tree holder out from the shed where she kept her bike. She didn't know who it had belonged to or how long it had been there. It was metal and rusted, but as she hadn't thought to buy a new one, it would have to do. She stood in front of the fireplace facing the front door and surveying the room. The sitting area was made up of couches, chairs, and a coffee table. One side of the great room was lined with built-in shelves which held books by North Carolina authors, a few pieces of maritime art and tiny ships in bottles made by her father, an array of local travel books, and a few of Leo's favorites. Housing copies of them on the inn's shelves felt like a small way to honor him and keep his presence alive.

The registration desk, which was two-tiered and movable, stood catty-corner in the room and in front of Pippin's small office, which was scarcely bigger than a walk-in closet.

A door on the right side of the great room led to what Pippin now called the game room. It also held built-in shelves, but her collection of books wasn't robust enough to call the space a library. She had games ranging from the traditional, like Monopoly and Stratego, to newer ones like Incoherent, 5 Second Rule, and Catan. There was a game table, decks of cards, and a few overstuffed chairs. Rain or shine, it was the perfect spot to curl up and read.

There was also a smaller room that, with Grey's help, Pippin had turned into a guest snack area. A small refrigerator held complimentary bottles of water, cans of soda and sparkling water, and two baskets on the counter held bags of chips, granola bars, and nuts. A designated section of wall in the great room held a sideboard where Pippin placed carafes of white and red wine and trays of cheese, crackers, and seasonal fruit each evening for the inn's happy hour.

The only place to put the Christmas tree—at least the only place that made sense—was in front of the gridded windows on the left side of the door. She walked across the room and spread a plastic garbage bag on the floor. She set the tree holder on top and a few minutes later, she and Grey had eased the trunk into the holder, screwed it into place, and Pippin had filled the holder with water.

She stood back, arms folded, evaluating the tree. "Turn it a little to the right," she said. Grey obliged, but it wasn't quite enough. "A little more."

After a few more adjustments, and some good-natured sibling ribbing, Pippin clapped her hands, her mouth curving into a smile. "Thank you, thank you, thank you! It's perfect, Greevie," she said, and it was. The scent of pine was faint, but even the thin ribbon of it sent her mind back to Greenville and her grandparent's home. Leo's parents had taken Pippin and Grey in after their son vanished and their house had become the twins' home. Memories of Devil's Cove had been relegated to a deep crevasse in Pippin's mind, resurfacing only after her grandparents were gone and

Pippin and Grey had learned that they had inherited the old sea captain's house.

"I brought my box of ornaments," Grey said, his words bringing Pippin back to the moment. He held it out to her.

"No tree for you?" she asked.

Grey shook his head. "I don't really need one this year since I've been—"

She waited, expectantly. "Since you've been...?"

He gave a lopsided shrug, one shoulder lifting up. "Not this year, but definitely next."

Right, she thought, because he'd be here with her on Christmas, but she didn't think *that* was what he'd been about to say. She dropped it, though. They'd never spent a Christmas apart. Neither of them had a family. They had each other, so of course he'd spend the holiday here. They spent the next hour unwrapping ornaments from the box Grey had brought, and from the one Pippin brought down from the attic. Bit by bit, they revealed memories of their childhoods. "Remember this one?" Grey said, holding up a Santa figure holding a fish. "Dad gave this one to me the year before he..."

He paused. For so long, they'd thought Leo had abandoned them. That he'd just walked away from his kids. There was no other explanation...until they'd come back to Devil's Cove...back to this house and had discovered the truth. Pippin held up a miniature replica of *The Hobbit*. She remembered Leo telling them the story of how their mother had found it for him their first Christmas together. Each year, she'd added to the collection with a new JRR Tolkien book ornament. One by one, Pippin unwrapped them and hung them on the tree from their thin strips of ribbon.

"Look at this one," Grey said. His voice had a note of melancholy as he held up a small placard with the words:

Baby Boy 1997 painted in navy blue. They fell silent, watching it swing like a pendulum from the length of ribbon looped around Grey's finger. Cassie had somehow escaped the curse, surviving after giving birth to Pippin and Grey. But she'd temped fate by becoming pregnant again. She had gone into labor a month early. Neither the baby nor Cassie had survived.

Why had she risked another pregnancy? Unless… "Do you think Dad thought he'd broken the curse when Mom survived…us?" she asked quietly. She knew they'd both wondered this very thing, but neither had ever voiced it aloud.

Grey didn't hesitate. "They must have," he said. He had his back to her as he hung the ornament on the tree. "I don't think they would have been cavalier about getting pregnant and taking a chance."

"So when she survived giving birth to us, they really did think they'd succeeded." It was the only thing that made sense. They would have been foolish to risk it otherwise. Only, they hadn't succeeded. She died, their baby brother with her.

"The question is: How will *we* ever know we've succeeded?" Grey asked. His question was more a musing than something that Pippin could actually respond to. It wasn't as if they were Harry Potter fighting Lord Voldemort, the defeat of the enemy evident at the end of the battle. If they recovered Dagda's cauldron somehow, were they supposed to just throw it into the ocean? Was there an incantation to speak? She remembered what had happened when she and Grey had tried to offer Titus's sword hilt into the ocean. The water of the Atlantic had whipped into a violent frenzy, nearly drowning Grey.

They were silent for a few minutes, focused on hanging

the ornaments. When he was empty-handed, Grey folded his arms over his chest and stared at the tree. She knew him nearly as well as she knew herself. Something big was bothering him. After a heavy silence, he cleared his throat. "I want to talk to you about something."

She could hear the dark undertones of his statement. "That sounds ominous."

Before he could respond, the front door opened. Brenda Naples, one of the inn's only guests, burst in like a tornado, her two daughters, Barbi and Brittney trailing behind. "Oh my heavens," she exclaimed, clasping her hands together. "The tree looks so beautiful!" She turned to her daughters. "Girls, girls, isn't the tree gorgeous! Now it *really* feels like Christmas. Pippin, I can't tell you how happy I am to see a tree. This is our annual mother-daughters holiday trip. We *love to* see the lights and trees and decorations on the island, don't we girls?"

Brenda's teenage daughters looked at each other and rolled their eyes, but Brenda was already prattling on. "The bookstore windows are stunning. Just stunning. And the coffee shop has all those twinkle lights. And the light-posts with the wreaths and garlands. Devil's Cove is magical." Her eyes fluttered closed for a second as she said it again, "Magical."

And then her face exploded with a smile, and she spun to face Barbi and Brittney. "Isn't it magical, girls?"

They each had their cell phones out, heads dipped, thumbs flying across the screens. "Magical, Mom," one of them said.

The other one smirked. "Yeah, totally magical."

Brenda was oblivious to her daughters' eye rolling. "Oh, Pippin! You should sell ornaments here! Little replicas of the inn with the year. Or without the year, since that might be complicated." She raised her brows expectantly, as if Pippin might magically produce such a sack of ornaments and hand her one.

"Yes, that's something to think about," Pippin said. It actually *was* a good idea.

"Holiday spirit and marketing, all in one," Grey said, reappearing. Instantly, Barbi and Brittney's hands dropped to their sides, their cellphones dangling, momentarily forgotten. They shot each other a look then circled around their mother until they were staggered next to her. Pippin bit back a smile as they each cocked a hip and lifted a shoulder coquettishly, batting their eyelashes. Grey, it seemed, was far more interesting than whatever Snapchat or Instagram or TikTok could show them. He was more than a decade older than them, but they didn't seem to mind.

Just like Brenda didn't seem to mind that Grey was close to two decades younger than *she* was. She put one hand on her hip and her mouth quirked up on one side in what Pippin could only describe as a come-hither smile. "That must be your truck out front," she said. Her voice had taken on a husky undertone. "Hawthorne Custom Woodworking." She tapped the center of her lips with the pad of one finger. "Hawthorne. So, you're—"

"Mrs. Naples, this is my brother, Grey," Pippin said.

"Oh heavens, just Brenda is fine. There's no Mr. Naples. Not anymore—"

Barbi and Brittney turned and gaped at their mother. "Mom!" they said in unison.

Brenda fluttered her hand at them. "Well, of course there *is* a Mr. Naples. He's just not *my* Mr. Naples anymore." She turned to Pippin and Grey, put the back of one hand to the side of her mouth, and lowered her voice to a whisper, "We're divorced."

"God, Mom!" Brittney squealed.

Barbi's jaw dropped. "You're being gross!"

Pippin could see Grey biting back a laugh. The front door opened again, and this time Ruby strode in holding Sasha's hand. "Good timing," he whispered. He seized the moment to divest himself from Brenda's flirtations by circling around the three Naples, nodding at Ruby, and scooping Sasha up into his arms with a grin.

"No I am not," Brenda snapped at her girls, but her face fell as she watched Grey whisper something to Sasha, who held up her stuffed penguin. "I'm going upstairs," Brenda said with a huff.

"Don't forget about happy hour," Pippin said cheerily.

"I certainly will not forget that fabulous wine," she said. She threw a forlorn glance at Grey before ushering her daughters toward the stairs. "Come on, girls."

Barbi and Brittney trailed behind their mother. They threw backward glances at Grey, who was still diverting his attention to Ruby and Sasha. He wasn't taking any chances.

"I come bearing gifts!" Ruby cheerfully announced once Brenda and her daughters had disappeared upstairs. Ruby lifted the cupcake carrier she'd been holding. "They're gluten free cranberry orange muffins. I've been working on new recipes for the café, and these are the winners. I think. I thought you could put them out for happy hour and get some feedback."

"Absolutely," Pippin said. She took the carrier and set it on the sideboard.

Sasha pointed at the Christmas tree, and her face lit up as she looked from it to Ruby.

"Pretty cool, eh?" Ruby stroked Sasha's chubby cheek with the back of her fingers.

Sasha's black spiral curls, identical to her Aunt Ruby's, bounced as she nodded. "Santa!"

Ruby's smile didn't quite reach her eyes. "She only talks when Grey's around," she said softly to Pippin as Grey took her to get a closer look at the tree.

"Baby steps," I said. Sasha's mother had died in a car wreck and Ruby had become Sasha's guardian. Up until a few weeks ago, the girl hadn't uttered a single word. It seemed Grey had a mesmerizing effect on six-year-old girls just as much as he did on waitresses, teenagers, and mothers.

Pippin handed Sasha the final ornament—a wooden spool with a white sheet wound around it, a list for Santa written in neat penmanship. Pippin remembered sitting with her grandmother, who had written down what Pippin had dictated. Looking at it now, her eyes pricked. The last line said: Mom and Dad. She would have given up Christmas gifts forever and ever if it would have brought her parents back.

After everything was cleaned up from decorating, Pippin put out the wine carafes and trays of cheese and crackers for happy hour while Ruby plated the muffins. Lily drifted downstairs wearing a long red corduroy skirt with buttons up the front, and a light cream sweater. Her loopy curls bounced lightly as she moved. She grabbed a glass of wine as she walked past the sideboard, lifted it in a toast, and took a hearty sip, setting it down again on the registration table. "Can I take Sailor for a walk?" she asked, taking the leash from one of the lower shelves.

The dog had been watching her as she'd descended the stairs. She couldn't hear, but the second she saw the leash, she knew. She hopped up, her tail whipping behind her. Lily leashed her up, grabbed a jacket from the coat tree, and they headed out.

For the next thirty minutes, Brenda Naples and her daughters gazed with unabashed adoration at Grey, but he kept his attention focused on Sasha.

Pippin and Ruby sat side by side on the couch. "She's glommed onto him," Ruby said to Pippin, nodding at Grey pointing at different ornaments on the tree as he spoke quietly to her.

"Who knew he was so good with kids," Pippin said with a stab of regret. If they didn't break the curse, Grey, like her, would never become a parent.

The evening passed, the melancholy lights of the Christmas tree twinkling in the old inn. It was only later that night when Pippin lay in bed half asleep that she realized Grey had never told her what he wanted to talk about.

CHAPTER 3

"*I have several times made a poor choice by avoiding a necessary confrontation.*"
~John Cleese

HAZEL SLIPPED her arms into her purple puffy coat, zipping it up with a decisive flick of the wrist. Pippin fell in beside her, a plate of cinnamon chip scones, fresh from the oven, in hand. As she stepped onto the porch, a burst of cold air hit her, sending a chill skittering over her skin. It had been unseasonably cold for December. Temperatures usually hovered in the mid-fifties during the day, the thermometer dipping into the forties after the sun set. But as dusk settled in, it was in the thirties. The sweater Pippin wore would not be warm enough, even for just a quick walk across the street and back.

"Hold this for a sec," she said to Hazel, handing her the plate, the scones secure under plastic wrap. She darted inside and grabbed a jacket off the coatrack in the foyer.

Back outside, Pippin clutched the sides of the coat together, bracing herself against the frigid air.

"Maybe we'll have a white Christmas," Hazel said, looking at the inky sky, just a few determined stars managing to flicker through the cloud layer.

Pippin didn't equate snow with the North Carolina coast. The juxtaposition of snowflakes circling the beaches in the sea wind, accumulating against the dunes, was enchanting. It did happen now and then, but for the moment, they had to contend with a light, freezing drizzle. Overhead, the inn's resident black crow glided by, apparently unaffected by the cold. The bird pecked on the windows sometimes, making herself a nuisance. Lore said that crows were a harbinger of bad luck, but Pippin had spent time doing research on the bird and found conflicting arguments. There was nothing definitive, but she chose to believe the articles which said crows were protectors. They were wise and a symbol of inner strength. The crow—Morgan, named after her ancestor—disappeared over the widow's walk and into the night sky.

A silver minivan cruised up the street, windshield wipers swiping side to side. It slowed and pulled up in front of the inn. Pippin stopped on the sidewalk to peer into the passenger window, but the second she heard Hazel clapping her hands with glee she knew it was Doc Wilkenson. It was a bit of a May-December romance, but it had been love at first sight for them both.

"Doc drives a minivan?" Pippin asked, stretching the sleeve of her sweater under her coat to cover her fingers.

"He does Meals On Wheels and he takes some of his invalid and hospice patients out once in a while," Hazel said. Her face practically melted with affection. "He's a good man."

Apparently, Doc Wilkenson was far more congenial than he seemed. Pippin had first met him when Lieutenant Jacobs had sent him over to care for one of the inn's guests. He'd presented as the quintessential small-town doctor from a British television show. He carried a black medical bag, had a receding hairline, large protruding ears, deep lines marking his forehead, and caterpillar eyebrows that started at the nose and arched sharply toward his grey temples. He was in his early sixties, putting a solid twenty years between him and Hazel, but their age difference didn't seem to bother either of them. Each time she saw him, Pippin thought he seemed a little less curmudgeonly than he had the time before. Hazel, it appeared, was good for him, and from the gleam in her eyes, he was good for her, too.

Hazel handed the plate of scones back to Pippin, who waved the two of them off before setting off across the street. She started up the walkway but stopped abruptly as someone called out her name. She whirled around. The streetlights emitted a dim light, but the mist kept visibility low. It was not a beautiful clear winter beach night. It was moody and atmospheric. Once the sun set, darkness fell fast. In her coat with a hood pulled up, she felt like Little Red Riding Hood venturing out into the deep, dark woods. "Hello?" she called into the darkness.

The faint thud of footsteps grew louder. "Pippin!"

Pippin peered in the direction of the voice. A dark silhouette slowly became clearer. A moment later, the person stood before her. A long, dark puffer jacket nearly dusted the ground and the faux fur trim on the hood shadowed the face. "Pippin Hawthorne, right?" It was a woman's voice. She pushed the hood back with one hand before extending her arm.

Pippin looked at the hand, then at the woman. She looked harmless enough, so she clasped the proffered hand in hers and shook. "That's right," she said with a question in her voice.

The woman heaved an enormous sigh of relief. "Oh, thank God. I was hoping it was you, but it's so hazy. It's like the world is a shadowland."

Pippin stared. The woman looked to be in her early to mid-thirties, had an ivory-complexion, and wore her straight, dark hair cut just above her shoulders and angling down in front. And Pippin had definitely never seen her before. "I'm sorry, who are you?"

"Oh! Moira O'Quinn," she said as she gave Pippin's hand a final firm shake. "I'm, um, a reporter for the Devil's Cove Gazette. I'm working, um, on an article for the paper and have a few, um, questions for you."

"You work with Quincy?" Pippin asked. Quincy Ratherford was one of the first people she'd met when she'd come back to Devil's Cove. He had started as a reporter for the local paper eons ago, and now he ran the whole kit and caboodle.

"Oh my gosh, he's the best, isn't he?" Moira exclaimed. "I just love him."

Pippin agreed. Quincy was quite lovable with his ginger hair, ruddy face, and doughy physique. He had an affinity for orange, plaid, and berets. He was also part of *Synkéntrosi*, a men's discussion group of which Jamie and Cyrus McAdams and Jed Riordin, were also part.

Another voice rang out in the darkness. "Pippin, is that you?"

This one Pippin recognized. She turned to see Hattie Juniper Pickle standing in her doorway waving a wild arm overhead. Hattie lived catty-corner and across the street to

Sea Captain's Inn. Her lavender and teal house perfectly represented her core character, which was unpredictable, colorful, and a little bit on the wild side. Pippin knew the abridged version of Hattie's life. She'd grown up on the island of Devil's Cove and in the very house in which she still lived. She'd been married three times, but husband one and three were the same man. She was being courted by husband number two, who had given her an adult tricycle, which Hattie had named Rizzo, of *Grease* fame. Eccentric was the best way to describe her.

She backed an unlit cigarette between her lips, leaving it dangling. She'd given up smoking long ago yet was rarely seen without a mangled ciggy.

"Yes! It's me, Hattie," Pippin called back.

Moira O'Quinn looked at the plate of scones. "Ah, you're hand-delivering. Nice."

"Someone with you?" Hattie called from her porch.

"Yes—" Pippin started, but Hattie broke in and hollered, "What in tarnation are you doin' outside in weather like this? Come inside! And bring your friend!"

Pippin didn't know Moira. She certainly wasn't a friend. Pippin also didn't know what the article she was going to be about but going inside sounded much better than standing out here in the freezing cold. She turned to Moira, raising her brows in an unspoken question.

Moira answered with a vigorous nod. "Yes, yes. Great. Thanks." She raised her voice so Hattie could hear. "Thanks!"

By the time they reached the front door, Hattie was indignant. "Good grief, you two are as slow as molasses—" She spied the plate of scones and her eyes grew wide. In one swift movement, her hand shot out and snatched it from Pippin's grasp and she stepped aside, holding the door wide.

"My darlin' girl, you shouldn't have." She gave an exaggerated wink, revealing green sparkly eyeshadow. "But I'm sure glad you did. Let's go, now. What are y'all waitin' for? In you come, outa the cold!"

The inside of Hattie's house was as true a reflection of the woman herself as the outside was. The living room walls were vibrant shades of green, blue, and purple. The chairs had a floral pattern while the sofa was plaid. Yellow pillows were the glue that melded together the mismatched furniture in the same way Hattie's Crocs tied together the chaos of her outfits.

The kitchen was even more colorful than the living room, if that was possible. The cabinets were a bold turquoise, and the walls were coral. The table, where Pippin, Moira, and Hattie now sat, was yellow with geometric shapes stenciled on top. Everything about Hattie and her house was visually loud. She was seventy-years-young. If she and Jamie's six-year-old, Mathilda, were the same size, they could have swapped clothes on the regular. They had the same bright Hanna Anderson primary color palette.

Hattie's snowy white hair was thin and hung above her shoulders. In honor of the holiday season, she'd dyed it in red and green chunky stripes. With her red tights, green polka dot skirt, and an admittedly simple white top, she could definitely get a job moonlighting at Santa's workshop. Hattie set the plate of scones on the table. "You shouldn't have," she said again as she pulled the plate closer to her.

Moira drummed her fingers. Whether she was nervous or impatient, Pippin couldn't tell. "I wanted to talk to you about—"

The sound of the front door closing cut her off. Hattie's eyes snapped up. "'Bout time, you old crone!" she hollered as Wenna, one of Hattie's oldest friends, blew in. A visible layer of moisture clung to her ever-present black cape. Her shoulders hunched and her face was a shriveled collection of wrinkles that told a thousand stories.

"Hello to you, too, Hattie," Wenna said with a smile. "Sorry to be late. This isn't our typical weather, is it?"

"No, indeed, but late is what I expect from you, Wen. You blow in like the wind and then you're gone again," Hattie said, pulling the scone plate a little bit closer.

"It keeps me young," Wenna said.

"This time you have a good excuse, at least. It *is* blowin' up a storm out there."

"It is," Wenna said, shaking off the rain like a cat.

Pippin scooted her chair over, making room. Like Hattie, Wenna had been around Devil's Cove when Pippin's mother had first arrived on island. She wanted to pick her brain for memories of Cassie, but the moment hadn't presented itself yet. Someday soon, she thought.

Wenna moved with ease despite her age. She took the empty chair next to Pippin, smiling her thanks, splitting her face into even more crevasses. She patted Pippin's knee affectionately. "My dear girl, it is good to see you."

"You, too," Pippin said. She was drawn in by the old woman's voice—both lilting and warm. She looked about a thousand years old, but she sounded youthful, her voice strong and melodic. Wenna moved her steady gaze to Moira. "And who is this?"

Moira extended her arm. "Moira O'Qui—"

Wenna let out a loud hacking cough that cut Moira off. Once it subsided, Hattie snorted. "And you said the cigs'd take *me* out."

"Getting old," Wenna said dryly, those two words saying it all. She patted her lips with a napkin she picked up from the table. Her voice didn't show her age and neither did her hands. From the looks of it, she hadn't worshiped the sun in her youth like Hattie had. "Pardon me. Moira, you said?"

Moira had drawn her arm back to her own space. She looked at Wenna, then at Hattie. Pippin could almost see the wheels turning. The two women were opposites in every way, so how had they formed such a lasting friendship? It was an unanswerable question. Who could explain why one person clicked with another? There wasn't a rhyme or reason to friendship or romantic chemistry. It just was.

"Right," Moira said. "And you?"

Hattie waved her unlit cigarette around. "That's Wenna and I'm Hattie," she said. "Where are your people from?"

"Oh, well my great-grandmother was adopted so I don't really know a lot, but I grew up in New York."

"The Big Apple," Hattie said with a shudder. "Horrid place."

It probably was for some like Hattie who had been born and raised on Devil's Cove.

"Right. Well...yeah. Okay. Well, nice to meet you both," Moira said, although from the pallor of her skin, she looked anything but pleased. Pippin sensed that, despite the cold, she would rather have not had an audience for their chat.

Hattie wasted no time with the scones. Her teeth sunk into one of them as Moira lobbed the first question, her voice betraying her nerves. "Well, as I said, I'm Moira and Hattie here was kind enough to ask me in. I'm writing a piece on Pippin and the inn."

Pippin looked at Moira as the woman spoke, gauging how honest she was being. Quincy Ratherford had already chronicled the decrepit old house Pippin and Grey had inherited and its transformation to the statuesque Sea

Captain's Inn it now was. "What's the interest in the inn?" she asked. "The Gazette already covered it."

Moira threw her arms up as if she were on the verge of being arrested. "Caught me!"

Hattie gulped down the hunk of scone, a sprinkling of cinnamon sugar coating her lips. "Caught you doin' what, honey?"

Moira lowered her arms and fiddled with her pen and notepad. "Okay, look. I'll be honest with you." She directed her explanation to Pippin. "I hear your name everywhere on the island. Every. Where. People think you're maybe a witch. Or something otherworldly with powers and stuff."

They weren't wrong, Pippin thought wryly. She *was* descended from Morrighan of the Tuatha dé Danann, after all. But only her inner circle—the people she trusted with her life—knew that. "That's ridiculous," she said.

"But the stories..." Moira trailed off, letting the idea of untold tales about Pippin and her magical powers circulating the island linger.

Hattie pshaw'd. "Stories, shmories. Anyone can spin a yarn. Tall tales are a dime a half-dozen 'round here. That don't make 'em true."

Moira threw up her hands again. "Hey, I'm with you. I'm still figuring out what angle I can take with the article. That's why I wanted to ask you a few questions, Pippin. To see if I can pin something down."

Hattie leaned back in her chair. "No time like the present," she declared, her unlit cigarette dangling from her fingers.

"Really?" Moira brushed a loose curtain of hair behind her ears, looking expectantly at Pippin.

Pippin sighed inwardly. She had wanted to drop off the scones then get back to the inn. She had research to do on how to break curses. But if she didn't answer Moira's questions now, the journalist would just track her down again at a later date. As Hattie had just said: No time like the present. "Yeah, it's fine," she said, resigned, and settled into her chair.

"Great! Thanks," Moira said, then launched into her questions without preamble. "How old were you when you first left Devil's Cove?"

Hattie elbowed Wenna. "Whoa, she's goin' way back."

"I admit, I'm curious," Wenna said. "I haven't heard your story, Pippin. Not from you, anyway."

There was a big difference between telling a story and answering questions. Pippin didn't consider herself a talker, so either way, Moira was going to get a summary rather than a blow-by-blow account. For Wenna's sake, she'd try to fill in the tale with a few added details. "Well, as you all probably know—I mean, at least Hattie does—my dad disappeared when Grey...that's my brother...my twin...we were nine years old. Our mom had died during childbirth a few years before that. Cassandra...or Cassie...and Leo. Those were their names."

Moira nodded vigorously, her hand flying across the page of her notepad. "So you were nine. Got it," she said.

"We went to live with our grandparents in Greenville."

"Okay, so, um, not too far from here," Moira said. "So did you visit? The island, I mean?"

"No. I think it was too painful for my grandparents. They held out hope that Leo had just walked off. That his grief over losing Cassie got the better of him. But they didn't want the constant reminder of the life he'd had on island."

"Right. Makes sense. What about the house? Did you know it belonged to you and your brother?"

"We didn't find that out until our grandparents passed.

They never told us. I guess we both just assumed they sold it."

"Right. So, you inherited. You and Grey. You could have sold it and made a pretty penny, don't you think?" Moira asked as she tapped the eraser end of her mechanical pencil on her notepad.

Grey had considered it, but selling it was never an option for Pippin. "I guess."

"So what made you want to keep it and move back here, then?"

Hattie and Wenna moved their heads in unison, as if they were watching a tennis match, the ball lobbing back and forth in a long rally. "We didn't know we were going to until we saw the house." She shook her head, remembering standing on the sidewalk in front of the decrepit house, instantly taken in by the combination of Cape Cod and Southern Coastal architecture; by the screened porch on the left side; by the wide sitting porch; by the widow's walk at the roof, which provided a view past the Roanoke Sound, the thin strip of barrier islands making up the Outer Banks, the Bodie Island lighthouse, and the Atlantic beyond.

Right off the bat, Pippin and Grey knew the place would need new paint, new shutters, and a lot of TLC, but it was the ghost of her mother on the widow's walk as she waited for Leo to come home from sea that choked Pippin. They couldn't sell that house. Their parents had lived there. They had lived there, and bit by bit, the memories would come back.

And they had, along with the discovery of their father's secret study and all his research and theories on how to break the Lane family curse.

Yes, she and Grey had transformed the house to a showcase both inside and out. Hydrangeas, hyacinths, and daisies bloomed all through spring and summer. They'd painted the house a crisp white with charcoal trim. It stood out amongst the colorful homes dotting the coastal landscape.

"So it was the memories of your childhood that made you move back?"

Moira's question brought Pippin back to the present and her hand automatically went to her neck. Instead of the touchstone of her mother's pendant, she found only the delicate necklace her grandmother had given her. "We couldn't stand the idea of selling the last...or maybe the *only* thing that connected us to both of our parents."

"That makes perfect sense," Wenna said.

"Right." Moira nodded. "It does. Perfect sense." She tapped the end of her pencil again. "So you moved in and fixed it up."

"And turned the old place into an inn," Hattie said. "Old Mother Hubbard is probably turnin' in her grave as we speak!"

Moira looked blankly at Hattie. "Mother Hubbard?"

"She was the last descendant of the old sea captain who built the place—during his rum running days and after a shipwreck." Hattie leaned forward. "She was murdered, you know. Pushed to her death."

Moira gasped. She put her hand to her mouth, then spoke through her fingers. "Is that true? Someone pushed her?"

"Sure it's the truth!" Hattie said, sitting back. "Why would I lie about a thing like that?"

Moira shook her head. "No, no, I didn't mean that. It's just such a...horrible story. And a coincidence, right? Because of the other deaths at the inn, I mean."

Pippin swallowed, thinking about how to respond to that. "You've done your homework," she said guardedly.

Moira shrugged and gave a little smile. "The job of a journalist. You have to have as many facts as possible going into a story."

"The deaths were definitely sad. And coincidental," she said, clearly indicating and end to the topic. And they hadn't all happened *at* the inn, but she didn't say that. "Any more questions?"

"A few," Moira said. She leaned in, forearms on the table, and dropped her voice. "There's a rumor about a secret room in the house."

The air in the kitchen turned heavy with tension. "Is that a question?" Pippin asked.

Moira chuckled. "Sure. Are the rumors true?"

Pippin had no intention of corroborating the rumors. "If there is one, it must be right next to my magic fireplace and looking glass," she said.

Wenna chuckled, but Moira frowned. "So that's a no?"

"That's a no," Pippin said, almost crossing her fingers to excuse the lie.

Hattie sprang from her chair as if a coil in her seat had suddenly been released. "Who wants a hot toddy?"

Pippin took the opportunity to stand. "Not me. I have to go. See you later, ladies."

She started for the door before any of them could try to stop her. Moira was quick, though. She was on Pippin's heels, waving her thanks to Hattie. "Nice to meet you both!"

"Pippin," Moira said, scurrying up beside her at the front door, notepad and pen in hand. "I only have one more question."

"What's that?" Pippin said.

Moira pulled Pippin to a stop in the open doorway, blocking the way. The frigid air spilled in and overtook the warmth of the house. "Tell me about the bibliomancy."

CHAPTER 4

"Life is full of fantasies. Life is full of realities. Fantasies bring fantasies and realities bring realities. You have a choice. Yes, an inevasible choice. To live in the world of fantasies or to live in the world of realities; your choice!"
~Ernest Agyemang Yeboah

THE BREATH BURST from Pippin's lungs with the speed of a balloon popping. In the back of her consciousness, she registered the scraping of chairs against the floor...the pitter-patter of curious feet...the sharp intake of a breath.

Pippin stared at Moira. Worked to keep her voice steady —normal, despite the collision of emotions spiraling through her. "What are you talking about?"

"I told you, rumors. Lots of rumors. I think island living is more small-town than the smallest of small towns," Moira said. She glanced over her shoulder toward Hattie and Wenna standing in the threshold to the kitchen then lowered her voice. "You never know who's listening."

Despite the cold, a chill skittered over Pippin's skin. Jed

Riordin had said the same thing to her recently. The walls have ears. "Moira, I don't know what you're talking about," she said again, mustering some indignation to mask the anxiety pooling in her gut.

She glanced over her shoulder, catching Hattie's eyes. She knew everything about everything and everyone. She knew about the curse and Pippin's bibliomancy. There was no keeping secrets from her, but she didn't want Wenna or anyone else to be privy to all the Lane family secrets. Too many people knew already, especially when she factored in the members of the Venatores group—the treasure hunters, some of whom had wreaked havoc on her life with their presence in Devil's Cove.

So how did Moira know? Had someone in Pippin's small group of trusted friends betrayed her? Talked about her? No, she didn't believe that. She worked hard to keep her face blank. "You shouldn't listen to rumors."

Her only thought was to get out of this house, away from Hattie and Wenna. The less they knew, the better. And she just didn't want to talk about any of this with Moira. She elbowed past Moira, hurrying down the porch steps, but Moira stuck by her side. She put a hand on Pippin's arm, pulling her to a stop once again at the end of the Hattie's walkway. Pippin tried to tamp down the agitation rising in her.

"Sometimes rumors are true," Moira said cryptically.

Pippin cupped her hand over her forehead with resignation. She wasn't going to be able to shake Moira. The woman would hunt her down until she got her answers. "So you think I use this...what did you call it?"

Moira tilted her head as she looked at Pippin, as if she was trying to get a read on her. When she spoke, she said the word slowly. "Bibliomancy."

"Bibliomancy. Right. What even is it?" she asked, trying to come off completely ignorant about her own gift.

Moira paused again, watching her with intensity. "It's an old divination," she said after a beat. Her face changed. The smile dropped. The lightness in her personality vanished. "A bibliomancer uses books to foretell the future and reveal things about the past. People say women from the Lane family have the ability. That means you. Your cousins. Your mom."

Pippin's blood ran cold. How did Moira know about her cousins? It was possible Moira had heard rumors and really was pursuing a story, but it was also possible—probable, even—that she wasn't who she said she was. That she was a hunter. A Venatore trying to find the ancient million-dollar coins her grandfather Edgar had brought with him from Ireland. Her heart ratcheted up until she thought it might explode right out of her chest. She summoned more disbelief. "What, like we're witches? Like we use magic? You were serious when you said that before?"

"I was. And yes, exactly like that, actually," Moira said.

Pippin started walking again, ducking her head against the wind that she was now heading into. Lightning sliced through the sky and thunder boomed like cannonballs being shot through the invisible sky. Again, Moira stuck by her. "That's crazy," Pippin said once she reached the inn's walkway. "There's no such thing as magic."

But Moira pulled a face. "Oh come now, Pippin. We both know that isn't true."

Pippin's head suddenly felt filled with bricks. She wanted nothing more than to escape from this woman's presence, but her need to find out what Moira knew was greater. Some invisible heat source in her body seemed to turn on. She didn't feel the rain coming down around her.

She was done being the mouse to Moira O'Quinn's cat. She crossed her arms and met Moira's gaze dead on. "And how do we know that?"

Moira drew her lips into a thin line but didn't answer.

Pippin scoffed. "You don't know what you're talking about."

Moira put her notepad into her coat pocket, shoving her hands in after them. "Can I come inside Pippin?"

"No, thanks. I'm done talking. And everything we've talked about, by the way, is officially off the record. I'll call Quincy in the morning."

Moira threw up a hand. "You don't have to do that. I won't print anything, I swear. I'm...um...I'm sorry about tonight. Maybe you're right. Maybe the rumors are just that. Rumors. Without evidence, there's no story."

Moira was saying all the right things, but Pippin watched her face for a clue about the subtext. She was more concerned about what the young woman *wasn't* saying. But Pippin couldn't read her. "Great. Good night, then," she said, and she turned and marched up the walkway, making a mental note to call Quincy Ratherford in the morning. She went up the porch steps and into the warmth of the inn, leaving Moira shivering on the sidewalk.

CHAPTER 5

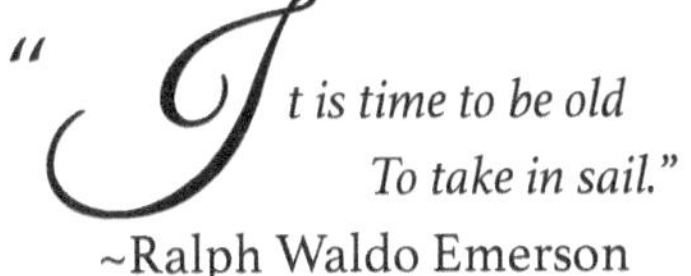

~Ralph Waldo Emerson

By MORNING, the storm had passed through, and Devil's Cove was quiet again. A winter chill hung in the air. Pippin had put Moira O'Quinn out of her mind for the time being. Pippin awoke at the crack of dawn to a text from Grey asking her to come over. She'd rolled out of bed and dressed. Downstairs, everything was in order, ready for breakfast. She left Hazel in charge of Brenda Naples and her daughters, grabbed her wallet, phone, and keys, slipped on her coat, and went out to the front porch, leaving Sailor still sound asleep in her dog bed.

The storm had left a mess in its wake. Small branches had been knocked loose from the trees and now cluttered yards up and down Rum Runner's Lane. The harsh rain and sleet had left pockets of mud. She crossed the street and turned so she could get a better look at the house she now called home. She and Grey had kept the underside of the porch ceiling haint blue, following the tradition of low country folk everywhere. The entire house seemed to sparkle in the dappled morning light. A storm shudder on the second floor hung askew. That would need to be fixed. Other than a few scattered branches, the house was unharmed.

God, they'd come a long, long way in such a short period of time. Moira's questions from the night before had churned up recent memories. When she and Grey first came back to Devil's Cove—less than a year ago—the place had been nearly uninhabitable. It had stood empty for twenty years, and those years had taken a toll.

She'd heard the tale of a 17th century ship carrying 'Devil's Rum', a potent Caribbean liquor. The ship had gone down in what was now known as the Graveyard of the Atlantic. A single survivor had taken a shallop and made his way from the harsh waters of the Atlantic to the Intracoastal Waterway, managing to land on the island. That lucky sailor had settled here, named the island Devil's Cove after the "Devil's Rum", and built the house Pippin's parents had bought.

The old house had withstood too many hurricanes to count. The piling foundation helped it stand firm against the wind, water, and sand that came with living on the Eastern Seaboard. Grey had put up lattice to ground the house, blocking the wide openness directly underneath the house.

The street was eerily silent, as if they were in the aftermath of the apocalypse. From where she stood, no trees had been felled by the wind. The houses were still standing. This storm had been nothing compared to any number of the big hurricanes that had unleashed their wrath on the coast over the centuries. Pippin left the branches in the yard to deal with later. She got into her old Jeep and took off across the island to the old farmhouse Grey had bought on the north side of the island. The ancient stone silo still stood empty. It was built in the late 1800s of glazed hollow blocks long before poured concrete was developed. Grey had followed his passion for woodworking, turning the barn into a design showroom. His workshop was in the back. As she drove, the salt and sea gave way to loblolly pines and forest. Her mind drifted to the boat.

That damned boat.

If Grey wasn't working on a contracted project, he was elbow deep in renovating an old boat he'd rescued. She tried to block out the memory of the first time she'd seen it. She'd shown up unexpectedly to find him chipping away at oysters and barnacles on the old wooden vessel.

This time, she'd come at his bidding. She pulled onto the dirt drive leading to the house and barn. A sign hung on the front of the barn announcing the business as Hawthorne Custom Woodworking. She bypassed the front parking spaces her brother had created in the front, instead pulling all the way around to the back of the barn, knowing that's where he'd be. She braced herself before leaving the car, knowing that the anxiety already pummeling her insides was going to multiply the second she laid eyes on that damned boat.

Grey, who never struggled with reading; who shared their father's love of the sea and everything that went with it; who always been so level-headed—he was going to put himself directly into the path of the curse once he finished refurbishing the thing. He was determined it would end up back on the water, and he'd be her captain. Pippin couldn't stop it from happening. She knew that. But seeing him work on it underscored that eventuality, renewing her purpose. They *had* to break the curse.

The first time she'd seen him working on the boat, he had a crowbar in hand, chipping away at the cemented on barnacles, trying to clear the hull. This time she found him on the forward deck of the boat. He was turned away from her. Despite the cold, he had on jeans and a short sleeve t-shirt, a vertical line of sweat marking the center of his back. In so many ways, they were like two parts of a whole. He was the yin to her yang. They grew up with their own secret language; finishing each other's sentences; knowing that they would always have each other. Even now, despite their separate pursuits—her with Sea Captain's Inn and him with Hawthorne Custom Woodworking—a strand of invisible silk filament connected them. His chestnut hair, so similar to their father's, was hidden beneath a cap, a local fishing tackle company's logo on the front. It took him only a few seconds to realize the shift in the air, her presence noted. He stopped what he was doing and turned. His lips curved under the rough beard he sported lately. Lines sprouted from the outsides of his eyes. His were gray-green, like churning seawater. "Hey," he said.

"Looks like you're making progress." She tried not to sound as disappointed by it as she felt. The boat's hull was sanded and stained and looked far too seaworthy.

"Slow and steady."

"Slow is good." She walked up to the boat, laying her palm on the wood planks. "At least that green slime is all gone. How old is this thing, anyway?" she asked, dismayed at the progress he was making. He released an audible breath as he flipped his cap around so the bill faced back-ward. Something about the way he hesitated made her radar go up. "Grey?"

"Pippin, I don't want you to freak out—"

She stared at him, her pulse instantly ratcheted up. "How can I *not* freak out when you lead with that?"

He cracked a smile, the tilt of his head and slight shrug conceding the point. "Okay, well don't freak out *too* much."

"Oh my God. What is it? Just tell me."

He maneuvered himself from the deck to the ladder leaning against the boat. A moment later, he was facing her. He laid his open palm against the hull the same way she had, but the expression on his face was one of reverence. "I found something—"

"Grey, what are you talking about?"

Instead of answering with words, he strode to his workbench, returning with a worn journal. The cover was wavy, as if water damaged. It was clearly old. Unfamiliar. And yet...

"I found this in the library at our grandparent's house when I was, I don't know, fifteen? Sixteen? Somewhere around there. It was hidden away behind a bunch of other books. I took it—and I've had it ever since."

Her head spun at this. He'd kept a secret from her for thirteen or fourteen years? "We weren't allowed in the library," she said, zeroing in on *that* fact as if it could disprove whatever bomb Grey was about to drop.

"Yeah, well," Grey said with a shrug, meaning he'd ignored the rule and had snuck in there anyway.

"*Okay.*"

"I put it away and forgot about until I bought this place and I was unpacking some old boxes. Peevie, it's one of dad's old journals."

Her breath caught. That explained the water damage. If it was Leo's, the odds were good he'd had it when he was on his boat. Their grandparents must have kept it as a touchstone to their missing son.

Grey continued, "It's just a lot of notes about his trips during that time. Some of his notes on Dagda and Morrighan, although I had no idea who they were at the time. There's some stuff about his crew. Some poems. And these..." He riffled through the pages until he came to two black and white photos. He handed them to her. She immediately flipped them over to look for notations on written on the back. *Edgar and the Blessed Siobhan* was printed in block letters on the first one. She turned it over. Her grandfather, Edgar, stood in front of the bow of a wooden sailing ship. *The Blessed Siobhan.* His face was serious, his mouth drawn into a tight line.

The second photo was much older. Artemis and Siobhan's names were written on the back in neat right-slanting cursive. When she flipped it over to look at the image of her somber-faced great-great-grandparents standing on a huge rock platform in front of a massive stone cross, her breath caught. Siobhan was clearly pregnant. Two toddlers clung to her long skirt. Pippin frowned. She hadn't know her great-great-grandparents had had *three* children.

But of course, they hadn't. Siobhan had died in childbirth, the baby with her. She dropped her arms to her sides, holding the photos tight, not wanting to let them go. "But?" she prompted Grey, because there had to be a 'but'.

"But when I found it again and started rereading it, I spotted something I hadn't before." He flipped open the worn journal to a page he'd marked with a strip of torn paper. He handed the notebook to her.

Leo's handwriting jumped above and below the lines as if he'd written while the boat lifted and fell on the waves. Dried droplets of water had distorted some of the writing.

Her eyes scanned the pages and then something happened. The letters and words seemed to move. They undulated and then a single sentence darkened, drawing her eye.

After his parents died, Edgar built a boat. Rose sold it. Contact:

SHE STARED AT THE WORDS. Looked at Grey. Back to the journal...and then to the boat itself. "Are you trying to tell me that this boat was built by Edgar? As in our *grandfather* Edgar?"

Grey dipped his chin in a single nod.

"That makes no sense. Why would our grandfather, who ended up dying from the curse, build a boat? To sail on the water?"

"Keep reading," Grey said.

Pippin went back to the open page. Reading didn't come easy for her. She worked through the pieces, putting it together.

Why would he build a boat when he was a Lane?

PIPPIN TAPPED her index finger on the sentence Leo had written. "Exactly! That's what I said."

"Doesn't change the fact that Edgar *did* actually build it."

She narrowed her eyes at him. "But how do you *know* he built it?"

"Because I contacted the guy I bought it from in Savannah, Peevie. And get this. *He remembers talking to Dad twenty years ago.* Dad died before he could go to Savannah to see it."

"But you did," she said quietly, placing her hand on the hull again to keep herself steady. "Are you *sure* it's Edgar's?"

"I'm sure, Peevie."

Pippin wanted to spread her free hand across her forehead, press her thumb and fingers against her throbbing temples. Instead, she held the notebook aloft. "How? How are you sure?"

He crooked his finger and beckoned her to the ladder. Pippin's skin turned to gooseflesh. "What?"

"I need to show you something," he said. She handed him the journal. He set it aside and held onto the ladder with one hand while she ascended it, swinging one leg over the side, then the other. Grey scurried up after her.

The boat's deck felt spacious because Grey had stripped away everything. It was a clean slate. He could make it whatever he wanted it to be. Pippin made a slow three-hundred-sixty degree turn, taking it all in. She stopped, face to face with Grey. "Okay, show me. How do you know?"

"This way," he said as he strode across the deck to the stern of the boat. He crouched down and waited for her to join him. Once she had, he grabbed ahold of a loose board, pulling it free to reveal the back of it. Pippin bent down next to him to get a closer look. She drew in a sharp breath. Ran her finger over the worn plank. "He really built it?" she asked, her voice scarcely more than a whisper.

"He really built it," Grey reaffirmed.

They both looked back at the piece of wood and the three words clearly engraved there. *Edgar Artemis Lane.* Their grandfather.

"There's more," Grey said, "only, this one I can't figure out." He led her below deck. The space was completely open, also cleared of everything save three small, smooth rocks laying there.

He picked up one of them and handed it to her. It was slightly larger than the palm of her hand, worn smooth from time. The others were slightly different in shape, but similar in size. "Where'd they come from?"

Once again, Grey squatted down and once again, he pulled a loose board from the inside wall of the boat. This time a crevasse was revealed. "They were in here."

Pippin bent down and peered into the dark hole. "That's weird." She looked up at him. "Right? That's weird."

"I think so. Did Edgar put them there? And if so, why?"

Pippin maneuvered until she sat on the floor. She leaned back, still cradling one of the stones. "There has to be a reason," she said. "He wouldn't just put them there for no reason."

"That's what I thought. I started researching. I Googled *Ireland* and *rocks*. It's just a bunch of geological articles and information about the different types of rocks in Ireland."

"So they're not valuable somehow? Like the coins?" she asked, referring to the ancient Roman coins now safely hidden away at the bank. Someone--their great-great grand-father, Artemis, they thought— had worked hard to disguise their true nature by adding a fleur de lis element with clay and silver plating them. But rocks?

"Not that I can figure out," Grey said. "I tried all kinds of search word combinations and nothing."

"Can you call the guy you bought the boat from? Maybe he knows about them," Pippin suggested.

"Worth a try." When she didn't say anything, his eyes widened. "Oh, you mean now?"

She gave a small smile. "No time like the present, Greevie."

Grey couldn't argue with that. He took his phone from his back pocket, scrolled through his contacts, and dialed, putting it on speaker. "Brent, Grey Hawthorne," he said when a man answered.

"Sure, sure, Grey, how is the old girl?"

Pippin raised her brows at the question and Grey pointed at the boat. Of course. Vessels were often referred to in the feminine.

"She's a beauty," Grey said. She could hear the reverence in his voice.

Brent clucked. "My old man always thought so. She's got good bones, he always said." They chatted about where Grey was with the refurbishing project for a scant minute before Brent said, "What can I do for you?"

Cut to the chase. Pippin liked that about this guy. They didn't have time for idle chitchat, and neither did he. "Yeah, I have a quick question for you," Grey started. He explained the cubby he'd found and the stones inside. "Any idea where they came from?"

Brent didn't hesitate. "I have no idea. Like I told you before, my father bought the vessel from a broker on the West Coast. As far as I know, once he got it to Savannah, he took it out only a handful of times. I never took to the sea like my old man, so when it came to me, I sold it. To you."

"So you never saw the stones."

Brent clucked again. "I certainly didn't put them there, if that's what you mean. And I can't think of a scenario where my dad would have."

Grey thanked him and hung up. He turned to Pippin. "And there we have it. Due diligence done and back to zero."

"Edgar *must* have put them in there." It was the only

thing that made sense in terms of *how* they got there. She cupped her hands and pressed her fingertips against her forehead. She couldn't come up with a single explanation for *why* he would have hidden the stones there, though. What did they mean?

"What are you going to do with them?" she asked Grey.

Her brother withdrew a small drawstring bag from his back pocket and slipped the stones into it, then handed it to her, along with the journal. She slipped the photos between the pages. "Put them in the safe, okay? Until we know more about them, I just want to keep them safe."

She agreed. She'd go straight to The Burrow and lock the stones and Leo's journal away. They climbed back down. Pippin took another long look at the seafaring vessel. "It must have taken him years to build this by himself," Pippin said. The boat was sturdy and strong, despite the fact that it had been crafted more than seventy years ago.

Grey ran his palm along one of the planks. "It's solid. Well made."

"Good bones," she said, echoing Brent's statement.

"Yep."

At her car Grey held the frame of the car door while she climbed in and started the ignition. "What time do you think you'll be coming over?" she asked, knowing he was bringing precious cargo to the inn.

"Leaving in—" He flipped his wrist to look at his watch. "—forty-five minutes, so let's say around two hours, there, two hours back. It'll be late this afternoon."

"Perfect." That gave her time to check things off her list at the inn. Grey started back to his workshop as she started to drive off. And then she remembered. She pressed her foot on the brake and cranked down the window. "Grey!" she called.

He stopped in his tracks and turned. "Hmm?"

She beckoned him over and he doubled back to the car. "There's a reporter--well, she *says* she's a reporter for the Gazette in town. She ambushed me last night," she said, because looking back on how the encounter with Moira O'Quinn played out, it definitely felt like she'd lain in wait, biding her time until she could corner Pippin.

"What does that mean, she ambushed you?"

She told him about going over to Hattie's when Moira appeared. "She was just suddenly there."

He folded his arms over his chest, shaking his head slightly. "And she went with you to Hattie's?"

"Not my idea, but yeah."

"So what did she want?" he asked.

"She had some basic background questions about the inn, how we inherited it. Stuff like that. But at the end she asked about the rumors around town."

"Shit. What rumors?"

"The ones that paint me as some sort of witch with magical powers."

His nostrils flared as he exhaled. "Not too far off the mark," he said wryly.

Exactly what she had thought. "She asked about my bibliomancy, though. She knew about *that*. I don't think she's just a reporter."

"You think she's one of them?" Grey asked.

The Venatores. "I didn't see a tattoo or anything," she said, referring to the V cradled in a circle, the face of a Roman soldier in the open space of the V. So far, every treasure hunter they'd encountered had the tattoo for the Venatores. "But yeah, I think it's possible."

"Moira O'Quinn." Grey muttered the name.

"What?" Pippin asked. She knew her twin almost as well as herself. An idea had sparked in his mind.

He exhaled. "I don't know. There's something, but...I don't know."

"Well, let me know if it comes to you," she said.

He gave one succinct nod. "Will do."

CHAPTER 6

"*If you're going through hell, keep going.*"
~Winston Churchill

"*WHERE THERE'S life there's hope.*"
~JRR Tolkien, *The Hobbit*

THE FIRST THING Pippin saw when she got home from Grey's was none other than Moira O'Quinn lurking at the house next door. It was a seasonal rental and currently unoccupied. Whether or not Moira was privy to that information, who knew, but she sat brazenly on the front porch wrapped up in her long, faux fur-trimmed coat. The second she saw Pippin drive up, Moira was on her feet and making a beeline for the front walkway of Sea Captain's Inn.

She waved her arm and Pippin gave her head a little shake. Did Moira think Pippin couldn't see her standing right there in front of her? The woman was too much. She headed toward the walkway, the drawstring bag with the stones swinging from her hand. "What do you want?" she asked, more gruffly than her usual tone, but she was suspicious.

"Look. I know I spooked you last night and I'm sorry about that, but we need to talk."

"We don't, actually." Pippin sidestepped around Moira, never breaking stride. "I'm really busy."

"Ahoy there!" Hattie's voice bellowed from across the street.

Pippin spun around to see Hattie and Wenna strolling up the opposite sidewalk toward Hattie's lavender and teal house. Pippin knew Wenna lived off island somewhere. With the storm, she must have stayed in Hattie's spare room. Now they walked side by side, To Go cups from Devil's Brew in their hands.

Staying to chat would give Moira another opening, something Pippin did *not* want to do. She transferred the gauze bag to her left hand. She waved as she started toward the porch steps again. "Morning!" she called. "Gotta run, talk later!"

She jogged up the stairs and quickly entered the code into the keypad on the door. She hadn't heard Moira's footsteps behind her. Good. Hopefully she'd gotten the message. She paused long enough to risk a quick look. She saw Moira walking down Rum Runner's Lane, heading toward Main Street and town. Hattie and Wenna had stopped and were watching her. Hattie caught Pippin's attention. "Strange girl!" she hollered.

Kind of the pot calling the kettle black, Pippin thought. She waved again and stepped inside.

∼

Lily had been staying in one of the bunk rooms on the third floor. She raced down the stairs, taking them two at a time, her long hair and skirt—gauzy this time rather than a heavy corduroy—billowing in her wake. "I saw Grey's truck pull up."

Pippin's heart did a little flip. With precious cargo. She stood behind the reservation desk. She closed her laptop and came around to join her cousin. It had been more than ten years since Lily had left Cape Misery. Ten years since she had left her sister behind. She'd gone on a quest for information, determined to find out who their father was. That quest had led her here, to Devil's Cove, to Jed Riordin, and to Pippin and Grey.

And now, Cora was here, too.

Grey had made the four-hour round-trip drive to the Raleigh-Durham airport to meet her, and now here they were. Pippin and Lily hurried out to the front porch and skipped down the steps, slowing only when they got to the brick walkway. Cora walked slowly, coming up the path. She wore a long jacket and clutched a tote bag in front of her. Like Lily, Cora's hair was blonde, but Lily's was wavy, and Cora had tight ringlets, the kind of curls women paid hundreds of dollars for at the hair salon. Cora came by hers naturally, though. Pippin and Grey had only met their cousins once, just after their father had vanished. They'd been sent to Oregon to stay with Aunt Rose. That is when Pippin and Grey first learned about the Lane family curse.

And now here they all were, together again twenty years later.

Grey came up the path behind Cora. Something in his expression sent up an alarm in Pippin. His lips were pressed into a line and his eyes were pinched, but he gave a tight smile.

Lily and Cora stopped a few feet from each other, each taking the other in. Slow smiles spread at the same time. Cora dropped her tote as Lily moved closer, stretching her arms out to pull her twin in for a hug, but she stopped suddenly. Pushed back, creating more distance between them. Grey stopped, watching, his expression still grim. Pippin moved closer

Lily stared at her sister. It took her a few seconds to find the words, and then she blurted, "No, no, no, no, no! Cora, are you pregnant?"

Pippin sputtered, darting right to get an unobstructed view of Cora. As soon as she saw the roundness of her belly, her blood ran cold. Grey's expression suddenly made sense, because if Cora was pregnant—and there seemed little doubt about that—then she would also soon be dead.

LILY CLAWED HER SCALP, the heels of her hands pressing against her forehead. She paced around the couches and chairs of the sitting area, making circles. Finally, she stopped and spun to face Cora. "H-h-how?"

Cora pulled a face. "You know *how* it happens."

"And you know exactly what I mean." She slowed her speech, enunciating each word. "How could you *let* this happen?"

Cora leaned back in the chair she'd taken, her hands interlocked and resting on her stomach. She closed her eyes and her nostrils flared. Pippin thought her chin quivered. "It wasn't supposed to happen," Cora finally said. "We took precautions, but they were strong little swimmers, I guess. Or I'm just a fertile Myrtle."

"That doesn't sound like you took the right kind of

precautions," Lily snapped. "And you're being way too flippant about it."

Cora lifted her head again and stared at Lily. "I'm not, actually. It wasn't planned and it doesn't matter how it happened. The fact is, it *did* happen. And to be honest, I am scared—no, I'm *terrified*."

"How far along are you?" Pippin asked.

Cora opened her mouth to speak, but the front door of the inn opened, and Brenda, Barbi, and Brittany Napels blew in, mid-conversation. "The boat leaves at 5 AM. I'm *not* doing that, Mom!" one of the girls screeched.

Brenda nudged her with her elbow. "Come on! When else are we going to get to go on a real fishing trip?"

Pippin's radar went up at the conversation. The fishing boats didn't usually go out at this time of year. It was far too cold. She needed to talk to her guests about it—make sure whatever they were planning was legit. It would have to wait, but she made a mental note to catch up with them as soon as she could.

"Oh!" Brenda spotted the four of them and stopped short. "Didn't see you all there!" Her smile thinned as she seemed to read the pulse of the room. She glanced at her daughters. "Come on," she said under her breath. "Let's go upstairs."

"I'd love to hear more about the fishing trip. I'll be up in a little while," Pippin said with a smile as they climbed the stairs.

"Sure, sure. Sorry to intrude."

Pippin waved away the apology with a smile. "Oh not at all! No intrusion." Although she did wish she and her cousins had settled in the kitchen instead of the great room. But Cora had collapsed onto the chair and Lily had started pacing. So here they were.

The second they heard the click of the guest door upstairs closing, all eyes swung back to Cora. "When are you due?" Lily asked, rephrasing Pippin's question.

"January 1st," Cora said. "I was thinking that maybe if I have a cesarean that I won't die. Maybe it only happens during natural childbirth."

Lily threw up her hands in exasperation. "You're willing to risk it on a maybe?"

Cora's lips twisted with frustration. "Well, Lil, I don't have too many choices here," she snapped. "The baby is going to be born one way or another."

Pippin felt her heart plummet. That night in Nags Head, months ago, she had felt the full weight of the curse pressing down on her, as is she were trapped under the weight of a crushing machine. She had almost lost Grey that night. Now, with Cora's news, the curse pressed heavily on her reality once again.

Pippin's mind raced, information and memories surfacing. They still didn't know what to offer to break the curse, or how. According to legend, Dagda was dead, mortally wounded during the battle with the Formorians. Cethlenn delivered the fatal blow. Dagda died later at his home at Brú na Bóinne. "It is said that you can consult with him where he was lain in the fairy mounds at Brú na Bóinne," Jamie had told them.

"Do we have to go there to break the curse? Find his treasures and offer them where he rests?" Pippin had asked, as if there was a definitive answer, which, of course, there wasn't. At least not one they knew of.

Jamie, though, hadn't been thwarted. "Brú na Bóinne is a series of Neolithic mounds approximately constructed in 3200 BCE," he'd said. "They're older than Stonehenge. Older than the Great Pyramids. The mounds are on the backs of the River Boyne. And this is interesting," he had said. "There is a mound—Newgrange—which, still to this day, represents how significant Dagda was. Or is. Newgrange is aligned with the sun, so it's symbolic, showing Dagda as master of the seasons, and master of day and night."

It was impossible for them to go to County Meath in Ireland to return Dagda's missing treasures to him. First, The *Stone of Destiny* was brought to England in the thirteenth century. It was said to be the Coronation Stone at Westminster Abbey. So there was absolutely no way to return *that* to Dagda.

Then there was the *Sword of Lugh*, also known as the *Invincible Spear*. Lugh was the first king of the Tuatha. The spear was akin to Zeus's lightning bolt, which was said to grow so hot that it had to be stored in a vat of water. They had no idea where it might be hidden, but likely in some watery grave somewhere.

The *Sword of Nuada* represented sacred knowledge and wisdom. And then there was *Dagda's Cauldron*. It made the most sense to find this lost treasure and return it to Dagda at the fairy mound at Newgrange. Their theory was that Titus, upon leaving Morgan, or Morrighan, as they now believed she was, had taken the cauldron with him. But how were they supposed to find such an artifact when it hadn't been seen for two thousand years? Pippin forced her thoughts to return to the present.

Cora closed her eyes. They'd all fallen silent after she'd announced the due date. It was only a few weeks away. It felt like a ticking time bomb had just been activated. A countdown to Cora's death.

"Our mother survived our birth," Grey said, breaking the silence. "You could survive."

It was true. An anomaly, perhaps, but true, nonetheless.

Cassie had survived. They had no idea how or why, but the reprieve from the curse had been short-lived. The curse had skipped over Cassie for a time, but in the end, it came for her with her second pregnancy.

Cora's eyelids fluttered open. "I don't really want to bank on the fact that I *could* survive. That hasn't worked out for anyone. They've all died, eventually. If we don't figure out what to do, my fate is sealed."

A strangled sound escaped from Lily. She spun around, her face pale, her expression resolved. When she spoke, it was through gritted teeth. "We cannot let her die."

Cora reached out her arm. Lily walked around the furniture until she was in front of her sister. She took her hand. Pulled her up. "You are not going to die, little sister," she said, and wrapped her up in a hug.

Pippin couldn't even smile at the twin humor. Grey was Pippin's big brother, but only because he'd been born seventy-three seconds before she had. Had their positions in the womb be reversed, *she* would have been the older one. She didn't know how much older Lily was than Cora, but it was enough to make her feel like the older sibling.

Pippin and Grey looked at each other. She knew her face held a combination of fear and panic. Fear that they wouldn't succeed, and panic at the inevitable loss if they didn't. Grey kept his emotions much closer to the vest, but she could see he was thinking the same things she was. Breaking the curse that had plagued the Lane family for two millennia was no longer about their abstract deaths at some unknown future date. It was urgent. They were running out of time.

Pippin reached for the pendant hanging from her neck but stopped when she touched the necklace her grandmother had given her. Her mother's pendant with the fleur de lis—and the Roman head—was locked away at the bank alongside Lily's. The delicate chain holding a heart-shaped locket was lovely, but it wasn't the same. It wasn't connected to Cassie. And right now, more than anything, Pippin wanted her mother.

CHAPTER 7

"*The most important thing a father can do for his children is to love their mother.*"
~Theodore Hesburgh

PIPPIN STIFLED a yawn as she made a fresh pot of coffee and cleared away the remains of the breakfast service. She'd given Cora her bed to sleep in, feeling pretty sure an eight-and-a-half-month pregnant woman wouldn't enjoy climbing two flights of stairs, which is where the only vacant bed was —next to Lily in the other bunk room.

Hazel's old room was fine, but Pippin wanted Cora to be comfortable. She shooed away the thought that these might be Cora's last nights, ordering herself to stop thinking that way. They *would* figure out how to break the curse. They *would* save Cora. There was nothing else to it.

Now Cora stared at Lily from her spot at the end of the long, reclaimed wood kitchen table. She sat in one of the rail-back chairs, one hand resting on top of the basketball inside her. She poked a finger in her ear, wiggling it around for effect. "What did you say?"

Lily leaned against the kitchen island, fiddling with the bracelets encircling her wrist. She slipped them on and off, turning them around and around. She looked at them intently, as if they were the most interesting thing on the face of the planet. When she spoke, the words were directed to the ground. "Our father. His name is Jed Riordin."

The chair creaked under Cora as she sat up straighter. She looked around as if the man himself would pop up from behind the counter like a life-sized Jack-in-the-box. "He's... he's coming here? Now?"

Pippin watched her cousins' expressions—Cora wearing a look of alarm; Lily looking reticent, which was out of character. Lily was usually vibrant and optimistic, as if positive energy were a tangible thing that vibrated around her. With the cooler weather, she'd traded her sandals, thin skirts, and crop tops for light weight sweaters, maxi skirts, and boots. The change of season had brought a change of wardrobe colors, but the impending death of her sister if they didn't figure out how to break the curse, had taken her spirit down a notch.

Finally, Lily looked up, meeting Cora's gaze. "He can help us. He's not the enemy."

Cora stared, disbelief replacing the shock on her face. "He got our mother pregnant, which, by the way, was her death sentence. Then abandoned her."

Lily took a step back as if Cora's words were a physical blow. "Okay. But he didn't *know* she got pregnant—"

"But he *did* know about the curse, so he knew it was a possibility. He went there to steal from her and Aunt Rose."

"He changed sides!" Lily's voice rose an octave. "Cora, he's taken me out on his boat. I *trust* him!"

Pippin watched them lob retorts back and forth like the hard serves of a tennis ball careening over a net—back and forth, back and forth. She thought about what Lily said. They only had Jed Riordin's word to go on, but Pippin's instinct told her Lily's assessment was on the money. Jed *had* changed sides and plus, Leo had trusted him.

Cora didn't believe it, though. "God, Lil, don't be so naïve."

The accusation of naiveté hit Lily like another blow, but this time, it didn't knock her down. Instead, she stood straighter. Her jaw tightened. "I am *not* being naïve. You haven't met him. I have."

"And you're such a great judge of character?" Cora snapped.

"Better than you," Lily shot back, pointing to her sister's swollen stomach.

Cora's face, pale from the overcast days in Oregon, lost even more color. Her eyes turned glassy and her chin quaked, but her voice was steady. "You don't know me anymore."

"And you don't know me, or *my* judgement," Lily said. "I am telling you, Cora, that Jed Riordin—*our father*—is not a bad guy."

Pippin could see from the storming of Cora's green eyes that she wasn't going to be easily convinced about Jed. Too many disappointments. Too many people had abandoned her. Her mother had died giving birth to her and Lily. Lily had left without a word for ten years. Aunt Rose was gone. Pippin knew the vast array of emotions her cousin was feeling. She'd been in that dark, lonely place herself, but she'd come through it and was on the other side. She had her community now. Her people. She'd started to believe in people again. She also knew that nobody could convince Cora that Jed had changed, and that Lily was back for good. She had to open herself up to people, and only *she* could make that happen for herself.

"When? When is he coming?" Cora demanded. As the words left her mouth, a knock sounded on the front door.

They all turned toward the sound. "Now," Lily said with a sigh.

Cora's face lost another layer of color. As Lily headed to the door, she put one hand palm down on the table, scooted forward in the chair, and started to push herself to standing. Pippin hurried to her side to help. "Give him a chance," she said softly. "My dad trusted him."

Cora started to say something, but a moan escaped instead. She collapsed back into the chair, one hand on her lower belly.

Panic surged through Pippin. This baby could *not* come early. "Cora? Are you okay?" Pippin asked. "Can I get you anything?"

Cora drew her lips into a circle and made a series of short exhalations.

Pippin stared, her gut tightening in fear. It was too soon! Cora wasn't due for another two weeks. Pippin dragged a chair closer and sat on the edge. She took one of Cora's hands in hers and looked her in the eyes, catching her attention. "Cora, it's too soon. Breathe. That's it. Just breathe through it."

"It's cramping like a...like a..." She closed her eyes as she drew in a breathe, letting it out in incremental puffs. "Like a claw."

Voices carried into the kitchen, growing louder. From the corner of her eye, Pippin saw Lily and Jed appear. Lily rushed around the table to them. She fell to her knees at her sister's side. "Oh my God, Cora. Are you in labor?"

"No," she spat in-between breaths. Finally, the grip Cora had on Pippin's hand loosened and she opened her eyes. "Oh my God."

"Are they gone?" Lily asked.

"They're called Braxton Hicks. I think that's what the doctor said. But these were stronger," she said. She looked down at her belly, patting the mound with her hand. "You have to wait, little one."

Yes. Good. The baby had to wait.

"Maybe flying so close to my due date wasn't such a good idea."

Lily lowered her head to Cora's lap. Her back lifted and fell, lifted and fell. It was a release of the sudden tension that had seized her, Pippin thought. After a few seconds, Lily looked up at Cora. "I'm sorry. I'm sorry for everything, Cor. If you don't want to meet him, you don't have to."

Cora's gaze traveled from Lily to Jed Riordin, who had stopped at the archway between the great room and kitchen. "It's a little late for that," she said wryly.

Jed gestured back toward the front door. "I can go—"

Lily sighed. Pippin could see from her expression how torn she was. She and Jed had been forging a tentative relationship, and now she was trying to do that with Cora, as well. She couldn't please them both. Pippin could see a moment of indecision on her face, but then she turned to Jed. "Another time might be better," she said, her eyes begging him to understand.

Cora held up a hand. "We might not have another chance," she said.

Pippin's skin pricked with anxiety. Cora couldn't give up. A minute had passed since the last contraction. Pippin braced herself, ready to help Cora through another contraction if that's what was coming, but it didn't. *Braxton Hicks, thank you!* she thought.

"And you're here," Cora said. "You might as well stay."

Pippin stepped back, leaving her chair for Jed. He was stocky, a little on the short side, and even when he wasn't smiling, lines sprouted from the outside corners of his eyes. His brown hair had been gray at the temples when they first met. That had been months ago now, back when she and Grey were just finishing the renovations to the house. It looked as if he'd aged ten years since then, the grey turning his dark hair salt and pepper. He circled around the table and sat in the vacated chair while Pippin moved to the sink to fill the electric kettle. She set the kettle on its base and pressed the switch down. After a few seconds, she heard the telltale sound of water beginning to heat. She took out a small container holding a variety of teabags. She pulled mugs from the cupboard and brought them to the table, one for each of the guests surrounding the table.

The conversation between Jed and his daughters was stilted. Awkward. "Cora," he said, looking intently at her. His eyes slipped to her belly. "I don't...I don't know what to say."

"You can start with why you're here," Cora said, her face not betraying any emotion. She didn't pull any punches and Jed's frown deepened. Pippin liked her cousin's directness, but in this moment, she felt sorry for Jed. She had come to believe that he really had changed and had been one of Leo's true confidants. She wanted Cora to give him a chance, but she didn't feel it was her place to intervene.

"Cora," Lily chided.

Cora looked up at her, unyielding. "What? I want to know why he's suddenly here in our lives after more than thirty years." She spun back to Jed. "Our mother left a journal, did you know that?"

Jed slowly shook his head. "No, but—"

"You didn't know," Cora continued, interrupting him, "because you used her then left."

Jed didn't have anything to say to that because it was true. He had been part of the Venatores, a treasure hunting group whose members traveled the globe in search of the ancient Roman coins Seamus Lane, né O'Dulany, had brought with him from Ireland. With Jamie's help, they likened the coins to the Aureo medallion of Massenzio coins, each of which was worth about a million and a half. People had died because of these coins, both of which now sat safely in a safe deposit box.

Pippin recalled the night Lily had confronted Jed, revealing her identity as his daughter. Lily had mentioned the coins that night, but they hadn't revisited the topic—at least not to Pippin's knowledge. Jed had been honest with them. He'd told them about the Venatores group. About how his father had been obsessed with finding ancient treasure and had come across the story of Morgan Dubhshláine and her Roman soldier. It had been a game to Jed, like Dungeons and Dragons, and his search eventually led him to Devil's Cove. There, he met Leo and started to understand the damage the Venatores had done. The damage they continued to do. When Pippin and Grey had come back to the island and encountered Salty and Jimmy Gallagher... that was when Jed really began to understand the lengths the Venatores were willing to go to. It was no longer a game.

When Leo told him about the curse, it had changed everything. Jed had tried to help Leo figure out how to break it. And then Leo vanished. After his friend disappearance, it seemed to Jed, the curse slept, only to be reawakened when Pippin and Grey had returned to Devil's Cove. For the cousins, though, the curse had never gone to sleep, especially when Pippin and Grey discovered the truth about their father. Words Jed had spoken to Lily still echoed in Pippin's mind. *"How could I show up on your doorstep without a solution to the problem I'd created for you? Because of me, Lacy died. Yes, yes, it was the curse, but I got her pregnant."*

Lily had been as angry then as Cora was now. She didn't want to hear that Jed had changed. That wouldn't bring Lacy back. Cora's sharp tone snapped Pippin out of her thoughts. "Did you find what you were looking for, or do you think *we* have it? Is that why you're here? Ready to use us like you used our mom?"

Pippin felt like an intruder listening to her cousins' conversation with their father. It was personal. Private. But everything about the Lane family...about the curse... impacted her, too. She stayed right where she was.

Jed laid his hand, palm down, on the table. "Cora, I know I have to earn your trust. I hope you can believe me when I say that I will do everything in my power to show you my true intentions and to break the curse before..." He trailed off as his eyes dropped to her belly again. "Before your baby is born."

His grandchild, Pippin thought. Cora was carrying Jed Riordin's grandchild. Jed stretched his arm until his hand reached Cora's. He lay it on top of hers for a mere second, then stood suddenly. He nodded at Lily with a sad smile, did the same to Pippin, and strode through the great room and out the front door.

CHAPTER 8

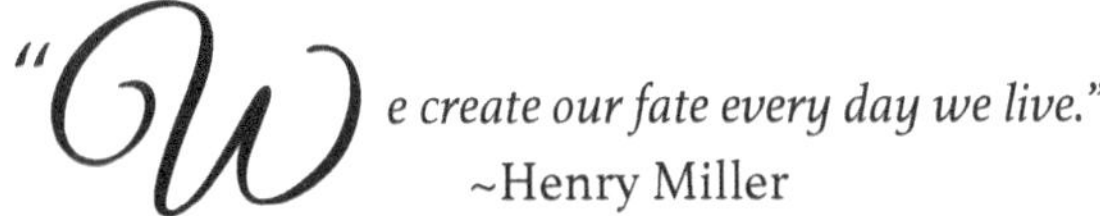

THE OPEN DOOR called to Pippin like no other bookstore or library on the planet possibly could. She'd grown up without books, so her strong connection to them now—both through reading (book club with Heidi!) and with her divination (bibliomancy!)—surprised her. Every time she picked up a book, she felt the history within the pages. She felt the lives of the characters written out, as well as the lives of those who had held that book in their hands.

The bookshop, owned by Jamie and his grandfather, Cyrus, was a mecca for literature fanatics. It was one of the specialty bookshops on the Outer Banks alongside Downtown Books in Manteo; Duck's Cottage Coffee & Books in Duck; Books to be Red on Ocracoke Island; and Buxton Village Books in Buxton on the way to Cape Hatteras. Each was unique from the others. Each drew in tourists and locals alike. Each was successful as independent bookstores because books and the beach simply went together.

Miss Havisham, the Open Door's longhaired gray cat, lay in a sliver of sunlight in the front window as Pippin walked in. She gave a haughty meow. "Hey kitty," Pippin crooned. Miss Havisham watched her with green translucent eyes. Pippin had grown up with two cats, but they'd both been temperamental and entitled. She absently touched one of the scars that marked her arm, a remnant from the two felines and gave Miss Havisham a wide berth.

The aroma of cinnamon and vanilla from a candle intermingled with the musty scent of old paper. Jamie had a good selection of new and popular books—the current best-selling titles that topped the charts, as well as an array of books penned by local authors—but the majority of books in the bookshop were used. The space was divided into two sections: new and used, with the used taking up a solid three-quarters of the floorspace. Shelves lined the walls, and freestanding shelves ran in rows in the center. The nonfiction section held memoirs, books on travel, poetry, religion, history, and celebrity biographies. Whatever subject piqued a person's interest, there was sure to be a title at The Open Door. The used fiction section was divided into hardcovers and mass-market and trade paperbacks. Mysteries; sci-fi; historical; romance; western; horror; classics. If you looked hard enough, you were sure to find something that appealed.

The juxtaposed spines of the books created abstract work of art. The books were of different sizes and widths. The covers were of different colors, shades, and tones. The vast number of books and the variety of titles never ceased to amaze Pippin. The thousands of stories the volumes told were almost unfathomable. What the authors had put down on the pages was just a small part of it. Characters and settings and plots from their creative minds were brought to life every time someone read the words. Complete lives were created. Mythical worlds were explored. Fantastical creatures existed. All of those things and more were there for readers to experience. They revealed worlds like Middle Earth, Hogwarts, and space stations orbiting Earth. They introduced talking spiders, bears who loved honey, and magic treehouses; they brought World War II, the Civil War, and Napoleon to life.

But the books were also so much more than all of that to a select few. If Pippin were to hold any one of these volumes, they would communicate something else entirely. They would reveal to her things about the past or foretell something about the future. Now, with Cora's due date fast approaching, Pippin felt the pressure of needing to solve a problem without having all the pertinent facts, and without actually having the answers.

At the checkout counter, she waited while Jamie helped a customer who, from the looks of it, was buying books for every person on her Christmas list. Noah, a high school student who worked after school and on weekends, stood next to Jamie wrapping each of the woman's books as individual gifts, a complimentary service the shop offered. Jamie finished ringing her up, ran her credit card, and left Noah to the wrapping. He crooked his finger and Pippin followed him into his office in the back. As soon as he shut the door, his mouth quirked up into a flirty smile. "Hey, you," he said.

This thing with Jamie was new. And exhilarating. But also scary as hell. She couldn't afford to find herself in Cora's position...pregnant and doomed. Steering clear of relationships was the best way to protect herself, which was exactly what she'd done her entire life. But she hadn't been able to deny her feelings for Jamie. Pandora's Box had been opened, her emotions released, and there was no way to hide them away again.

Jamie had told her he would stand by her. That he would help break the curse. That he wouldn't give up. Pippin chose to believe him. To believe they really could change her fate. Cora's pregnancy had increased the urgency. She had filled Jamie in on Cora's bombshell and now, twenty-four hours later, here she was.

"Hey," she said. He opened his arms and she stepped into the embrace. The feel of his hands against her back sent a shiver through her. She had spent so much of her life with only her grandparents and Grey. Since coming back to Devil's Cove, her world had grown. She'd reunited with Daisy, her oldest friend. They'd played together as young children, before Pippin's mother had died. Pippin didn't remember, but Daisy had photos of them together. Of their mothers together.

And she had Ruby, who owned Devil's Brew. The coffee shop shared a wall with The Open Door. An archway doubled as a pass-way between the two businesses. Ruby's life had become exponentially more complicated when she'd become Sasha's guardian, not to mention busier, but she and Pippin had formed a friendship through it all. Hattie Juniper Pickle was like everyone's favorite zany aunt. She was unpredictable and fun and definitely danced to the beat of her own drum.

And then there was Jamie. And his girls, Mathilda and Heidi. His mother Erin. And his grandfather, Cyrus.

These were the people she chose to be in her life. The people who made it a full and rich life. The relationships she wanted to protect.

Jamie pushed her back, his hands on her shoulders. He

looked at her as if he knew every thought fluttering around in her mind. "We're going to do this, Pip," he said with confidence.

Her eyes burned with unshed tears. She had to believe they could break the curse, otherwise what was the point? She forced a smile and nodded. "I know. I know we can. We have to."

He dropped his hands and went to his desk, which was neat and orderly with trays to corral loose papers and printed invoices. She followed, standing next to him. He picked up a book, flipped it open to a page marked with a sticky note and held it out to her. She recognized it as one of the books Connell Foley had possessed when he died in the bookshop's rare books room recently. Connell had been a friend of Leo's. Another confidant, like Jed Riordin. Another person Pippin's father had trusted. Connell had been working with Leo to break the curse. Both men had died before they were able to accomplish that goal, but both had left clues. With copies of *Treasure Island* and *Captain Blood*, Connell had led Pippin to a book written by Seamus O'Dulany, who they discovered was her ancestor. He'd written the book *Dagda and the Curse of Morrighan*. Connell had found it and hidden it. Jamie had dated the book based on the gold tooling on the spine, the golden edges of the pages, and the mottled treatment of the leather. They were typical to 17th century bindings. The green and white endbands and the embellishments, including the cord attached near the spine and the pasteboard and endpapers, all supported the date.

But it wasn't Seamus's book that Jamie had handed to her. That volume was in the safe deposit box Pippin and Grey had opened, along with the two coin necklaces they believed their great-great grandfather, Artemis, had brought with him from Ireland.

The book Pippin now held was called *The Kingdom of the Barbarians*. Connell Foley had it with him when he died, but so far they hadn't been able to make a connection between it and the curse.

"What's it say?" Pippin asked, looking at the open pages.

"It's the story of the Alani."

She remembered Jamie mentioning them once but hadn't given them much thought. "I don't remember anything about them," she admitted.

"I didn't know much either, but I've been thinking about why Connell Foley had this book. He had a reason behind everything he did. He came here to talk to you, but he died before he was able to. He had Seamus O'Dulany's book, but he also had this one." He tapped the pad of one finger on the open book. "I've been doing some research and I think it has to do with the Alani people."

"You think they have something to do with my family? With the curse?"

Jamie leaned back against his desk. "I think it's possible."

She clasped her hands together, waiting. Excited. In truth, Jamie was the smartest person she'd ever met. He'd studied at National University of Ireland in Galway, and had two doctorates from Maynooth in County Kildare, one in Medieval Irish Literature and the other in anthropology, specifically the conquering of the Irish. He was a bonafide brainiac. If he thought he had figured something out, he probably had.

"Here's what I think. Keep in mind it's just a theory," he said. "The Alani were a nomadic people. Merchants and mercenaries who lived northeast of the Black Sea."

Pippin called up her high school geography. The Black Sea might as well be a lake, from her recollection. It was bordered by Ukraine and Russia and Turkey and...she couldn't remember the other countries, but she knew the Emerald Isle was *not* one of them. "So, nowhere near Ireland," she said.

"No, not even close. But—" He drew out the word and paused, pointing to *The Kingdom of the Barbarians*—"this book talks about two Roman historians who first placed the Alani in the west, so potentially in or around Rome, in the first century."

Pippin's eyes pinched as she considered the impact of what Jamie was saying. "You think Titus was connected to them? With the Alani?"

Jamie shrugged at this. "I don't have any way of proving or disproving that. Seamus O'Dulany alluded to it in his book, and Connell Foley must have been digging into the idea. Why else would he have that book?" he asked, nodding at the volume Pippin held.

She lined up the pieces of information, drawing a conclusion. "So if Titus sailed from Ireland to Rome, and the Alani people made their way *to* Rome and somehow came across Titus—"

"And if the Alani people were thieves and warriors—," Jamie continued.

"And if Titus had Dagda's Cauldron, then..."

"Then it's very possible the Alani people stole it," Jamie said at the same time Pippin said, "They stole it from him."

"Right."

Pippin stared at the open book in her hands. She moved to Jamie's side. He turned, watching her as she closed the book and set it on its spine. She spoke aloud, as if she were saying a prayer. "What can you tell me about the Alani people and the curse on my family?"

She let go of the sides. The front and back covers dropped. Pages fluttered briefly, and then the book settled on an open page. It was the same page Jamie had marked. She concentrated, scanning the lines, the words, the letters. The print of one sentence grew darker. Undulated. Seemed to lift off the page, but just barely. It was as if this book wasn't particularly interested in her divination, only giving partial effort. The words settled back into place. She pointed at the sentence, letting her finger rest there.

> Other groups of Alani ventured out along the familiar paths of Indo-European migration, reaching Central Europe in an initial phase so that they were present in Dacia, on the northern bank of the Danube, in the first centuries BC and AD.

THE LONG SENTENCE made Pippin's head swim. She reread it, thinking about what it was saying, first, then how it could relate to Morrighan, Dagda, and Titus.

Jamie jumped in before her head exploded from the effort. "The indo-European migration routes might have led the Alani toward Greece and then on to Italy. They were pastoral people. Horse breeders. They would have followed the river, staying close to good pasturelands. The historians place them in Rome. I mean, look, we'll never know for sure, but it certainly makes sense. Especially if that was how Connell Foley interpreted what Seamus wrote about the Alani in his book."

Pippin's shoulders sagged. She hadn't held out much hope that they'd be able to find Dagda's Cauldron, but now any sliver of that dream was gone. "That means the cauldron really is lost to history."

Jamie nodded his agreement. "Afraid so."

Without Dagda's Cauldron, they had nothing to offer to the fairy mound where he lay, which was almost a moot point since finding that which Dagda sought and making an offering at Brú na Bóinne, all before Cora gave birth, seemed impossible.

And that left them back at ground zero. Pippin had a lingering thought: Did Hugh have answers to some of the unanswerable questions they kept bumping up against?

If only she could summon him, she could try to find out.

CHAPTER 9

"*Urgency creates decision making.*"
~Kevin Brady

A LIGHT RAIN started again during the walk back home from the book shop. Pippin hurried through the waning afternoon light, mulling over the dilemma of Dagda's cauldron, the Alani, and how exactly to return something to the Tuatha dé Danann chief when they'd never be able to find it. By the time she mounted the porch of Sea Captain's Inn, her hair hung in wet strands. A shiver passed over her as she keyed in the code on the door lock and let herself in. She pulled up short, nearly running into Joelle Menendez and Zac Bush, guests Hazel had checked in while Pippin had been gone. They'd been two of the inn's first visitors and had rebooked for a week less than six months later. "Those are the best kind," Hazel had said when they'd taken the booking. "They're repeaters, so they know the drill. They'll be easy and non-demanding—knock on wood." She'd gone on to rap her knuckles against the counter of the registration desk with a wink.

Zac was tall and lanky. He kept his dirty blond hair short and combed back. Nothing could hide the receding hairline, but he had a good face and an even better smile. Joelle was a few inches shorter than Zac, but her energy filled the room. "There you are!" she exclaimed. "Hazel didn't know when you'd be back, but we *had* to wait for you."

A momentary thread of alarm wove through Pippin at the ambush and her thoughts scurried through possible problems. Had the toilet overflowed? Did the bed frame break? Did one of them have an allergy they hadn't told her about? None of that was earth shattering, and each was something Hazel could easily have dealt with. Plus, Joelle seemed happy, not as if something were wrong. "Oh? Is everything alright?" she asked anyway, tucking her wet hair behind her ears and stripping off her damp coat.

Zac stayed back as Joelle took a step toward Pippin. The next second, she had Pippin's hands cradled in hers and she looked earnestly into her eyes. Pippin nearly yanked her hands free, but she resisted. Something big was propelling Joelle's actions.

"Don't worry, everything is fine," Joelle said with a wide smile. "Better than fine, actually. Remember when we were here at Sea Captain's Inn after you first opened? Zac proposed to me then." She released her left hand and wiggled her fingers. The small diamond on her ring finger was shiny and full of hope.

Pippin remembered. The young couple had told her about the engagement after the proposal, thanking her for being such an instrumental part of their romance, although all she'd done was provide their lodging.

Now Joelle glanced at her fiancé, her smile growing wide. She looked back at Pippin. "We want to ask you something. Now, it may sound crazy, but please think about it. Like I said, the magic of this island and this inn is now part our history. *You* are part of it." She paused, clasping her hands together, holding them to her dipped chin. She looked at Pippin though her lashes. "We would like you to marry us."

Whatever Pippin expected, it certainly hadn't been this. She wanted to poke a finger in her ear and jiggle it around, to make sure she had heard right. "What?"

"We want you to marry us."

She'd anticipated getting strange requests, but this one had not even been a crumb of an idea. "You want *me* to officiate your wedding?" she asked in surprise, pulling one hand free and pressing her palm to her chest.

Joelle glanced at Zac again. They both nodded. Joelle clasped her hands together. "We know it's a big ask, but please say you'll think about it! It would be icing on the cake. A perfect way to start our marriage, you know? And don't worry, it won't be until summer. We want it to be a year from when Zac proposed. So romantic!"

Pippin's mind raced. Was this even possible? First, she'd have to do whatever it took to get certified as an officiant. But she could manage that. You could do that online, couldn't you? The bigger issue was whether or not she'd have successfully broken the curse by then. Would Cora and her baby live? Would the Lanes all be free? Would she have the bandwidth to focus on something else?

But, she reasoned, she had to think positively. She had to manifest. The curse *would* be broken. Cora and her baby would be just fine. And having a wedding here would mean business for the inn. There would be no vacancy during the wedding week, she was sure. But more than that, Pippin and

Sea Captain's Inn would be permanently embedded into Joelle and Zac's life, and that was a lovely thought indeed. She drew in a breath—manifesting!—before she smiled and nodded. "I'd love to."

Joelle squealed, jumping up and down and clapping her hands. "I knew you'd say yes. I just knew it!"

Zac wasn't as effusive, but his grin said everything.

Joelle launched into the details but stopped abruptly at someone pounding on the front door. "Pippin! Open up! Pippin!"

Pippin hurried to the foyer and yanked the door open. Hattie stood there wrapped up in a bright orange raincoat, the hood pulled up over her red and green hair. "I need help!"

Pippin's head nearly spun around from the urgency in Hattie's voice. She could have been a doctor in surgery saying, "Scalpel, stat!" to the surgical nurse. "Um, okay. Come in."

She held the door open, but Hattie shook her head with as much vehemence as her voice held. She clapped her hands impatiently. "No time! Vodka! Vodka! Pronto!"

Pippin gaped. "That's the emergency? You need vodka?"

Hattie rolled one hand to hurry Pippin along. "When you need it, you need it!"

What could Pippin say to that? Resigned to her friend's eccentricities, she turned on her heel and hurried to the kitchen. A few seconds later she was back at the front door, a bottle of Blue Shark Vodka in hand. Of all the vodka choices in the world—and at the ABC store just over the bridge in Sand Point—she chose Blue Shark because the bottles reminded her of the marine art her father had made. She had several of his ships in bottles displayed around the inn. The small batch Vodka company based in Wrightsville

Beach used glass blowers to hand craft little sharks. Each bottle had one rooted to the inside base. The blowers crafted the bottles around the sharks, each becoming a unique collectable. Pippin didn't drink enough vodka to start a Blue Shark bottle collection, but she loved the story of father and daughter founded business. It resonated with her.

At the moment Hattie didn't care about the shark or the hand-blown glass. She grabbed the bottle's neck, held it up like a trophy, and scurried down the house's two sets of stairs. Pippin stepped out to the edge of the porch, but the rain stopped her from going further. "What's going on, Hattie?" she hollered.

"Wenna's on her way and I had a hankerin' to make Harvey Wallbangers," she yelled.

Almost nothing Hattie said could surprise Pippin. This was no exception. The sudden desire for a specific kind of drink was par for the course.

"Have one for me!" Pippin called.

Hattie waved the Blue Shark bottle around overhead—an acknowledgment that she'd heard Pippin—but she didn't turn around. A minute later, she disappeared into her house and Pippin retreated back inside hers. Joelle Menendez and Zac Bush stood in the foyer wearing befuddled expressions. "She's as jumpy as a lightning bug," Joelle said.

That was a good way to put it. And all that jumpiness was without an added charge of caffeine. Pippin gave a wry shrug. "When Hattie has a hankerin' for Harvey Wall-bangers, I guess nothing'll stand in her way."

Pippin and Hazel got to work setting up the daily happy hour. Pippin had spent hours and hours decorating both the inside and outside of Sea Captain's Inn. She captured the joyfulness of the holidays with poinsettias and garlands, plus the lovely Christmas tree Grey had brought. She'd hung handmade wreaths on the front door and above the rustic mantel of the fireplace, installed by her brother during renovations. A few decorations dotted the built-in bookshelves, but Pippin had gone with the less-is-more concept. She didn't want to overdo the decorations, and everything she put up could fit into a few plastic bins which she could easily store in the shed next to the house. Happy hour during the holidays was a festive hour during which everyone's troubles, whatever they might be, were suspended.

Joelle and Zac lingered, enjoying the holiday vibe of the inn. They were the first to pour glasses of wine. Brenda came in, dragging Barbi and Brittney behind her. They gathered around the snacks, filling small plates with cheese and crackers and fruit. Lily and Cora came in from the reading nook area of the kitchen, arms linked. Lily filled up a glass of the red blend while Cora stuck to a can of sparkling water. Once the small group was situated, Joelle picked up a knife from the sideboard and tapped it against her glass. "Excuse me?"

The low chatter of side conversations stopped as everyone looked at Joelle with varying degrees of curiosity. Zac ran his hand over his face, hiding his smile. It looked like he was used to his future wife's theatrics.

"I want to make a toast to Pippin Lane Hawthorne, the most amazing innkeeper I..." She gestured to Zac then amended, "*We* have ever met."

Heat pricked at Pippin's skin. She could feel it staining her chest under her sweater before it crept up her neck and to her cheeks. She smiled at Joelle and raised her own glass to the engaged couple. "To you both," she said.

Joelle's grin grew. "Listen y'all, Zac and I got engaged

right here on Devil's Cove six months ago." An orchestra of *oohs* and *ahhhs* came from the guests. Several people clapped. Joelle blushed. "Aw, thanks. See, this is why we love it here. Everyone is so lovely."

Hazel raised her glass. "To the young couple."

Glasses clinked as Brenda tossed out her congratulations. "Cheers!"

"There's more," Joelle said excitedly. "Pippin has agreed to be the one to marry us. It's going to happen in six months, exactly one year from the day Zac proposed." She beamed at her fiancé. "If any of you are able to come back to Devil's Cove in June, we'd love for you to attend."

Another cascade of *oohs* and *ahhhs* came from the guests. Brenda squeezed Barbi's hand. "How fun! Don't you want to come back for that, girls?"

Barbi extricated her hand and gave a thin smile, but Brittney's reaction was sincere. "A wedding!" She leaned in front of her sister to speak to her mother. "I definitely want to come."

Joelle bounced on the balls of her feet, excitement coursing through her. She shared a few more details about their summer nuptials. After an hour, Pippin and Hazel started cleaning up. Joelle and Zac bundled up and left for a dinner reservation. Brenda convinced her girls to go with her to wander around the island and experience the holiday decorations and festive vibe. Devil's Cove did the holidays with verve. Despite the shorter days and longer nights, the shops stayed open later. The already old-fashioned streetlights were strung with garland and wreathes adorned the corner street signs. Each store window displayed a merry arrangement, and the restaurants featured holiday-themed food and drink. Even the Brewery, Charcuterie, and the Chocolatier offered special items just for the season.

The excitement of the engagement, the request from Joelle and Zac, and happy hour had pushed thoughts of the curse to the back of Pippin's mind, but now, once the activity settled, the thoughts resurfaced. Doc "James" Wilkenson had shown up and he and Hazel sat side by side on the couch. She snuggled up against him, listening as he read to her from *A Christmas Carol*. Whenever he was around Hazel, the doc's curmudgeonliness softened around the edges.

Pippin left them to their canoodling and retreated into the kitchen. Sailor lay on her bed, completely zonked from the walk they'd taken earlier. Pippin had rescued the deaf dog, but in truth, it was really Sailor who'd rescued Pippin. She had become a comfort and companion. Even a sounding board, despite the fact that Sailor couldn't actually hear Pippin's voice. The dog felt the sound vibrations when Pippin put her face next to Sailor's. Her tail wagged with unbridled excitement. In these moments, Pippin's heart bloomed.

She was about to crouch down to get Sailor's attention when someone pounded on the front door again. "Pippin!" It was Hattie again. She hollered at the very top of her lungs. Surely, she hadn't finished off the vodka already. Pippin hurried back to the foyer, beating Hazel, who looked like she hadn't wanted to leave the snuggly spot she'd been occupying next to James.

Pippin threw open the door, catching Hattie by surprise mid-knock. Her fist continued its trajectory, taking her off-balance. One look at Hattie's pale face told Pippin that this was *not* another vodka run. She wasn't wearing her orange jacket. A layer of mist coated her hair. "What's wrong?"

"That newspaper woman—"

"Moira?" Pippin asked.

Hattie touched her fingers to her nose. A mangled

cigarette broken at the filter, barely hanging on. "Wenna—" she started, but broke off.

"Yes," Pippin prompted.

"She was coming over for drinks…"

Oh God, had something happened to Wenna? "Right. The Harvey Wallbangers. Hattie, what happened?"

A caw sounded in the darkness outside. Hattie glanced over her shoulder. The black crow with its tuft of white feathers glided past her. A harbinger of bad luck. The thought was in and out of Pippin's head in an instant. Hattie turned back. Her lips, usually stained with bright pink lipstick, were pale. Pippin felt her pulse skitter. "Hattie, what's going on?"

"She called. Wenna. Wenna called. They found her—" She trailed off, clutching her heart and breathing heavily. She didn't smoke now, but her years of inhaling tobacco had taken their toll.

Pippin connected the dots of Hattie's scattered words. An icy chill instantly swept over Pippin's skin raising goose-bumps. "They found…Moira?"

Hattie bent over at the waist, hands on her knees. She dragged in big gulps of air. "They found her on the beach at the pier."

The inside of Pippin's head felt as if it was filled with fuzz. Hazel and Doc Wilkenson where both by her side in an instant. Hazel's hand pressed against Pippin's back, as if she knew Pippin needed the support. She fought to stop her knees from buckling. "What happened? Is she alright?"

Hattie stood up straight and slowly shook her head. "No, no, no! She's very *not* alright. She's dead."

CHAPTER 10

"Confront a corpse at least once. The absolute absence of life is the most disturbing and challenging confrontation you will ever have."
~David Bowie

Moira O'Quinn couldn't be dead. She simply couldn't. Pippin had spoken to her...when was that? A day ago? Two? How could she now be dead?

The very idea was like a dark shroud pressing its heavy hand down on her, pushing her down, nearly suffocating her. Death was inescapable, not only for her, as a Lane woman, but for everyone on Devil's Cove. Everyone everywhere. And now for Moira O'Quinn.

By the time Hattie had made her announcement and careened down the porch stairs, Hazel had already disappeared. She reappeared not three seconds later, shrugging on her heavy green sweater, which had been hung on a hook in the mudroom. She thrust out her arm, Pippin's navy peacoat hanging from her clutched hand. "You're going, aren't you?" she said, shaking the coat when Pippin didn't immediately take hold.

"I don't think—"

"Pippin Lane Hawthorne," Hazel said. She wasn't a mother, but she certainly had the tone down pat. "You talked to the woman. She sought you out. Don't you want to find out what happened?"

"Lieutenant Jacobs isn't going to appreciate a bunch of looky-loos," Pippin said as she reluctantly reached for her jacket.

Hazel clasped Doc Wilkenson's hand. "James is a doctor, not a looky-loo. He *should* be there."

James flipped his wrist to look at his watch. "I should *already* be there. Let's go."

With that, he strode out the door, Hazel by his side.

Pippin quickly scooped some kibble into Sailor's bowl and checked her water. "Be back soon," she said as she gave the dog a pat on the head. Seconds later she locked the front door with a touch of her finger on the keypad and rushed down the porch steps after Doc and Hazel.

Pippin usually walked or rode her coral Electra cruiser bike when going to town—the island was small, after all— but the doc had a minivan, which he'd parked in front of the inn. He had the engine running and Hazel sat in the front passenger seat. They'd left the back door open for her. She climbed in, and before the automatic door was fully closed, Doc was driving. Before she'd buckled, he was flipping a sharp U-turn, nearly tossing Pippin off her bucket seat. Hazel glanced back and lifted her eyebrows. Pippin wasn't sure what that was supposed to mean, exactly, but she lifted hers back as if to say, "yeah" in response.

Minutes later, Doc rolled by the pier. They all swiveled their heads to look at the crowd gathered behind the strip of yellow crime scene tape that had been strung across the entrance onto the pier. Doc drove past, pulling into a parking spot at Dolphin's Landing Marina, which was just down the street.

"Guess we're not the only looky-loos," Pippin said as they started walking quickly back to the pier.

"Death draws a crowd," Doc Wilkenson said. "Always has, always will."

The marine layer was light, but ominous. From somewhere in the distance, a dog howled. A murder of crows glided by, circling back a few seconds later. A shudder passed through Pippin. She didn't like being out when the fog hung close to the ground and visibility waned.

She didn't have a good feeling about this and did not want to be involved in yet another murder, but she stayed next to Hazel, pushing forward. The low rumble of hushed conversations hung in the air all around them. As the Doc said, Death drew a crowd but it also brought a sense of melancholy and soft voices. With Doc leading the way, the crowd parted to let them pass. Pippin and Hazel stayed close in his wake. Pippin picked up snippets here and there—*"She drowned..." "I heard she fell..." "She was a busybody..."*

Pippin whipped her head around at the last statement, but she could't identify where it had come from or who had spoken. A second shudder washed over her, but the idea that Moira had died because she'd been butting her head into something—something related to the Lane family— shook her at her core. They stepped up to the cordoned off area. A group of the island's law enforcement stood in a dense cluster, blocking whatever was beyond them from view.

Not whatever...Moira. They were blocking Moira's body.

Doc Wilkenson put his thumb and forefinger in his

mouth, emitting a sharp whistle. Several of the officers turned. Lieutenant Roy Jacobs was one of them. As was the case every time Pippin had seen the man, he wore his navy-blue uniform. The lieutenant was fastidious about his uniform. She would bet the inn that his pants had a crisp line ironed into them, and that his shirt was wrinkle-free. He was portly and had a strong presence. He demanded respect. He said something to a younger officer who was Jacobs' opposite—tall, and lanky, compared to the older man's beefier physique. Blond hair to Jacobs' gray. Tanned skin to the lieutenant's splotchy aged complexion. A moment later, the younger officer loped across the pier. "Come on in, Doc," he said in a heavy North Carolina accent.

The officer held up the crime scene tape for Doc to duck under. Hazel started to follow but the officer dropped the tape and held up his hand. "Just the doc, ma'am."

Hazel brushed back flyaway strands of her short blond hair and took a defiant stance. She was smitten with the doc, but at the moment, Pippin thought her interest in being on the pier was more about her curiosity than sticking close to James Wilkenson.

Seconds passed, then minutes. Finally, the officers dispersed, making room for the paramedics. The crowd watched as four police officers left the pier first, dividing the growing crowd into two sections, creating a pathway for the medics. A *beep beep beep* sounded. People stepped back even further to give the ambulance more room as it backed up to the pier's entrance. A hush fell as one man jumped from the driver's side, circled around, and opened the rear doors. As the other medics wheeled a gurney laden with a covered body over the uneven, bumpy wooden slats of the pier. They paused, and after a silent communique, they lifted the gurney to make it smoother for poor Moira. It was their way of showing reverence for the dead woman. The silence grew heavy as they slid the bagged body into the vehicle and closed the doors. Only the discordant *caw, caw, caw* of a murder of crows sounded in the distance as they drove off with the deceased Moira O'Quinn.

CHAPTER 11

"*And the family you choose? That's the strongest love of all.*"
~G. N. Solomon, Blood So Black

PIPPIN CURLED up under a blanket in The Burrow. Sailor was in her bed underneath the family tree Leo had neatly printed and hung on the wall. Pippin stared at her father's books, not seeing any of them, distracted by the thoughts swirling through her head. Moira O'Quinn was dead. She couldn't wrap her mind around it. The authorities said the woman had fallen from the pier. Leaned over the railing too far and lost her balance. The fall rendered her unconscious and she had drowned in the water. Her death had been accidental. A drowning, but that made no sense. It was December, so why had she been at the pier in the first place?

"The tide came in quick," Lieutenant Jacobs had said when Pippin had asked that very question. "She never regained consciousness, and then it was too late."

Accidental. It was possible, of course, but deep in her

gut, Pippin knew there was more to it. She knew it had to do with *her*. With the Lanes. With the curse.

Moira had been curious. She'd known about the book magic, the bibliomancy. "How?" Pippin said aloud to the ghosts in her mind. "How did you know, Moira?"

She grabbed her phone from the little occasional table, scrolled through her contacts until she found Quincy Ratherford's number and dialed. He answered after the second ring with a clipped, "Devil's Cove Gazette. You've got Quincy, here."

"Quincy! It's Pippin. Hawthorne," she clarified, although there was only one Pippin on the island and it was her.

"Pippin, my dear girl. What can I do for you?" Quincy Ratherford was a good-natured fifty-something year old man whose plaid pants, pastel shirts, and berets set him apart from the ordinary islander. He was exuberant and jovial, but today his voice was subdued.

"I'm calling because...I'm just so sorry about Moira. I only met her briefly, but she seemed nice enough." She omitted the fact that Pippin had cut Moira off at the knees, refusing to talk to her anymore. It was a decision she now regretted. If she'd let Moira come inside like she'd wanted to, she might have found out more about her. Maybe that simple decision, to invite her in, would have created a shift in the fabric of Moira's life. Maybe she'd still be alive.

"The young woman at the beach," Quincy said. "Very sad. I'm working on her obituary now, but I don't understand why you are calling me with your condolences."

An alarm bell went off in Pippin's head. She uncurled her legs and sat up. "Because she worked for you."

Quincy was silent for a beat, which was all Pippin needed to fill in the blanks. He confirmed her realization a moment later. "I don't know where you heard that, but she didn't work for the paper," he said.

"Are you sure?" she asked, knowing what an idiotic question it was. Of course he was sure. He ran the local newspaper, singlehandedly keeping it afloat when others like it had gone out of business. He would know his own employees.

"Quite sure," he said. "I've been trying to find out about her, but no one seems to know anything. Do you know her?" He cleared his throat. "Er, did, I mean."

Pippin's thoughts careened against each other. Moira was dead. Moira had lied. She didn't work for Quincy. That explained why she'd quickly backtracked when Pippin had said she would call Quincy in the morning. "You haven't found any of her people?" she asked.

"Not a one. She was staying at the The Marina Motel," he said, referring to the refurbished vintage motel across the street from Devil's Cove Marina. "That's all I've been able to find out. I'm holding the obit for a few days, until the police track down her family."

Pippin thanked Quincy and hung up. She sank back into her chair, uneasy, her gaze settling on the family tree. Her father's writing was a like a comfort. Familiar and reassuring. He'd left as much information as he could for her and Grey to pick up and carry on. But of course, Moira would have been a child when Leo first vanished. There was no connection there.

If Moira hadn't been working for Quincy, then the idea that she was part of the Venatores seemed all the more possible. Probable, even. Except she hadn't asked about treasure. Hadn't searched Pippin's neck for the pendant. She came back to her first question. How *had* Moira known about the bibliomancy?

Pippin's gaze traced the branches of her family. She and

Grey and their baby brother who had not lived stemmed from Leo and Cassie. Cora and Lily came from Cassie's sister, Lacy. Pippin should add Jed Riordin as their father, now that they had that information. It was one blank that could be filled.

Lacy and Cassie branched from Edgar and Annabel Hart. Edgar and Aunt Rose were the children of Trevor and Emily Davis. And Trevor was the son of Artemis and Siobhan O'Quinn.

Her breath caught as she bolted upright. *Siobhan O'Quinn. O'Quinn. Moira O'Quinn.* She remembered Grey musing after she told him about Moira. The name had sounded familiar to him. Now she knew why. It was the same as their great-great-grandmother who had died on the passage from Ireland to America so long ago.

Moira O'Quinn was family.

THIRTY MINUTES LATER, Pippin walked into the lobby of The Marina Motel. A twenty-something man sat behind the counter at the registration desk. As she approached, he stood, looking like a Loblolly tree sprouting to life and growing to full size before her eyes—albeit a thin, lanky one that looked like it might snap from a strong wind. He had to be at least six feet five inches tall. Maybe taller. She had to tilt her head back to look at him. He pushed a chunky pair of clear plastic-framed glasses up the ridge of his nose. He wore a white button-down shirt beneath a navy crewneck sweater and his name tag read Ty Rhodes. "Welcome to The Marina Motel, where vintage meets modern. Do you have a reservation?"

Pippin smiled big and launched into the speech she'd

prepared on the short drive from the inn. She introduced herself, then said, "I run an inn over on Rum Runner's Lane. We're island colleagues."

Ty's eyes went wide behind the thick lenses of his glasses. He put his hands on the counter and leaned forward, looking down on her, his excitement almost palpable. "You're *the* Pippin Hawthorne? Of Sea Captain's Inn?"

Her smile wobbled. Everywhere she went on island, people knew her name. Her family's reputation was apparently a thing of legend. There were several stories that had become lore. The first was when Pippin had been four or five years old. They'd been at the pier, her mother gazing out to sea, searching the horizon for Leo's boat. They'd headed back to their old house, her mother crossing the street catty-corner to avoid both the bookshop and the library.

Pippin had only a vague memory of the incident on Main Street, but Cyrus McAdams, the sole proprietor of The Open Door, as his grandson Jamie was just a wee lad at the time, had filled in the blanks. The way he told it, an old, hunched woman had been crossing the street. Darkness was settling. The woman dropped a copy of a book that Cassie, not thinking, had bent to pick up. She called after the woman, but she had already been swallowed by the mist. Cassie's bibliomancy had kicked into gear, the book opening and a passage from the book darkening. Lifting from the page. Cassie had collapsed in the middle of the street because the passage she read had foretold Leo's death. From that moment on, Cassie had hated and feared her bibliomancy. If she steered clear of books, they couldn't reveal anything of the past or foretell the future.

And then there was the mystery of Leo's disappearance and its resolution. When Pippin and Grey had first come back to Devil's Cove, so many ubiquitous questions were answered, and many things were brought to light. Most importantly, the narrative of Leo as a man who had abandoned his children, was rewritten.

It made Pippin uncomfortable to be known by so many, when she knew relatively few people in comparison. She forced her smile to remain intact. "That's the one," she said. "It's nice to meet you."

Ty's white teeth gleamed. "Oh no, it is nice to meet *you*! Truly exciting. You and your brother. You're real live celebrities!"

She waved away the proclamation. "No we're not. We're just regular people." Who were destined to die early deaths, thanks to an ancient Irish curse. What would people think if they knew *that*?

"Yo, you are so *not* regular people. You're my competition, but I have to give you props for how you fixed up that old house. And all that stuff with your dad and how you figured it out? I mean...epic."

Epic wasn't the word she would have used to describe the discovery of her father's murderer, but she wasn't going to argue the point with Ty. "We're just glad we got to the truth," she said.

He pressed his lips together and gave a knowing nod. "I get you. For sure, good to know the truth."

There was an awkward pause. Pippin cleared her throat. "So listen," she said. "I was wondering if you could help me with something."

"A ha! More truth seeking?" Ty asked.

"Exactly." Pippin rested her elbows on the counter making her expression as earnest as possible. "It's about Moira O'Quinn."

"That woman they found at the beach? Man oh man.

She was staying here, you know? Like, I met her. A couple of times."

So, it looked like getting Ty to talk was not going to take any convincing. Pippin released the breath she'd been holding. "Yeah, that's what I heard. That's why I stopped by."

"What'd'ya want to know? I can't give you her credit card info or anything like that. That shit is all encrypted."

Plus, unethical. Pippin waved her hands and shook her head. "No, no, I don't want her credit card information. It's nothing like that."

Ty looked her in the eyes and gave a single nod. "Excellent. Then shoot."

Pippin hadn't expected such easy cooperation, but here Ty was, eager to help. She cut to the chase. "Could I see her room?"

"Nah," Ty said.

She deflated and her shoulders sank.

Ty saw her reaction and backtracked. "Whoa! It's not that I *won't* show you. It's that someone else in it now. Anyway, the cops took everything they needed and the maid service cleaned the room."

"That makes sense," Pippin said. It wasn't like The Marina Motel was going to set up a shrine to Moira O'Quinn. She turned to leave. "Thanks anyway, Ty. I'll see you around."

"Yo, wait. Where are you going?" Ty circled around the registration desk. His massively long shoes slapped against the laminate floor as he walked.

"That's all I wanted. To see Moira's room."

"But, yo, I told you the cops took what they wanted, but who knows who her next of kin is. I sure don't." He gestured vaguely to somewhere behind him. "I have her stuff."

Pippin was silent for a beat as Ty's words registered. "You still have Moira's things?"

He shrugged. "Whatever the cops didn't take."

She had no idea what Lieutenant Jacobs and his people would have kept given that Moira's death was considered an unfortunate accident. Certainly not murder.

But Pippin thought differently. "Can I see it? Whatever was left?"

Ty swept his long arm out, ushering her to an office to the left of the registration desk. In the back was another door. "Our lost and found," he said, yanking it open to reveal a smaller room about the size of a walk-in closet. Pippin stared. Several suitcases were lined up like soldiers against the side wall. Two clear rubber storage bins with light blue lids sat in the back, one stacked on top of the other. A chair held a pile of clothing, most of it buried underneath an ochre-colored coat.

"People leave all this stuff behind?" She had found the occasional rogue flipflop, the top half of a bikini, a few books, and the odd piece of costume jewelry. Never an expensive jacket or a whole suitcase.

He shrugged. "Over the years. Three years is my cutoff, and that's only because a man came back three years after staying here. He left a camping stove behind. He was from Missouri, so it wasn't like he could come back to get it. He didn't want to pay to have it shipped. I just hung onto it for no particular reason, then one day, in he comes. I didn't recognize or remember him, but he described the stove right down to the massive dent on the front. So now I keep things for three years...in case someone shows up looking for whatever they left behind."

"Wow. That's amazing."

"One time? This lady called completely stressed. Said

she left her wedding ring by the sink in the bathroom. She was sure it was there, and when I told her the maid service didn't find it, she went off on me. Accused the maid of stealing it. Then accused me. Said she was going to report us to the cops. She was seriously batshi—" He caught himself, apparently deciding he shouldn't swear in front of her anymore. "Erm, ballistic."

"Did you ever find it?"

"She never lost it! Her husband called fifteen minutes later to say he'd seen it and put it in his toiletry bag to give back to his wife later. He forgot about it until he heard her go crazy on the phone."

The woman did sound crazy. And mean. "Did she apologize?"

Ty shook his head, his lips pressed together as if he still couldn't believe it. "Nope. Just the husband."

"Wow," Pippin said again.

Ty turned and pulled a black suitcase out from among the others. The one he retrieved had a black and white checked length of ribbon tied to the handle. Ty laid it flat on a small table pushed up against the wall. He unzipped it and flipped the top up, stepping away to make room. "Thank you," Pippin said, moving into the space he'd vacated.

"Yep. There's a coat, too."

Pippin turned, stunned. "A puffer jacket?"

Ty moved the ochre coat revealing a puffy bundle with faux fur trim. The same jacket Moira O'Quinn was wearing the night they met.

CHAPTER 12

"*Develop your eccentricities while you are young. That way, when you get old, people won't think you're going gaga.*"
~David Ogilvy

PIPPIN STARED AT THE COAT. "Why would Moira have been outside at the beach, in December, without her jacket?" Pippin asked the question aloud, but it was a rhetorical question—something she was mulling over. Ty Rhodes had an answer for her, though.

"That night? Because she ran outa here like a bat outa hell."

Pippin draped the coat over one arm and spun to face Ty. "What do you mean?"

Ty stood with his skinny legs spread, his long shoes rooting him to the spot. "She came to the lobby looking for an extra bath towel, then she got a call on her cell phone. I remember she said, 'Right now?', then she said she was on her way and took off."

"In her car?"

"Nah. I saw her go toward the pier. I mean it's only a three-minute walk."

"It's been so cold, though. Why wouldn't she go back to her room to get her coat?"

"Can't answer that," Ty said with a shrug, "except to say that she was in a serious hurry."

It was a long shot, but she asked, "Did she happen to mention anyone's name? Like, whoever called?"

Ty shook his head. "Nope."

Pippin thought back to her conversation with Moira outside Sea Captain's Inn. She'd known about Leo's secret room. She'd known about the book magic. The bibliomancy. And she hadn't been working for Quincy at the Gazette.

An idea struck her. Hugh. What if Moira had gone off to meet Hugh? The man always seemed to be around when bad things happened. And no matter what their familial connection was, Pippin still didn't trust him. But would he have killed Moira? And why? What had Moira really been after, especially if she was a descendant of Siobhan?

"Did you still want to look at this stuff?" Ty asked, bringing her out of her thoughts.

"I do, thanks. You can go back to work if you want. I'll just be a few minutes."

Ty seemed to consider whether or not it was a good idea to leave her on her own. After a pause he said, "I guess it's okay."

The second she was alone Pippin laid the long puffer coat on the row of suitcases. Moira had been wearing it the night they'd met. She felt along the sides, searching for the pockets. She stopped when her hand landed on something hard. Bulky. A jolt of anticipation shot through her. She knew what it was before she reached into the pocket. Moira's notepad. She withdrew it, quickly feeling in the pocket for anything else. There was a small pack of tissue and a pen, but nothing else. She fanned through the pages of the notepad. Half of the pages were filled. She flipped back to the first page and started to read, but Moira's handwriting was a mix between print and cursive and would take Pippin some time to decode. Her reading skills had improved over the last six months, but she still wouldn't say it was easy. She saw some of the letters backwards and it was sometimes hard to make sense of the words, but bit by bit, she was getting better.

Moira's notes, however, would take time. She glanced at the door to make sure Ty wasn't lurking there. The coast was clear, so she slipped the notepad into her crossover bag then put the coat back on the pile of clothing Ty had taken it from. She turned to the open suitcase. The contents were a jumbled mess. It looked as if whoever had cleared out Moira's room at the motel had just shoved everything together, not bothering to fold or organize. One by one, Pippin took out Moira's clothing. A pair of jeans. Two long-sleeve button up blouses. A wad of underwear, socks, and a bra. There was a toiletry bag, but it was unzipped and contained only a razor, a bottle of acetaminophen, and a travel sized bottle of lotion. Everything else that should have been in the bag had been tossed into the suitcase. Make up, from foundation to mascara; a toothbrush; a squished tube of toothpaste; a brush, the bristles filled with Moira's dark hair; a small container of face cleanser. Pippin put all of it into the toiletry bag and zipped up the compartments. The rest of the suitcase was more of the same. A few more clothing items. A pair of shoes. A paperback book. The only thing that might tell Pippin anything about the dead woman was the notepad.

Pippin took a few minutes to fold Moira's clothing. To organize her things. It felt wrong to leave everything in a jumble. She closed up the suitcase and slid it back into its spot along the wall. She scanned the room and turned to leave but stopped abruptly. The book.

The book! She did an about-face and yanked the suitcase from the line of bags and heaved it back onto the table. She unzipped it and flipped open the top. She'd slid the book, spine down, pages up, against the left side. She pulled it out and tucked it under her arm, zipped everything back up, and slid the case back into place again. Only then did she look at the cover. She caught her breath. It was a well-worn copy of The Hobbit.

Pippin tucked the book under her arm and hurried out of the back room. She waved at Ty. "Thanks again!"

He watched her zip by, slack jawed at her hasty departure. "Don't be a stranger," he called after her. She felt his eyes on her through the windows as she circled around to the driver's side of her Jeep and slipped in. She took the Tolkien book and set it on the passenger seat and was in the process of taking Moira's notepad from her bag when there was a clack on her window. She jumped and spun around, but the parking lot was empty.

Her nerves were getting the better of her. She shook them away, deciding to look at the notebook at the inn, and drove off. Twenty seconds later she started to pass the fishing pier. She swiveled her head to look then cranked the steering wheel to the right. The old Jeep screeched from the torque. The tires skidded. For a split second, she lost control. Her heart jettisoned to her throat. She white-knuckled the steering wheel and turned it hard the other way, straightening the tires. The Jeep jerked, pitching her forward as she slammed on the brakes. She chastised herself even as her throbbing pulse calmed. Foolish to have made the turn like that.

She was here now, though. The parking lot was nearly deserted. Thankfully, or she would have careened into a parked car. She drove slowly now, her hands trembling, and found a spot close to the pier. She couldn't say what compelled her to take a closer look at the place Moira had been found, but she needed to. It felt visceral, like a rope was pulling her from her car and onto the weather-worn planks of the pier. Getting out of the Jeep, she veered left, stopping to look at the wet shoreline. The tide was coming in. She glanced at the time on her cell phone. 6:45. It was close to the time Moira's body had been discovered. "Who were you meeting?" she asked aloud. The breeze carried the question away.

"I'll tell you what I saw."

Pippin spun around at the raspy voice. A woman appeared, as if she were a ghost gliding along the wooden slats of the pier rather than moving her feet. She recognized her as the woman she'd run into a few months ago in front of The Open Door. Hugh had appeared and he'd given her a slip of paper with Seamus O'Dulany's name. That had been the catalyst for so many discoveries about the Lane family and the ancient Irish curse. The woman had told her how Hugh stared out across the Sound as if he were lost in another world. She remembered the woman's words exactly. *"Like he can see past the barrier islands straight to the Atlantic."*

The recollection made her wonder again if Hugh could have been the one Moira was meeting. The woman was bundled up in layers of clothing and a warm coat. A hood was pulled over her head, shadowing her face, but she flipped it back revealing shoulder length steel gray hair that flipped up on the ends. Her skin was leathery and mottled. "Were you here?" Pippin asked. "When it happened?"

"Sure I was here. Where else would I be?" The woman was one of those people with a built-in smile, which took the edge off the surliness of her words.

Pippin shrugged helplessly. "I have no idea. Where do you live?"

She notched her head in the general direction of the marinas but gave nothing more specific.

"What's your name?"

"You ask too many questions. My name's Olive. Now. Do you wanna know what I saw or not?"

"I do," Pippin said. "Anything you can tell me, Olive. Was she...Moira O'Quinn, the woman who died...was she alone?"

"At first she was, yeah." She lifted her arm and pointed as if she were one of Charles Dickens's ghosts. "Right there. Climbed up on the railing. She was leaning over the railing searching for something."

"Or someone?"

"I didn't see no one, but could be," Olive said. She angled her back and stared up at the hazy sky. "Yeah, could be."

"So what happened? How did she fall?" Pippin held her breath, waiting for the answer.

"It was the dang birds."

She thought she'd heard wrong. "Wh—what do you mean, the birds?"

Olive slowly brought her gaze around again. "They spooked her."

An image of a Hitchcock movie came to Pippin's mind. "Did she lose her balance?"

"And fell." Olive nodded solemnly. "She flipped over."

Pippin closed her eyes for a beat, trying to picture the scene. Moira standing on the railing, looking for whoever she was supposed to meet. A swarm of birds suddenly circling. Spooking her. Moira's body tumbling over. Could she have been saved? She opened her eyes again, zeroing in on Olive. "Did anyone try to help her?"

Olive's weather-beaten skin scrunched into rough wrinkles. "There was no stoppin' it from happenin'. I'm the one called 911," she said, practically slapping her chest with her palm. "'Course it was too late by then."

Pippin moved to the railing. Peered over. Stared at the dark water below, the tide swirling around the pier's pilings. What...or who...had Moira been looking for? A shudder wound through her. If Olive hadn't seen the whole thing happen, who knows when or where Moira's body would have been discovered? She turned around again wanting to thank Olive for not allowing Moira to be swept out to see with the receding tide, but the woman was gone without a sound.

CHAPTER 13

"*Worry does not empty tomorrow of its sorrow. It empties today of its strength.*"
~Corrie Ten Boom

PIPPIN SAT at the up-cycled desk Grey had refinished for her in her small office off the foyer. She slipped Moira's notepad and the paperback copy of *The Hobbit* from her bag, flipping through the first several pages. It looked as if she wrote each entry with the same pen, putting her notes in lists and abbreviated words, all of written in a blend of cursive and print. She studied the entries, expecting to see information about articles she'd written. Instead, each page held information about the Lane family. About Irish history. About Pippin and Grey. About Cassie and Leo.

What had Moira been after? Even if she was a distant relation of Siobhan O'Quinn, she wouldn't have been impacted by the curse. Unless...

The idea struck Pippin with the force of a battering ram. The air left her and her chest felt suddenly tight, like a belt was wrapping around her heart, squeezing, squeezing, squeezing.

No, surely not.

"Had Moira been a Lane?"

This notion gave Pippin a new lens to look through. The singled-out words and clipped phrases took on clearer meaning. Moira was interested in Pippin and Grey and the curse because she had been a victim of it, too.

This made it easier, in some ways, for Pippin to decipher Moira's words. She picked things out and inferred their meaning in a larger context, looking at everything through the lens she thought Moira had been writing through--the lens of the Lanes and the curse.

Moira's notebook was equal parts writing and sketching. She flipped through, a feeling of awe deep in her gut at the simple beauty of the pen and ink drawings scattered throughout the pages. A few were pencil drawings, edges softened by soft graphite and fingertips.

A bed of flowers blew across the bottom of one page. A landscape with an enormous cross sprouting from the earth below was on another. On another pair of pages, Loblolly pines grew up on either side of the center seam. Page after page were sketches of the pier, the beach, birds swooping low over choppy waves, a lighthouse built on a tall platform. And then there were a series of portraits. The collection looked like a compendium of all the people Moira had encountered on Devil's Cove. She'd drawn indiscriminately, men, women, and children taking up equal space. Some Pippin recognized. Collette from the cheese shop. Jamie's mother, Erin. Hattie Juniper Pickle. Wenna. Hazel. Heidi and Matilda leaning over a table, their faces close as if they were sharing secrets. Ruby behind the counter at Devil's Brew. Grey holding a proffered cup and saucer. Jamie carrying a stack of books. Even Pippin was there, her long curls blowing in the ocean breeze.

A stab of anger pierced her heart. First at herself for shunning Moira. Then at the curse. Moira had been too young to die. Her artistic talent had died with her. Whatever she'd learned had also died with her.

She went back to the notes. She had lists of Irish words. Snippets of conversations. Just random bits and bobs that, by themselves, didn't paint a whole picture.

—Devil's Cove

—Dagda, lain to rest at *Brú na Bóinne* under a fairy
    mound

—Morrighan

—Tory

—Blessings and curses

—HMS Wasp

Moira had known so much more than she'd let on.

Next to Dagda's and Morrighan's names were small portraits, Dagda with a beard and Morrighan with long, flowing locks. They were at the center of everything, and Moira had known it. She kept skimming Moira's notes.

—Moira—>Liam—>Saoirse—>Moira

—The Lane cousins

—The coins

—Cassie and Leo

SHE STOPPED FIRST at Moira's own name written twice, along with the others—Liam and Saoirse. These had to be the people in Moira's family line. Another Moira...

And then an idea sparked. She closed her eyes. In her mind's eye, she saw the photograph of a pregnant Siobhan and her two other children. She assumed the baby had died on the crossing during childbirth, but what if...

She paused, thinking it through. What if that baby had lived? Gone on to marry and have children. What if Moira came from that line? She looked again at Moira's notes.

—Moira—>Liam—>Saoirse—>Moira

THERE WERE two girls named Moira. The first one could be the baby Siobhan had been pregnant with. Moira had told her that her great-grandmother was adopted. Siobhan died on the voyage, but Pippin imagined a scenario where a mother died in childbirth, the baby was assumed dead, but had actually been spirited away and given to another couple. It was certainly possible.

Artemis couldn't have known. She couldn't imagine him leaving his cursed child out there on her own, left to suffer the consequences alone.

A shudder wound through Pippin. Moira was a Lane. The *first* Moira. Her son, Liam, and his daughter, Saoirse. And then Moira O'Quinn. The fact that she had taken Siobhan's surname told Pippin that Moira had known her own history.

She kept reading, stopping again at her parents' names. At the mention of her family and the coins. So, Moira had also known about the treasure. Pippin fanned through the pages again looking for anything else that might help her, anything that might direct her in how to break the curse. But deep down, she knew that the answer didn't lie in Moira's notebook. If she'd known what to do and how to do it, she wouldn't have been seeking information from Pippin.

With a heavy sigh, she closed the notebook and picked up *The Hobbit*. Maybe the book had something to tell her. She set the worn book on its spine and closed her eyes. This had become part of her ritual. "What do you have to tell me?" she asked aloud, as if the book had ears and a mind and understood what she said.

She let the sides go and it fell open. Immediately, the words of a paragraph darkened, rose off the page, and created a shadow beneath them.

"Go back?" he thought. "No good at all! Go sideways? Impossible! Go forward? Only thing to do! On we go!" So up he got, and trotted along with his little sword held in front of him and one hand feeling the wall, and his heart all of a patter and a pitter."

SHE READ IT AGAIN, but the meaning was clear. There was no going back. There was only forward. Going back...or standing still, for that matter...meant defeat. It meant that Dagda won. That the curse would live on. That's what the curse felt like—a living thing whose only goal was to destroy every descendant of Morrighan and Titus.

"Okay," Pippin said—to the book...to the air...to whoever

or whatever was listening. "I will go forward." She held up her hand, clutching an invisible sword. "On we go," she proclaimed, channeling Bilbo Baggins. If the little Hobbit had the courage to face the unknown, so did she. "On we go."

PIPPIN SPENT the rest of the afternoon doing chores around the inn. She needed to keep busy. Keep moving. She dragged a step ladder around the Great Room, moving the books and knickknacks on the shelves of the built-ins while she dusted. It was mindless work, and it gave her time to think. If she closed her eyes, she had a vague memory of following her mother around the house, play cleaning while Cassie did the real work. Her mother had tried to live a normal life with Leo and her twins. She had tried so hard to pretend the curse didn't exist. To deny her bibliomancy, as if the pretense would make it true somehow. Had Cassie tried to break the curse before she'd given up?

Leo had spent years with the effort. Had Cassie helped him, or had she been in denial about that as well? For about the millionth time, she wished she had her mother's journal. Hattie said she had seen Cassie writing in a lovely cloth-covered book when Cassie had rented a room from her, but it had never been found—at least not to Pippin's knowledge. It had either been lost over the years or Cassie had destroyed it. Either scenario meant Pippin would never be able to know her mother beyond the few memories she had.

She went back to the question of whether or not Cassie had been in denial. She thought the answer was probably *yes*. Why else would she have risked pregnancy—twice?

When had she told Leo about the curse? That was another question she'd never have an answer to.

She dragged the stepladder to another area, beginning at the top shelf and working her way down to the bottom. Her rag was practically clean even after tackling half the area. It didn't matter. She kept going, and once she finished that task, she grabbed a broom and went onto the front porch to sweep the planks and whisk away nonexistent cobwebs.

Across the street, her neighbor, Kimberly Cox, wrestled her three young boys into the back of a minivan. The kids' father, Aaron, had the hood of his old truck up. The man was always tinkering with his cars or playing poker. He notched his head up and gave a quick wave as his wife drove off, then went back to his truck.

Pippin's mind moved on to replay her encounter with Moira, Ty's account of the phone call Moira got while she was in the motel's lobby, and the story Olive had told her about Moira climbing up onto the railing searching for something. She imagined the fall. Was she supposed to meet whoever had called her on the peer, or down below? There wasn't much of a beach around the pier, and the riptides were notoriously dangerous around the pilings, so it was an off-limits area. But Moira wasn't an islander. She might not have known how dangerous the water beneath the pier could be. If she had, she might have taken more precaution when she'd stood on the railing.

Someone tapped on her shoulder. She screeched and spun around, wielding the broom as a weapon.

Hazel jumped and scurried back, throwing her arms up in apology. "Good golly gosh! Sorry, Pippin. I didn't mean to startle you."

Pippin's heart had shot to her throat. She doubled over,

letting it settle back into place. "It's okay. Guess I'm a little on edge."

That was quite an understatement, but if Hazel thought so, she didn't comment on it. "Joelle and Zac asked for late checkout. Just wanted to let you know."

"Perfect. Thanks. Everything else is good?"

Hazel started to answer but broke off when a voice bellowed from the sidewalk. "Ahoy, girlies!"

Pippin and Hazel turned to see Hattie bundled up and strolling up the sidewalk, arm in arm with Wenna. Their walks had become a daily event. Even wrapped in coats, they were opposites. Hattie had a bright orange puffy jacket and Wenna wore her typical black. Seeing them wrapped up and warm, coupled with the lull in her chore, made a chill race through Pippin. Adrenaline had kept her blood heated, but it was beginning to fade. She waved. "Ahoy," she said, but without Hattie's enthusiasm.

The two older women made a sudden right turn to head up the walkway to the porch. Hazel disappeared inside, popping out a minute later with Pippin's peacoat.

Pippin slipped it on. "You're a lifesaver."

Hazel flicked her brows up. "Among other things," she said then disappeared back inside.

Hattie and Wenna climbed the final steps. "Cold day to do outside chores," Hattie said.

"It's a cold day to be taking a walk," Pippin pointed out.

Hattie smiled, a smudge of pink lipstick on a tooth. "Touché."

"I admit, I dragged her outside," Wenna said. "I love a brisk walk by the water. How many memories it calls to mind." Her voice filled with nostalgia as she remembered. "Oh, how lovely that was. The Dingle. All the beehive huts, and the crashing waves—"

"E-yo, let's go!" Hattie said. "This cold is making me ready for a hot toddy," Hattie said.

Wenna had a black scarf tied around her wiry gray hair. She tilted her head to one side and considered Pippin. "You have something on your mind. The reporter at the pier."

She was perceptive. "Among other things," Pippin said, repeating the very words Hazel had spoken a minute earlier.

Wenna nodded to the rocking chairs. "I am a very good listener. Shall we sit?"

"E-yee, not me!" Hattie exclaimed. "That hot toddy is calling my name."

Wenna released her arm from Hattie's and waved her off. "You go make them. I'll be along. I want the fresh air for a few more minutes."

Hattie plunged her hands into her jacket pockets. "Suit yourself, but I'm not staying out here so I can freeze my patootie off."

Wenna chuckled. "Some people swear by cold showers. For me, it is the cold air. It keeps me healthy. And young." Mischief twinkled in her eyes.

"If you snooze you lose. Stay too long and I won't be able to resist having your drink, too."

"Ten minutes," Wenna said.

Pippin propped the broom in the corner then leaned back against the porch railing. "I can make you some hot tea..." she suggested.

"No need."

Looking at Wenna, Pippin's thoughts went back to Moira O'Quinn. They, along with Hattie, had been with Moira just before she'd died. To see someone alive one day, and to find them dead the next was sobering. Wenna and Hattie and Pippin shared this experience. It was a connection weaving them together.

"You will be okay," Wenna said.

Pippin sighed. She'd grown up schooling her expression, keeping her emotions off her face. Now, though, they were surfacing, there for everybody to see. "I don't know…"

"Worry does not change the future, you know. It only affects you today."

"I'm not worried…" she started, but her eyes pricked and Wenna's open expression and words sent her thoughts tumbling. "I mean, I am. It was all so long ago, and…and my mother and father…and now Grey and the boat…and what if we can't…? I mean, what's going to happen? And poor Moira. She was…" She almost told Wenna about her theory that Moira was a descendant of Artemis and Siobhan. That she might have been yet another Lane who had surfaced… and died. But Wenna didn't know about the curse or the bibliomancy. She didn't know any of it. It was better that way. "Moira was here, then gone. I…it's so hard to make sense of it." She buried her face in her hands. "I'm sorry. Ignore me," she said through her fingers. "I'm just…I'm tired."

Wenna considered her. Cocked her head. "Time is but a distance between the past and the present."

She thought for a moment, trying to figure out what Wenna meant. *Time is but a distance between the past and the present.* "I don't understand."

"Worry, Pippin, is based on past experiences. As I said, you can't change the future. All you can do is be in the present. There is nothing else but now."

"But that's not entirely true," Pippin said. "At least not what I'm talking about."

"Is it not?"

"What I do now *will* either change the future…or it won't." She spoke cryptically, not wanting to reveal the details of how she would or wouldn't be able to break the curse.

Wenna didn't pry. "So you try and then wait, yes? You can't see the future, so what else *can* you do?"

Only, she *could* foretell the future with her bibliomancy. If it would let her. If she could ever figure out exactly how to break the curse, maybe she could use her divination to figure out if she was successful. The problem was, she still had no idea how to break the curse or truly master her divination. "I guess."

Wenna pushed herself up from the rocking chair. "If I want a hot toddy, I had better go."

"Have one for me."

Wenna gazed at Pippin as if she could see right into her soul. "Do you believe in fate?"

Pippin couldn't afford to believe in fate. If she did, then she had no chance of breaking a curse set into motion at what felt like the beginning of time. "I don't," she said. "I believe we can change the future."

Wenna pulled her cape tight around her. She considered her. "Is that what you're trying to do, my dear? Change your fate?"

"I have to," Pippin said with as much conviction as she could.

Wenna gave a sad shake of her head. "A person's destiny, Pippin, it is written."

No! She didn't believe that. She *couldn't* believe that. "It's not."

Wenna clucked. "Your future, it will unfold however it's meant to. You don't know what's going to happen, so how can you change it? No one *knows* their fate, so whatever you do now, well, that's part of how things are meant to unfold."

"But I do," Pippin said. "I do know my fate. My—my—

my mother. She...died in childbirth with my baby brother. We all... That is my fate, too."

Wenna offered a sad smile. "When a parent dies young, it is a common fear that the child will not make it past that age. That's what it is, Pippin. A fear."

"It's more than that," Pippin said. "Moira...she was...she was..."

She left the sentence hanging, unable to tell Wenna that she thought Moira was family...and another victim of the Lane curse.

"You weren't there, my dear. You couldn't have helped her," Wenna said.

She wanted to blurt out that she should have talked to her that night at Hattie's, or the next day when she'd been waiting for Pippin to return home. She wanted to say that Moira was a Lane, but none of that meant anything to anyone other than Grey, Lily, Cora, and her. "I should have, though. I should have listened. I should have helped her."

CHAPTER 14

"$\mathcal{A}$*nd before my Soul took me to task I was hard of hearing; I heard only tumult and uproar. But now I am all ears listening to the silence and its choirs singing the hymns of time, intoning the praises of the firmament, revealing the secrets of the invisible."*
~Khalil Gibran

THE BRINY MIST weighed down the air as Pippin left Devil's Brew, a To Go cup of hot green tea cradled between her hands. The island temperature had swung from freezing to a more average temperate level causing the marine layer to thicken. Pippin felt as though she were walking through a cloud. She had told Grey and Cora and Lily...and Jamie... about Moira. About her theory that Moira's great-grand-mother was the infant thought to have died during Artemis and Siobhan's voyage to America.

It was sobering for them all. Moira didn't die in child-birth, but death was tied to the Lanes and the curse. Pippin felt deep in the marrow of her bones that some nefarious force was at play.

It was late afternoon, but the tourists still ambled downtown, holiday shopping in full swing. High season sustained the island businesses, but the holidays brought good revenue, too. Pippin waved to familiar faces. The storm had passed through, leaving a heavy breeze behind. The wreaths hanging from the light posts swayed and the branches of the island's stalwart loblolly trees danced.

As Pippin started up Main Street in the direction of Rum Runner's Lane, a figure appeared, as if out of thin air. Recognition hit immediately. Hugh—or his Gaelic name, Aodh, which when pronounced was nothing more than a grunt. He appeared like an apparition, materializing fifty yards ahead of her.

Of course, it was just the heavy fog that made his appearance seem so mystical. He walked out of the mist toward her, a shadow whose outline grew sharper and darker the closer he got. She remembered what Olive had said about Hugh vanishing, as if into thin air. She had the fleeting thought that maybe he wasn't who he said he was at all but, instead, was one of the Tuatha dé Danann. What if he had come to her in this form to spy on her and Grey, to stop them from breaking the curse? What if he was Dagda, come back to life?

She pushed the thoughts away, dismissing them as crazy. Why would the Irish deities walk among them here on this little island? No, the original explanation made the most sense...that Hugh was a descendant of Aoife.

Pippin stood rooted to ground. She hadn't seen the man for months now.

Now he was back.

She remained motionless, just watching him, as pedestrians weaved around her. Waiting for him to notice her standing on the sidewalk. Or maybe he already knew she was there. His translucent eyes, nearly glowing in the dusk, sent a shiver down her spine. She imagined his direct ancestor, Aoife, with the same clear eyes. The feeling that it—or he—was supernatural came to her again. But then, she was, too, wasn't she? She had Morrighan's blood coursing through her veins via her daughter Aisling. She had a magical gift.

Time stood still for a minute. Hugh walked slowly, yet a few seconds later he was in front of her. "Hello, Pippin."

"Hugh," she said drily, resisting the urge to call him Aodh. At the moment, she wanted to keep her knowledge about the truth of his lineage close to the vest. She didn't know what it meant in connection to the curse. Surely, he wanted it broken, too. After all, he'd somehow known about Seamus O'Dulany. Without him, she might not have made the connection when she'd found Seamus's book at The Open Door. She just didn't know the *why*.

"You're back," she said.

"Did you miss me?"

Like an elephant misses a poacher, she thought. "That's not how I'd put it, but I am glad to see you."

He spread his arms wide. "Here I am." He was dressed the same as he always was, in black and white, this time with black slacks, a white turtleneck, and a black sweater under a black jacket. "I see you've been busy."

Pippin tilted her head to one side trying to discern what he might mean by that comment. "The inn is doing well," she said.

"So I have heard, despite your recent problems."

She stared at him, waiting.

"That business with Camille Gallagher..." He trailed off with a tsk and a shake of his head. "Ugly situation, that."

"That's one way of putting it." Another was that Camille Gallagher was connected with him through the Venatores, which made the man doubly mysterious. And possibly dangerous. If he wanted to steal the ancient coins...if that's what he'd been searching for that first time she'd met him, when he'd been upstairs at the inn...then he could easily see both Pippin and Grey as liabilities. But he didn't know where they were. Or exactly *what* they were. And even if he did, he didn't have access to their secure safe deposit box at the bank. If he was after this treasure, he needed Pippin and Grey alive.

And if he wanted to break the curse and was depending on them to work out how, then he needed them for that, too.

The fact that Camille had called Hugh by his Gaelic name bothered her, though. How did she know it, and why address him by it? It didn't make sense to Pippin.

He looked around at the people milling around town. "We need to speak," he said in his slow Southern drawl. A drawl she was beginning to suspect was as fake as a politician's promises.

A chilling breeze kicked up. Pippin overlapped the two sides of her coat and held them together with folded arms, her hot tea still clutched in one hand. "We *are* speaking," she said, but inside, she was secretly glad he'd brought up the need to talk. She had questions for the man.

His mouth lifted into a slight mirthless grin. "We need to speak properly," he amended. "Privately."

"Like another rendezvous in the library?" she asked, thinking about when he'd told her they were distantly related, and when he'd lied to her about how.

"I believe the library is currently closed," he said, not reacting to the sarcasm she'd embedded into her words.

Pippin rolled her wrist enough to see the face of her watch. Five twenty-three. He was right about the fact that it was closed. During the shorter winter days, the hours changed. They closed at five o'clock. "Where were you coming from? Were you at the inn? To see me?"

"Not everything is about you, Pippin, is it?" He paused just long enough to let the judgement hang over her, and then he changed the subject. "Your brother is refurbishing a seventy year old boat. That's very interesting."

As Hugh usually did, he answered a question with a question, only this felt more rhetorical. Clearly he knew about the boat, but how? Grey didn't go around town talking about it, and he certainly hadn't shared how he'd tracked it down through one of Leo's old notebooks. She watched him, not speaking. She would neither confirm nor deny.

Hugh didn't seem to care that she hadn't responded. "We can talk at the pier."

Before she could say yay or nay, he strolled past her. She could ignore him and keep going toward the inn, but the truth was, she wanted to talk to Hugh. But—and it was a big but—she wasn't about to let him create the narrative of their encounter. There would be anglers on the pier fishing for flounder and whatever else they could catch in the December waters, but not enough people to feel safe with a man she didn't trust. There was also the fact that Moira had died just beneath it, leaving it haunted with her memory.

No, *she* would set the terms of their meeting. "Not the pier."

He stopped in his tracks, realizing she wasn't in step behind him. He slowly turned until he faced her again. His clear eyes drilled into her. Waited.

Pippin didn't speak. She turned on her heel and walked the short distance back to The Open Door. Hugh would either follow her...or he wouldn't.

She thought he would, but she didn't wait to see. She pushed through the door and stopped short. Miss Havisham sauntered past, her tail reaching to the ceiling, an air of indifference about her. Like all cats, Miss Havisham did *what* she wanted, *when* she wanted. Once the cat was out of the way, Pippin let the door whoosh closed behind her. Jamie looked up from where he rang up a purchase. He smiled. "You're back," he said, but his smile faded as he registered her somber face. "What's wro—" he started, stopping short as the door opened behind her. He looked past her, his expression clouding. Pippin had described Hugh, but this was the first time Jamie was seeing him up close and personal. "Mam," he said to his mother, "take over here, would you?"

Erin had been straightening books on the new release table. "Of course, my love," she said with her Irish lilt. She went behind the counter and waited while Jamie finished the transaction he'd been handling. The couple took their bags of books, passing by Pippin and Hugh as they left. The next person in line stepped up. Erin took over and Jamie came out from behind the check-out counter. He lowered his voice when got to Pippin. "What's going on?"

She notched her head to indicate Hugh. "We need a place to talk."

CHAPTER 15

"*The power of one, if fearless and focused, is formidable, but the power of many working together is better.*"

~Gloria Macapagal Arroyo

JAMIE TOOK a moment to adjust his horn-rimmed glasses as he looked from Pippin to Hugh. And then, without another word, he nodded. "This way."

He led them to the back of the store. A door led to the rare book room, and another led to a stairwell up to the second floor of the building. Jamie's grandfather, Cyrus, lived in a flat there. But Jamie passed by both doors and took them down the hallway, past the customer restroom, and into his office. He led them to a small round table, an addition from the last time Pippin had been in here. A hardcover book sat squarely in the center. He quickly picked it up and deposited it on his desk. Back at the table, he pulled a chair out for her before taking his own. "Have a seat, Hugh," he said.

Hugh held Jamie's gaze with his translucent eyes in a game of chicken. Who was the alpha? Jamie didn't blink. "He is staying?" Hugh said to her.

"Yes," Pippin said. Hugh's brows narrowed, so she added, "He knows everything."

His upper lip curled into a sneer. "Fine," he said, finally sitting.

Pippin jumped right in. "What do we need to talk about privately?"

"I do like that about you, Pippin. No fluff."

"I don't have time for fluff."

He dipped his head in a slight nod. "Nor do I, nor do I."

Pippin drummed her fingertips on the table, impatient. Being in the same room with Hugh gave her the heebie-jeebies. She trusted him about as much as she trusted a Great White gliding through the sound. "So?"

Finally, he spoke. "We have a common enemy. It is time we worked together to overcome it."

Pippin shot her gaze to Jamie, holding it for a long second. A series of thoughts ricocheted through her mind. Hugh was leapfrogging ahead, but she needed to hit reverse. Her first meeting with him had been disturbing. He had infiltrated her house...her space...only to leave the hilt of Titus's sword for her to find. After that, he'd summoned her to the library where he'd told her that they shared Titus's ancestry. Not entirely true, as it turned out. And then he'd cryptically passed her a slip of paper with the name Seamus O'Dulany written on it. "Whoa, whoa, whoa," she said. "Let's back up. I need some answers first."

The nostrils on Hugh's aquiline nose flared. He sighed. "Fine."

She'd thought about what to ask him when she encountered him again. She wanted to know why he'd left the hilt.

Why he'd provided her with Seamus's name. She suspected he had gotten as far as he could in trying to break the curse, but she wasn't sure he would admit that. She cut to the chase. "The story you told me, about Titus going back to Rome and the child he had there…it's not true."

He didn't speak. Didn't blink. Just stared at her with those eyes.

"Let me tell you what we know," she continued. She used her fingers to count off the information. "First, Morgan Dubhshláine had an affair with the Roman soldier, Titus."

"I concur."

She tapped her second finger. "But we believe that Morgan Dubhshláine was actually the Morrighan, goddess of war and wife to Dagda."

Pippin watched his face, looking for any reaction, but his face remained impassive. If he was surprised by this revelation, he wasn't showing it. She tapped her next finger. "You led us to Seamus O'Dulany and his book, *Dagda and the Curse of Morrighan*." She didn't bother asking how he knew about Seamus. She was pretty sure he wouldn't answer the question. "That book told us something."

A muscle in his face twitched. "You found the book."

Finally! A reaction.

She laced her fingers together, tapping her thumbs. "I did." She plowed on. "Based on Seamus's book, Morrighan became pregnant by Titus." She put her hand on her chest. "I am descended from them. From her. From the Tuatha dé Danann." She leaned forward, elbows on the table, meeting Hugh's eerie gaze head-on, gaining confidence. Strength. "But here's the thing, *Hugh*. Morrighan had *two* children. Twins named Aisling and Aoife. In a rage, Dagda wrapped Aoife in a leather-skin bag and pushed her out to sea. She became the 'forgotten child'.

But she survived that ordeal, grew up, and had children of her own."

That got a bigger reaction. A strong and unmistakable muscle twitch. She went back to counting on her fingers, moving to the thumb of her other hand. "And something else, *Aodh*," she said, grunting his name, "Dagda discovered Morrighan's betrayal and cursed the babies. We believe you are a descendant of Aoife's line—which means you are directly descended from Morrighan." She dropped the final bomb. "Which means *you* and *all* the descendants of Aoife are also cursed."

She sat back and folded her arms, ready for him to deny it. Or to berate her. Instead, the color drain from his face. "No," he said in a hoarse whisper.

Not the reaction she'd expected. She leaned forward again. "You didn't know."

"That we're cursed? Yes, of course I know that," he snapped. It was the first sign of actual emotion the man had ever shown in Pippin's presence. "What I didn't know was how. I have long speculated that Seamus O'Dulany's book held the answer. It seems I was right. Aoife."

She didn't know how long it would take Hugh to process this new information. She didn't want him to abort their conversation, so she plunged ahead, asking him a question that had been bothering her. "How is it that Camille called you by your Gaelic name? In fact, why do you even *have* a Gaelic name?"

The question snapped him back to his ordinary self, all emotion erased from his Romanesque face. "Because," he said, "my grandmother preferred that. It dates back to Saint Aodh, who my grandmother claimed was an ancestor. I could never figure out how that could be if I descended from Titus and his Roman wife. Everyone thought my grandmother was mad. Delusional. Everyone but me. Over the years, I have come to believe the story of Titus and his pregnant wife in Rome was fabricated."

Jamie had been watching him closely. "Why? What made you believe that?"

Hugh's jaw drew taut. Pippin thought he might clam up, but he continued. "The family history did not make sense. There were holes. Missing pieces. I have spent decades researching. Searching for the truth. Titus left Ireland on a Roman ship. Nothing I have found indicates it completed its voyage. I believe it went down in the Black Sea. My research led me to a Venatore. She told me about the curse laid upon the Lane family. It made me wonder."

Jamie shot Pippin a look with a raised eyebrow, then looked at Hugh. "Your Southern accent has taken on an Irish lilt," he said. Not a question, just an observation.

Hugh shrugged. "No more need for pretense."

"So you're actually very Irish," Pippin asked. "Like, from Ireland, I mean."

"I am. Another reason for my questions. My family comes from Ireland, not Italy, yet the move from one country to another in the family history was never explained. Too many lies. Too many people pretending to be something...or someone...they are not." He swung his gaze to Pippin. "You must understand what that is like. Pretending to be something you are not."

She bristled under his scrutiny. "I'm not pretending anything."

"Oh, but I disagree. You tied on an apron and set up house, but you should be mastering your divination."

She glared at him. Yes, she had moved into her parents' old house. No pretending there. And she *had* been practicing her divination. She just didn't think it was ever something that could be fully mastered. She wished her bibliomancy could tell her something more about this man. About this distant relation. She didn't know what he wanted. Whether he was here to help or hinder. "What exactly do you want?" she asked.

"Like the Lane family, the Molloys have suffered loss at the hands of that ancient curse. Now I know why. Or rather, how."

"So you're Hugh Molloy," she said.

"A derivative of Ó Mail Aodha. Technically I am Aodh Ó Mail Aodha. Hugh Molloy is far easier."

"That's about as Irish as they come," Jamie said.

He watched her with as much scrutiny as she watched him. "Camille,"she said. "She's from here. Why would she call you Aodh?"

"The Venatores. Most now are nothing more than hunters. Vultures..."

"*But,*" she prodded.

"But there are still some who believe the history of Tuatha dé Danann. The origin story, if you will. She was one of those. The Venatores were direct descendants of the early Romans. They sought to reclaim what they thought was theirs. Treasures. Over the centuries, that interest has been diluted. Those, like Salty Gallagher and his son, had no connection to the past. They were treasure hunters, plain and simple. Camille dug deeper. Her interest stemmed from Irish lore. From her own family's culture. "I made the mistake of revealing my true name to her. She used it from that moment on."

Jamie shifted in his chair. "I have a question for you. How does Camille even know you? Know who you are?"

"The Venatores' research goes back six or more centuries. Different people have different parts of it. Salty and Jimmy Gallagher didn't care about the history. As I said, they wanted the treasure, which I assume you have safely hidden away."

Pippin didn't take the bait. She didn't know if Hugh had knowledge of the two Roman coins, or not, but she wasn't about to confirm their existence to him.

When she didn't speak, he continued. "Camille was the smart one. She found the history Salty discarded and realized there was something more."

The two Roman coins were worth a fortune. What more could there be? "Like what?"

"That, I do not know."

Pippin shook her head, flabbergasted. Hardly anyone was who they seemed. "Why not tell me all of this from the beginning?" she asked. She still didn't trust him, but this conversation made her fear him less.

Hugh's clear eyes were bright. "Would you have believed me?" he asked.

She thought about it. Just as Grey had been skeptical, she probably would have been, too, had he simply pulled her aside and said, "Pippin, your family descended from first century Ireland, oh, and by the way, you're all cursed. My family is, too, but I don't know how...or why. Plus, you're a bibliomancer."

He was right, she would have called him nuts. She hated to admit it, but she and Grey had had to discover the truth about their family on their own. Even then, it took Grey some time to accept it. "Do you know how to break the curse?" she asked.

His gaze bore into her like two laser beams. "If I did, I would not be here."

True. "So what now? What do you want?"

"Isn't it obvious, Pippin. We can work together to break the curse on both the Lanes and the Molloys."

She caught Jamie's side eye. He was just as suspicious of Hugh as she was. But she was smart enough to play along, and honestly, until she got all the answers she needed, she didn't have much choice. In the end, though, Hugh left and they had no plan on how, exactly, he intended for them to work together.

CHAPTER 16

"You know how you let yourself think that everything will be alright if you can only get to a certain place or do a certain thing. But when you get there you find it's not that simple?"
~Richard Adams, *Watership Down*

AN HOUR LATER, Pippin was at Jamie's quaint island cottage. He paid the babysitter who'd spent the afternoon with Heidi and Mathilda, as well as Sasha.

The girls stayed upstairs. Alone in the kitchen, Jamie slipped a book from his satchel and showed it to Pippin. It was the hardcover volume he'd moved from the small round table in his office earlier. It held everything one might want to know about curses. How to make blessings, cast curses, and, most importantly, how to break them.

The two of them sat at the table in his kitchen, the book open in Jamie's hands.

"Do you really think this will work?" she asked.

Jamie gave a noncommittal one shoulder shrug. "Your guess is as good as mine."

His uncertainty felt disquieting. He was usually so sure of himself. So sure of what he knew and confident with the vast breadth of his knowledge. To hear his hesitancy...well, it left Pippin thinking that it couldn't possibly work. There was no proof. No empirical data.

"Don't overthink it," Jamie said, finding her hand and giving it a quick squeeze. "We're talking ancient magic here. A year ago, I didn't believe any of this was possible. Bibliomancy? A real live curse? I'd have said you were crazy." He gave a quick laugh, as if he still couldn't believe it. "But here we are. And it's all real."

Pippin had experienced the same mind-blowing emotions. But, as he said, here they were. It was very real. Too real. She blew out a breath. "Okay. So, let's walk through it."

Jamie read aloud. "Step one is to evaluate. Are you sure there is a curse?"

It was rhetorical, but she answered anyway. "Yes, I'm very sure."

"Do you know who cursed you?"

Morrighan had been disloyal to her husband...Dagda had exacted his revenge. "Yes," she said.

He frowned. Thought. Adjusted his glasses. "We don't have incontrovertible proof, so for clarity sake, it's probably better to say you suspect."

This wasn't science. Did they really *need* incontrovertible proof? She didn't think so, but she nodded. "I am ninety percent sure," she amended.

"Do you know *why* you are cursed?" Jamie continued. "Or why the family is cursed?"

"Betrayal," she said without hesitation.

Jamie's eyes scanned the open pages. One fingertip moved over the words. "Okay, what about the effects of the curse."

"Death during childbirth for the women and death at sea for the men."

"Right." Jamie turned the page. "Next is about reflecting. It suggests sending the curse back to the one who cast it."

"Back to Dagda? He's dead, so that's not going to work," Pippin said. Already, she felt a sense of defeat pressing down on her. It had seemed farfetched in the first place. Now she felt more doubt creeping in. None of this might work in the end.

"Right. Even if we could find the cauldron, returning it to *Brú na Bóinne* before Cora gives birth is a long-shot. However, we have to try everything we can." He flipped forward a few pages. "The next step is to use a breaking spell."

Pippin cupped her hand at her forehead. "I'm not a witch."

"You have Morrighan's blood in you, Pippin," Jamie said, "so you are, in a way. Your bibliomancy...that's a divination. Maybe it's not modern witchcraft, but it's a *power* you have."

She turned on her heel and paced around the kitchen. "That doesn't mean I know how to cast a spell. I'm not Hermione!"

Jamie scanned the page and gave a little shake of his head. "I don't think any of these will work," he said.

Pippin came back to the table. "What does it say?"

"Simple things like go to a natural source of living water. A river, the ocean, a lake."

"Grey and I did that in Nags Head," Pippin said, recalling the desperate night they'd tried to offer the hilt of the sword they'd found at the inn back to Lir only to have it hurled right back out and onto the beach. "Still cursed."

"Next suggestion. Burn a bay leaf, first at dawn, then at sunset."

"Like smudging with sage?"

Jamie nodded. "Exactly. Let the smoke waft over you, then let the ashes blow away in the wind."

Pippin couldn't imagine that this simple act would break the two-thousand-year-old curse. "What else?"

"Use selenite—"

"Which is...?" she asked.

He traced his finger down the page until he found a footnote. "It's a crystal with gypsum in it. You're supposed to use it to cleanse the energy field around you."

"And that'll break the curse?"

"Soak in an epsom salt bath—"

"No."

"Use water infused with special herbs to clean your house—"

"No."

"Then throw the water out the back door."

She pressed her hands to either side of her head, clawing her fingers into her scalp. "No, no, no! None of this is going to work."

He squeezed her arm. "It's okay, Pip. We're going to figure it out."

She looked down at the book. "Does it say anything else?"

"The last step is to use brute force."

"Oh my God." She spun around and paced again. She had a vision of Professor Dumbledore touching the tip of his wand to Harry Potter's temple, then slowly drawing out his thoughts and memories in a ribbon-like stream. She chased the image away. That was fiction. This was life. *Her* life. "Brute force. What does that even mean?"

Jamie started to read, listing the necessary tools: air drying clay; water warmed by the noonday sun; paper and red ink; a bay leaf; a black candle; a ceramic bowl or some other fireproof container; a hammer; a carving tool.

As crazy as it sounded, it actually felt more tangible than the other options. "Do you think it's possible this could work?"

"No idea. Maybe it's worth a try?" he said.

She didn't know what other option they had. "Grey has to be part of it."

"And Lily and Cora," Jamie said. "At least I think they'd need to be there since they're cursed too."

Pippin nodded. "Yes. I agree." And Hugh, she thought, but he was as unpredictable as the wind. He appeared unexpectedly, and disappeared without a trace. If she couldn't find him, she'd have to trust that the whole thing would work without him. After all, they were going to attempt to break the curse against the entire family...against *all* the descendants of Morrighan and Titus. He'd benefit whether he was there or not.

She found her phone in her purse and sent a group text to her brother and cousins telling them what she and Jamie had found, asking them to meet at Sea Captain's Inn the next evening to fill them in and get started on their plan. That gave her enough time to find air drying clay, bay leaves, warm up some water—even though it was December and the sun wouldn't really be able to do the job sufficiently, and gather the other tools.

Grey replied to her text with: sounds hokie.

She couldn't disagree.

Mathilda's voice bellowing through the house, followed

by her pounding footsteps. "Daddy, Dad, Dad, Dad!"

Pippin closed the book and slipped it into her bag as Mathilda bounded into the kitchen. Jamie patted the air with his hands. "Whoa, squirt. You're way too loud."

Sasha was on Mathilda's heels. She reached for her, but Mathilda grabbed ahold of her dad and spun herself just out of reach. "Safe!" Mathilda panted. "Daddy's safe!"

Sasha skidded to a stop. She juked left, then right, trying to trick Mathilda, but Jamie's youngest had the advantage of her dad as a barrier. Jamie glanced at the analog clock hanging on one wall, then he put a hand on Sasha's shoulder to stop her back and forth movements. At the same time, he managed to find Mathilda's wrist, taking hold of it and gently pulling her front and center. "Okay, you two. Ruby's going to be here any second. Mathilda, help Sasha get her things together."

"But *daaaaddd*."

Mathilda drew out the word as only a six-year-old can but Jamie gave it right back. "*Tiiiillll*. It's five o'clock. Your mom's going to be here in an hour, and you still need a bath."

Mathilda stomped a rainbow Croc'd foot. She criss-crossed her arms, her hands grabbing opposite shoulders. "I don't wanna go with Mommy."

Jamie crouched down until he was eye to eye with his daughter. "Till, you'll have fun. She's taking you to the new Pixar movie. You've been wanting to see that."

Mathilda's grumpy expression softened. "Will she get us popcorn?"

"I'm sure she will," he said. He ruffled her hair as he stood. "Now, go help Sasha."

Sasha had been standing there, quietly watching Mathilda and her dad and wearing a heavy frown. Pippin always wondered what went through the little girl's head. She had uttered only a few words since the accident and she kept the worn penguin with her at all times ever since. It was her safety blanket in the form of a stuffed toy.

Mathilda disappeared, returning a few seconds later with Sasha's red coat and a bag. The coat was lightweight—warm enough for island winters without being overbearing. Sasha handed Mathilda her penguin, trading it for the coat. She slipped into it and took back the doll just as there was a knock on the door.

"Perfect timing," Pippin said to Sasha. "I bet that's your Aunt Ruby right now."

Jamie strode from the kitchen to the family room. He threw open the front door, but it wasn't Ruby standing there. It was Grey. The second Sasha spotted him, her face lit up, as if a bulb inside her little body had clicked on. She was a-glow. "Waddle!" she said, her smile wide and bright.

Grey scooped Sasha up into his arms. She flung her free arm around his neck, holding tight onto her doll with her other arm.

"What are you doing here?" Pippin asked.

"I was at Devil's Brew. Ruby wasn't feeling well, so I offered to come pick up Sasha."

"Is she sick?"

Grey frowned and shrugged. "A little stomach bug, she said."

Sasha's smile fell. "Auntie?"

"She's okay, baby," Grey reassured.

"And what's with Sasha calling you *waddle*?" Pippin said, circling back to Sasha's word for Grey.

"Ever since I found her penguin that night at the inn, she's called me that," he said, his lips quirking up. Pippin could tell he liked it. Once again, sadness washed over her.

With the curse solidly in place, he couldn't take the chance of becoming a father, only to doom his own child to the same fate from which the four Lanes currently suffered. But Grey would have made an excellent dad, just like Leo had been to them, and just like Jamie was to his girls.

Her resolve grew. They *had* to break the curse.

"See you tomorrow?" she asked.

He cocked a skeptical brow. "Is it gonna be like a séance, or something? I'm serious, it sounds ridiculous."

"Maybe, but we have to try everything. It's worth a try," she said, echoing what Jamie had said earlier. "It's a curse-breaking ritual."

"Mmm-hmm."

"Yeah," she said. In those two words, they communicated everything they needed to.

"Listen," he said, but he hesitated. Stopped. He gave his head a little shake. "Never mind."

"Everything okay?" she asked, the question excluding the obvious things that were definitely *not* okay, like the curse and their fate.

"Yeah, yeah. We can talk later." He waved, picked up the bag, and left with Sasha.

A minute later, Heidi came out of her bedroom, three books tucked under one arm.

Mathilda eyed her with a gaping mouth of utter disbelief. She spoke dramatically, emphasizing words as if she were stomping an invisible foot at the same time. "We're *going* to the *movies*, Heidi! We're getting *popcorn*! You don't *need* books." She swung her gaze to Jamie. "She doesn't *need* books, Daddy. We're going to the movies."

"It's fine, squirt. She can bring them if she wants to."

Heidi ignored Mathilda, instead looking at Pippin. "I chose our next book."

She was referring to the book club of two that Pippin and Heidi had formed. Pippin flashed a big smile for Heidi. It wasn't that she was excited about reading. Reading for pleasure was a difficult and slow task, but she loved that Heidi wanted to spend time with her. Her adoration of Jamie's girls was completely separate from her adoration of him. Heidi was a precocious and studious pre-teen. She'd taken to wearing her hair down, was taking time to curl it, and she dressed with more attention to her outfits than she had just months before. Jeans and t-shirts and blouses with buttons had been her standard for the first six months Pippin had known her, but adolescence had knocked on the door and Heidi had opened it wide. The subtle changes she was going through just underscored how young, colorful, and carefree Mathilda was by comparison. That made her even more annoying to Heidi. From Mathilda's frown, the feeling was mutual. She scurried off to take her bath, completely uninterested in whatever book Heidi had chosen. "Make sure you pack your jacket," Jamie called after her.

"Aye aye, Captain," she said, stopping long enough to throw up a salute, then she disappeared up the stairs.

"So, what're we going to read?" Pippin asked Heidi.

Heidi shuffled the books she carried before holding up a battered copy of *The Hobbit*.

Pippin started, a million thoughts running through her head at the same time. It felt serendipitous that this was the same book Moira had been reading. On top of that incredible coincidence, she and Grey were both named after Tolkien characters. Grey's namesake was Gandalf, and Pippin's was Peregrin Took, fondly known throughout Lord of the Rings as Pippin. Pippin had often thought Leo had gotten it wrong by naming her Peregrin. The name meant traveller, and that did not describe her at all. She was a homebody. She'd seen Sea Captain's Inn and fallen in love, and she hoped never to leave it or the island of Devil's Cove. Her parents' history started here, and that was something she was slowly uncovering. She'd be in one of the rooms and a memory would spark. There were moments when she could almost see Cassie and Leo in the shadows at the inn.

She'd been named after Peregrin Took, but she'd never read any of Tolkien's books. It was high time.

"Do you need a copy?" Heidi asked. "We don't have any at the store, but Dad can probably order you one."

"No need. I have my dad's copy," she said. And Moira's. "I'll start it right away."

"This one doesn't have Pippin in it," Heidi said, "but I thought the Lord of the Rings trilogy would be too much. A lot of people like it better than *The Hobbit*, though."

"What about you?" Pippin asked, sure that Heidi had an opinion.

She put her copy of *The Hobbit* back with the other books she still held and tucked them all back under her arm at her side. She chewed her lower lip for a few seconds before answering. "I like them both—*The Hobbit* and *LOTR*—for different reasons."

Pippin glanced at Jamie, who watched his daughter with a fascinated smile.

"*The Hobbit* is simple. It's joyful," Heidi said. "Did you know Tolkien wrote it for kids? Grown-ups like it, too, but it's really a kid's book. *Lord of the Rings* isn't. My teacher says that *LOTR*—that's what fans call it—has a lot more to do with war and power, but mostly death and immortality."

Pippin had a flash of her father's enthusiasm when she watched Heidi talk about the book. She remembered Leo growing animated when he described the reverse quest in the trilogy. "Frodo doesn't want treasure," her father had said. "Instead he wants to destroy what others thought was treasure—the One Ring. That is his quest, the reverse of what most others would do. Well, until he can't resist it anymore and he puts it on, but then Gollum bites it off his finger. But Sauron loses his power, so it's all good. But isn't that cool? A reverse quest?"

As a child, Pippin hadn't fully understood, but now she suddenly saw the parallel between Frodo trying to destroy the ring and her trying to break the curse. Hers wasn't a reverse quest, like the hobbit's was, but still... both the ring and the curse caused many souls to suffer, and both had the tendency to exert control over their bearers, and adversely affect their lives. They both had to stop that from continuing.

"We'll definitely need to read the trilogy," Heidi said, bringing Pippin back to the moment. "But *The Hobbit* is easier, so it shouldn't be too hard for you." Jamie frowned at her and Heidi hurried on. "I mean, it'll be easier since you're dyslexic, right? I didn't want to choose something too difficult."

"Heidi," Jamie scolded, but Pippin held up her hand. "It's okay. She's right." She looked at Heidi. "You're right. I mean, I've never been diagnosed, but I might be dyslexic. Maybe. Probably, even."

"So you don't need this copy of *The Hobbit*?" Heidi asked, lifting her shoulder to indicate the books under her arms again.

"Nope, I'm covered."

Pippin hurried off before Miranda McAdams, Jamie's ex-wife, turned up to pick up the girls. "See you tomorrow," she said, waving to Jamie from her Jeep.

He smiled. Nodded. "Definitely."

CHAPTER 17

"*A sister is both your mirror and your opposite.*"
~Elizabeth Fishel

PIPPIN SPENT the night tossing and turning, reviewing the steps they planned to take to break the curse. Together with Grey, Cora, and Lily, maybe they had a chance. If she envisioned it as working, it would work. She manifested, repeating it over and over. *It will work. We will break the curse. It will work.*

After serving breakfast to Brenda, Barbi, and Brittney Naples, and to Joelle and Zac, she took her car to run a few errands, looking for, but never spotting, Hugh. She stocked up on wine from Oak Barrel tasting room. She swung by the post office to collect her mail from her PO box, and picked up another couple of poinsettias to up the festive vibe of the inn. Finally, she bought clay and bay leaves.

Back on Rum Runner's Lane, she drove past Wenna striding down the sidewalk at a brisk pace, heading toward Main Street. She looked like Little Red Riding Hood, but in black. The hood shadowed her face. They hadn't spoken since Wenna's advice to Pippin on fate, which still rattled her. Could she change hers?

Pippin waved to her, but Wenna kept her head straight, focused on her brisk stride. Pippin pulled into her driveway to the right of the inn. The moment she stepped out of her car, Hattie Juniper Pickle called to her from across the street. Hattie stood on her porch with another woman whose hair —a mixture of fire-engine red and carrot orange—glowed, visible from afar like the beacon on one of the Outer Banks's famous lighthouses. Pippin looked left and right. Wenna was gone, enveloped by the thickening mist. The coast was clear so Pippin strode across the street and up the steps. Up close, she got a better look at the candy apple hair of the stranger. The front swept across her forehead like an ocean wave and the rest was pulled into a bun in back. Her lips were stained vermillion and, like Hattie—and Mathilda—, she wore Crocs on her feet.

"Dabba, this is Pippin." She swung out one arm dramatically. "Pippin, *this* is my sister."

Pippin did a double-take. For starters, she didn't know Hattie *had* a sister. And second, now that she was looking, the resemblance was...unmistakable. They hair color was different, but the bone structure, the smile, the height, and their fashion sense looked the same.

Hattie's sister gave a wide grin revealing a smudge of lipstick on her teeth. Sisters, indeed."Hattie's told me all about you."

Pippin almost spouted, "*Well, she's told me nothing about you.*" Instead she smiled right back at her and said, "Nice to meet you, em, Dabba was it?"

"She was a Flintstones fan," Hattie blurted with a chortle.

Dabba scoffed. "Hattie J, this girl is too young to know the Flintstones."

Hattie touched the cigarette tucked behind her ear. "It *is* an old cartoon. Fred Flintstone would say Yabba-Dabba-Doo. Deborah—" She hitched a thumb in her sister's direction. "That's her real name—Deborah. She went through a phase where she wanted us to call her Wilma. That's Fred's wife. She just loved Wilma. Look at her hair."

Pippin hadn't grown up watching the show, but she knew about the cartoon with its stone age setting and the romanticized life of the Flintstones and the Rubbles. She called up an image of Wilma as she looked at Dabba. "I can see it."

"We called her Yabba-Dabba-Doo growing up—" Hattie started.

"—But eventually everyone shortened to just Dabba," Dabba finished. "I've been called it ever since."

"As nicknames go, it's pretty cute," Pippin said.

Dabba mouth tugged down in an exaggerated nonchalant expression. "Works for me."

Pippin's cellphone rang. She fished it from her back pocket and saw Grey's name. She held up a finger. "It's my brother."

In unison, Hattie and Dabba waved her away. She cracked a smile. They operated like she and Grey did, finishing each other's sentences and doing the same actions. "Hey," she said, turning away from the Pickle sisters and hoping Grey wasn't backing out of the curse-breaking session.

"Hey Peevie," he said. He paused as if he was considering what to say. "Listen, I want to talk to you about something."

She didn't like the sound of that. Her mind flashed back

to when he'd told her he didn't believe in the curse. Surely he wasn't back to that. "You're coming over tonight, right?"

"Yeah, of course, but I have something to talk to you about before that."

"*Okay.*"

"Not over the phone. Can you come here?"

Her stomach clenched. "What's wrong? Just tell me."

"It's…" He hesitated. "Peevie, just come over."

They hung up and she turned back to Hattie and Dabba. "I have to go."

"An emergency with Grey?" Hattie asked. She swung her hand around, her unlit cigarette now dangling from from between two fingers. She ushered Dabba toward the steps. "Let's go."

"Wait," Pippin started, but Dabba slung a massive tote bag over her shoulder, and the sisters scurried past her and jogged down the porch steps.

"It's high time I met this Grey Hawthorne," Dabba said, throwing the words over her shoulder. "I need to put a face to a name."

"It's a good face," Hattie said, flashing a tooth-stained grin at Pippin. "Looks a lot like his dad, and you, my dear, look just like your mother."

Pippin had heard that before. People told her she had her mother's hair, though hers was more strawberry and Cassie's had been more copper. The same smile. The same Kelly green eyes. The same fair complexion. Grey had inherited their father's height, his dark hair, and his olive complexion. Hearing it as a child and teenager had been painful. Her eyes would prick with tears and her mind would go fuzzy. As an adult, it made her feel closer to her mother. Something Wenna said came back to her. People who lost a parent young often feared they would not live longer than the tragic year their mother or father died. Cassie had been twenty-nine years old when Cassie had become pregnant with Pippin and Grey's baby brother. She had been thirty when the curse took her from them.

Thirty loomed like a dark cloud for Pippin. She *did* hold that fear close to her chest, worrying that she wouldn't live into her third decade.

She pushed the thought away and quickly unloaded her shopping bags and wine from the Jeep. Sensing it would be futile, she didn't even try to talk Hattie and Dabba out of coming with her so she just took them along. Dabba rode shotgun and Hattie sat in the middle of the backseat.

"I could tell you some stories about this old place," Dabba said as they approached the dirt road leading to Grey's place.

Pippin turned to look at her. "Oh yeah? Like what?"

Dabba looked around, her eyes pinched. "We had country parties out here, don't you remember, Hattie J?"

Hattie rattled her head in a half shake, half nod. "Out here? You sure 'bout that?"

Dabba gave a wry smile, as if a specific memory had popped into her mind. "I'm a thousand percent sure."

Hattie stared out the window as Pippin drove toward the house. The glazed hollow blocks of the ancient silo that stood like a stalwart barrier at the corner of the barn dated back to the 1800s. The barn itself was the workshop, a rough living space, and a design showroom for Grey's custom woodworking. When he had time, his plan was to renovate the farmhouse that stood off to one side of the property.

She pulled up to the barn and they piled out of the Jeep. Hattie and Dabba trailed behind in their matching Crocs and puffer jackets. Pippin knocked. Two seconds later, the door flung open and Grey stood there. His eyes were pinched with worry but shifted to confusion as he spotted the Pickle sisters behind her. He looked back at Pippin. She gave him a *sorry, I couldn't help it* look. "Grey, this is Hattie's sister, Dabba."

His brows drew together and she knew he wanted to ask about the name, but he just nodded. "Okay, then. Nice to meet you, Dabba. Hattie."

Dabba leaned toward Hattie. "Right you are, it's a good face."

Grey rubbed his chin with one hand, pretending he hadn't heard. Normally he would have smiled at that. Even flirted. The fact that he'd done neither sent another jolt of concern through Pippin. He stepped back and held the door open for them. One by one, they filed past him into the showroom. Grey had a few pieces of handcrafted furniture on display, as well as slabs of reclaimed wood countertops and mantels. Dabba peeled off from the group and wandered around, oooing and ahhing as she wove around the pieces, trailing her fingers on the polished wood.

Pippin knew Lily and Cora were safe, curled up on the couch in the great room of the inn. For a while, they wanted to believe that everything was normal. That Cora's baby would come and the curse would not rear its ugly head.

As the sisters wandered the showroom, Pippin pulled Grey aside. "What's wrong?"

He instinctively glanced toward the door that led to the workshop. A sign above it read: Employees Only.

The only employee was Kyron Washington. He had worked with Grey renovating the inn and Grey had hired him on the spot once he decided to open his own business. As if Grey had sent a silent summons, the door opened a crack. Pippin had expected to see Kyron. Instead, Ruby's niece Sasha scooted out. She headed straight for Grey and wrapped her arms around one of his legs. "Waddle," she said softly. Lovingly. His hand found her shoulder and he gave a little squeeze.

"Are you babysitting?" Pippin asked, but as she finished the question, Ruby appeared at the door looking sheepish. She was tall and slim and her hair was a riot of black coiled curls. She held them back with a headband. Sheepish was never a word Pippin would have used to describe her friend. Confident. Determined. Generous. Those were the words she associated with Ruby. So why was she looking so uncomfortable?

Even as she asked herself the question, a few things clicked into place, like the cogs of a machine. Grey comforting Sasha with her toy penguin. The little girl, still traumatized over losing her mother in a car accident and not speaking for months, glomming onto Grey. He'd carried Sasha to Ruby's car. Him picking up Sasha from Jamie's. She recalled Moira's sketches—one of Ruby handing a cup of coffee to Grey. Had something started between them?

Grey hadn't been dating the waitresses he usually did. He'd given *her* advice on love. He'd gone over to Devil's Brew when she'd gone to The Open Door. To see Ruby, she realized.

She looked from her brother to her friend. And smiled. "Are you two--" She wagged her finger between them... "an item?" she asked.

Ruby gave a shaky smile, but this was good! Pippin started forward, but stopped short at the worry painted on Ruby's face. Ruby strode straight to her and wrapped her arms around her. "I'm sorry, Pippin. I'm so sorry."

Pippin pushed Ruby back. Stared at her. The clenching in her gut tightened. "Sorry about what?" She looked at

Grey. Her voice rose, fear of what they might tell her taking root. "What's she sorry about, Grey?'

Ruby moved next to Grey on the other side of Sasha. She slid her arm around her niece's shoulders, crossing over Grey's.

"You're dating," Pippin said, but she was happy about that if it made them happy. That wasn't what this was about.

"For a while now," Ruby said.

Grey pulled Ruby and Sasha a little closer. He smiled down at Sasha. "Since that night on the deck at the inn."

Pippin remembered. The night with the penguin. That stuffed doll was Sasha's lifeline. Grey had been the one to find it, instantly bonding with Sasha. It looked like that bond had only grown stronger.

Pippin turned at the sound of crunching and chewing. Her jaw dropped. Hattie and Dabba had pulled up chairs at Grey's sample dining table. Popcorn spilled out from a bag laying flat on the table. The sisters sat side-by-side, each leaning onto the table on one elbow, munching on handfuls of popcorn. She had completely forgotten about them.

She started to ask where the popcorn came from but then she caught a glimpse of bright orange. Aha. Dabba's tote bag. What else was hidden in that thing?

Grey saw them, too, and shot Pippin a *what the hell* glance. She shrugged because all she could do was shake her head. She turned back, registering Grey's expression shift to a rueful smile. Ruby's hand on her stomach, her other arm around Sasha. Sasha's arm wrapped around his leg.

Pippin blinked. She had a flash of Cora with her hand resting on her bump. She looked at Ruby. At her hand. Oh no. No, no, no. Her knees felt weak. She stared. "You're not... you're pregnant?"

Their silence was enough of an answer. Fury rose in her. She wanted to lunge at Grey. To pound her fists against his chest. To shout: *Why? Why? Why?* Finding out Cora was pregnant had been like steam ready to explode from a pressure cooker. Her impending due date meant the clock was ticking. Ruby wasn't blood, but Pippin had no idea if carrying Grey's baby—a baby with cursed blood—put her in the line of fire. Right here, *this* was proof Wenna was wrong about changing fate. In a single moment, Ruby's future was altered, because her child with Grey would be cursed, and from their distraught expressions, she and Grey both knew the significance of that. It suddenly felt as if the minute hand was racing around the clock face double-time, increasing the weight of Pipin's burden—of *their* burden—ten-fold.

"How long?" she asked, barely keeping herself coolheaded.

"Close to ten weeks," Ruby said. Her voice quavered. It dropped to a whisper and she looked at Pippin as if she had all the answers. "This thing tonight. Will it stop the curse?"

Behind her, Pippin heard Dabba whisper to Hattie, "Curse?"

Hattie shushed her with a curt, "Later," and a crunch of popcorn.

"I don't know, Ruby," Pippin said, helplessly. Vexed. Angry. "I honestly have no idea."

Unfettered energy pulsed through her. She turned. Paced around the room to give herself time to think. Time to calm down. How could Grey be so careless? It was as if every time she turned around, he was willing to put himself at risk, tempting fate. Taunting the curse. But this time he'd put Ruby and his unborn child at risk. She whirled around.

Stalked over to him. Spoke through clenched teeth. "How, Greevie...how could you do this?"

He threw up his hands. Blew out a frustrated breath. "We were careful—"

"Clearly not careful enough—"

She stopped when Ruby said, "It was an accident. An honest to God accident."

Pippin clawed her fingers through her hair, yanking out the banana clip that had been holding it up. Her stomach roiled and she let out an embittered laugh. Accident or not, the consequences could be dire. "It doesn't matter, does it?" she said, because it had happened, and now the ticking clock had turned into a ticking bomb.

CHAPTER 18

"If there is magic on this planet, it is contained in water."
~Loren Eiseley

THEIR EFFORT TO break the curse had taken on new importance. They had to save Cora and her baby, but now they also had the weight of Grey's and Ruby's future to think about. The four of them—Pippin, Grey, Cora, and Lily—stood in The Burrow facing Jamie. Jamie had moved the small side table to the center of the room, placing a yellow ceramic bowl in the center of it. He stepped back, standing with his back to the built-in shelves, and opened the book on curses. "Ready?"

"Ready," Lily said at the same time Cora said, "So ready."

Pippin gave a nod and Grey pursed his lips. They were as ready as they'd ever be.

Jamie cleared his throat. "Okay, we're going to try to break the curse using brute force."

They all stared at Jamie as he read from the open page.

"It says the spell works better under a waxing or waning gibbous."

They all turned to look out the window but the moon was hidden from view. "We're heading for an unusual lunar experience," Lily said. "A waning crescent moon means time for reflection. A waxing moon signifies new opportunities. Optimism. That would be a good time to attempt something like..." She waved her arm around... "Like what we're going to attempt, but this is even better. On Christmas, we're going to have a bright Full Cold Moon," she said. She registered their bewilderment and clarified. "A Full Cold Moon happening just after the winter solstice is rare. Really rare."

Pippin didn't know if everything had to be perfect for this thing to work, but she was glad to have the symbolism of the moon in their favor, and a special lunar experience seemed serendipitous.

Jamie directed them to pass around the solar water. It hadn't become warm from the sun, but it was the best they could do. "Anoint yourself with it," he said.

"Do you think it was in the sun long enough?" Cora asked. None of them could actually answer that question.

"I guess we'll see," Grey said.

"Pip, light the candle," Jamie said, moving on to the next step. As she struck a match and let the flame ignite the wick of the single tapered candle, Jamie handed them each a pencil and a slip of paper. "Now, write down how this curse has effected both you and the entire family."

"I don't think this little bit of paper is big enough for that," Pippin said. "I need more."

Lily held out her hand. "Me, too."

Jamie tore a sheet of paper into quarters, handing them each one, trading them for the small strips. They each found a spot in the cramped room and started writing. The words flowed from Pippin's mind to her hand.

The curse kills the women and men in my family. It killed my mother, Cassandra. It almost took Grey. It means I can never have children. It means Grey can never be a father without risking the lives of his children. It cost my father his life. Aunt Rose is gone. Maybe IT is the reason the Venatores formed and are hunting us. It has caused the death of too many people, even outside of my own family: Max Lawrence; Monique Baxter; Connell Foley. And Moira O'Quinn.

Pippin looked at Grey. At Cora. At Lily. They were all each other had. They were family.

"Done," Lily announced.

Cora held up her paper. "Me, too."

When Pippin and Grey were finished, Jamie handed them each a dried bay leaf. "Put that in the center of your paper and fold it up," he instructed, then went back to the book. "Okay, now you need to light the paper and let it burn."

Grey took the matchbook, The Brewery's logo emblazoned on it, and ripped off a match. He pressed his thumb against the head and then dragged it across the dark strip on the matchbook. It sparked, then a small flame ignited. He held the burning match to the corner of the paper until it caught, then dropped the flame into the bowl.

He passed the matchbook to Cora, then Lily. They each lit their folded paper, letting them burn alongside Grey's. Pippin was last. She struck a match and held it so the flame licked the paper until it ignited. She held it up, watching her notes about the curse burn with the bayleaf. Finally she dropped it into the bowl, adding it to the smoking pages written by her brother and cousins.

The five of them stood around the table, watching the last of it burn. Waiting for the ashes to finish smoldering. They stood in limbo until the ashes were cool enough to handle. "Now what?" Grey asked.

Jamie went back to the book. "You each take a piece of clay—big enough to mold and inscribe," he said, nodding toward the small piles Pippin had put on one of the bookshelves. They each took a mound then returned to the ceramic bowl atop the table. "Now each of you anoint the clay with a drop of the solar water, then mix in some of the ashes."

They followed Jamie's directions, dividing the ashes into four sections then scooping them out and folding them into the clay. Pippin flattened the clay between her palms. She then folded it in half, worked the clay with her fingers, then folded it in half again, as if she were kneading bread dough. Finally, it was mixed enough and she mashed it into a ball. She rolled the clay between her hands, smoothing it out. Following Jamie's instructions, she pressed it into a disc.

"I hope these work," Jamie said as he picked up the four sharp-tipped wooden skewers he'd brought with him, giving one to each of them. "You need to inscribe these words into your clay: **No more befouled, again unbound, again unbidden**."

He repeated the phrase. Pippin dug the pointed end of the wooden skewer into the clay, carefully printing the words just as Jamie had read them. Once they had each finished, he instructed them to turn it over. "Now you're supposed to draw something that represents the curse."

"Like what, a coffin?" Cora said wryly.

"A gravestone?" Lily said, her own voice mocking, as well.

"A boat," Grey said.

"Hey." Pippin looked at each of them in turn. "This is serious."

"I don't know about this." Cora looked skeptical. "Seems a little *Practical Magic* to me."

"I love that movie," Lily gushed.

Pippin had never read the Alice Hoffman book, but she'd seen the movie and Lily had the bohemian flare of Gillian Owens. "We have to believe," she said.

"It can be a sigil, like the fleur de lis on the coins," Jamie continued, referring to the ancient coins their grandfather had disguised, "or it says it can just be a doodle. Once that's done, you have to let them dry, then set them outside in the sun. After that, you carry them with you."

"And that's it? The curse is broken?" Grey asked, his brows pinched together.

"They're supposed to absorb the energy of the curse. Then, when the moon either waxes or wanes crescent, you're supposed to take it and smash it to pieces."

"Rendering the curse useless," Lily said, nodding. "It makes sense."

Lily practiced taro and believed whole-heartedly in old magic. To Pippin, this kind of magic felt different than the curse, though. She didn't want to mirror Grey's skepticism. She felt it rising and shoved it back down, away from her conscious mind.

They fell silent as they used the skewers to draw on the backside of their clay discs. Pippin drew a design of a circle filled with interlocking curved lines. "It's a Celtic symbol of Tuatha dé Danann," she said when she was done. "Or, it's supposed to be." To her it looked to be a bit of a mess, but it's the best she could do with a disc of clay that was just two inches in diameter.

"I drew a sword," Grey said.

"I did a cauldron." Lily held hers up. "Like Dagda's."

They all looked to Cora to see what she'd drawn. "It's a raven," she said. She turned to Lily. "Remember that raven that hung out by the cemetery when we were little?"

Lily's eyes grew big. "I do! It used to perch on the gravestones. I used to think it was the cemetery's guardian."

"They're all buried there," Cora said. "The women, anyway. Rose is. Our grandmother, Annabel. Our great-great grandmother, Emily, and our great-great Aunt Ruth." Her voice caught in her throat. Her hand found her bump. She lay her palm against it. When she looked up again at Lily, then at Grey and Pippin, her eyes had turned glassy. "I don't want to die," she whispered.

In an instant, Lily was by Cora's side. She wrapped her arms around her, her hands rubbing Cora's back in soothing circles. "You're not going to die," Lily said. "You're not. We're not going to let that happen."

Cora's fractured breaths grew calmer. She spoke into Lily's shoulder, her voice muffled, but audible. "I'm not going to die. I am *not* going to die."

Pippin murmured the words, as if they were an incantation. "You're not going to die, Cora. You are *not* going to die. We're going to destroy this thing once and for all."

CHAPTER 19

"In our obscurity - in all this vastness - there is no hint that help will come from elsewhere to save us from ourselves. It is up to us."
~Carl Sagan

After a busy morning tending to the baking and tidying and merry-making with the inn's guests, Pippin's skin crawled. She had to get out. To think. "Go," Hazel said, clearly picking up on her mood and shooing her off. "I've got things handled here. Seriously, you're going to give me an aneurysm if you keep pacing like that."

Pippin threw a glance up the stairs, peering as if she could see through the walls and right into Lily's bunk room. She should wait for her cousin, she thought, just as Cora ambled out of Pippin's room, her blond curls haphazard, dark circles under her eyes.

"You, too, huh?" Pippin had asked.

"What?" Cora said mid-yawn.

"You look like you slept about as well as I did," Pippin said.

"Not for lack of trying." Cora raked her hand through her hair, making some of the curls stand on end. "I just keep having nightmares. I see my grave in the family cemetery, the raven watching over me."

That was all it took for the image to fill Pippin's mind, too. They talked. Reassured each other. Cora patted the pocket of her robe "I have it here," she whispered about her clay disc.

Pippin wore a light sweater. She put her hand against the pocket. "Me, too."

She convinced Cora to go back to bed. To get some rest while she still could. Then she resumed her pacing.

"Go!" Hazel's command brought Pippin back to the sounds of the kitchen—Sailor crunching on her kibble, the dishwasher running through its cycle, the caw of a bird outside the window, the bubbling of the water in the electric kettle. "I'll check on Lily," Hazel said, "and I'll keep an eye on Cora. You're a phone call away. Go have lunch with the professor."

Pippin called Jamie. Twenty minutes later she was browsing the new releases at a rectangular table near the checkout counter while Jamie gave instructions to his mother. "Winds are kicking up. It might knock out the WiFi. If that happens, you can't process credit cards."

Erin knitted her brows together. "And if that happens, love, what do I do?"

"Cash only," Jamie said.

"Not ideal, to be sure, but Mother Nature is Mother Nature," Erin said.

Pippin frowned to herself. Except when it's not. The visceral memory of Grey nearly drowning surfaced. She'd bet her life that wasn't Mother Nature, but that was already on the line. She shuddered, then felt Jamie's hand on her shoulder. "Hey. Are you okay?"

She shook away the memory of that night. "Yeah, yeah, I'm good." As good as she could be under the circumstances, anyway. "Ready?"

He looked at his mother. "You good?"

"Cyrus is upstairs and Noah is here." She smiled at the high school boy whose hair fell like a curtain in front of his face. He angled his head sideways, just enough so he could see Jamie. "We got it," he said.

Erin doubled down. "You two go have a good time. You certainly deserve it."

Guilt bubbled up inside Pippin. They were going to lunch at Shakespeare, a little place with big taste. With Heidi and Mathilda with their mother, it was just the two of them. Jamie slipped his arm around her as they ducked their heads and walked the two blocks to the restaurant. The wind was at their back, blowing in from beyond the barrier islands. They passed The Chocolatier, then Charcuterie. The latter was run by Colette de Maurin, a French woman from a family of cheesemongers who had fallen for an American in Europe. They'd come to the U.S. and opened the cheese shop, expanding the traditional definition of charcuterie to include fruits, nuts, and cheeses, rather than just meats.

Colette was in her mid-fifties and looked like she might have stepped out of pages of a classic Vogue magazine. She was chic and sophisticated—sort of an anomaly in a beachy town. People often said Colette had a certain *je ne sais quoi* about her, but to Pippin, it was obvious. She had style that transcended time. She stood in the threshold of Charcuterie peering into the sky. She wore a silk scarf tied around her head, holding back her wavy hair, looking even more French than normal, if that was possible. When she spotted them, she smiled and waved. "*Bonne après-midi!*" She pulled a cream wool jacket tighter against the cool breeze. "*Sauf pour le vent,*" she said, waving her hand around. Except for the wind, the gesture said.

Pippin had picked up a bit of French since meeting the cheesemonger. She returned the greeting with a simple, "*Bonjour,* Colette."

"*Bonjour, bonjour, mes chéris.* The wind, it is too strong," she said, her accent turning every syllable into something musical.

"Another storm's brewing," Jamie said.

"*Mais pas de pluie.*" She stretched her arm out, palm up, then looked to the cloudless cerulean sky again. "But no rain," she said. "I am coming to the bookshop tomorrow. With bells ringing?"

With bells ringing? She thought, then Jamie said, "You'll be there with bells on."

"Tell me the right way to say things," Colette had told them recently. "Otherwise, how will my English get better?"

"Yes." She tapped her head as if cementing the idiom into her gray matter. "We will be there...*mais*, no...I will be there with balls on—"

"Bells," Pippin said through a laugh. "You'll be there with bells on."

"Oh, but I know," she said. "I just wanted to make you smile. Every day I see you, you look so...mmm...*désespéré.*"

Pippin frowned. "Desperate?" she asked.

Colette shook her head. "No, no. Desperate is not quite right." She tilted her head to one side. "How do you say in English?" she mused. She looked up, as if the churning gray sky could give her the answer, and then it seemed to have because she snapped her fingers and looked back at them. "Forlorn."

Forlorn did seem to fit the way Pippin had been feeling. Each day that passed brought Cora's baby closer to being born. Truth be told, she was a little desperate, too.

Colette reached for one of Pippin's hands, cupping it between hers. "You have the gift of *bibliomancie*. You will do what must be done. Remember Nostradamus."

Colette had grown up in Provence, the same place the famous truth seer hailed from. Because of this, she'd known what bibliomancy was. Colette had become an instant friend and confidant. She already believed in the divination that, once the curse was broken, would vanish from Pippin's life. She would be sad about losing this gift, this one thing she shared with her mother, but if this was the sacrifice needed to free them all from what Dagda had done to them, then it was a sacrifice she was willing to make.

"Nostradamos," she mused, half under her breath.

Colette gave a succinct nod. "*Mais oui. Avec...*mmm...with your *bibliomancie*. The book told you, did it not?"

She recalled one passage from *Les Prophèties:*

Tomorrow at sunrise I shall no longer be here.

Pippin had interpreted that to mean that they had to work quickly. That time was running out, because the curse would take them all. But what if the 'I' in the sentence referred to the *curse,* and not to her? What if it was fore-telling the future, telling her that she would succeed in unloading the burden she and Grey and their cousins all carried heavy on their backs?

Not only them, she thought with a jolt. The revelation of Moira's and Hugh's familial connection meant there had to be others. There was a whole lost family line that suffered from the curse as they did.

"Ah, the wind!" Colette's voice faded into the wind.

"Go inside before you blow away," Pippin urged as Jamie took her hand.

"*Au revoir!*" Colette called after them as she ducked back inside her cheese shop.

Pippin and Jamie hurried the half block to Shakespeare. Inside, with the door closed behind them, the sound of the wind faded, replaced by traditional Christmas carols. The hostess showed them to a semi-private table. "Have you heard anything about Jed? Has Cora seen him again?" Jamie asked the moment the hostess left them with their menus.

"Not that I know of," she said.

A twenty-something man dressed in khakis and a white button-down strolled up to the table. A minute later, he strolled away again with their order committed to memory. She wondered if he did that parlor trick if he was serving more than two people, but the moment he was out of sight, he was out of mind. "I'm worried about Lily. If we can't...if something happens to Cora..." She trailed off, unable to finish her thoughts.

They spent the next ten minutes talking about business at The Open Door, the guests at the inn...about anything that was a distraction from the curse and looming danger, even if just for a little while. Their food was served and they tried to keep the conversation light. Being with Jamie was the only time she could manage that. He was beginning to feel like home to her. Whenever they were together, her burden lessened, and she felt supported, like a pier that is held up with beams and pilings.

A blur of red…or maybe pink…outside the restaurant's window caught Pippin's eye. She glanced up just as the eatery door flung open, the wind catching it and slamming it against the wall. A figure—a woman, Pippin thought—in a bright raincoat, face obscured by the hood pulled up over her head to protect against the rain and wind. She took a frenetic step inside.

Pippin did a double take. She knew that raincoat. She stared, watching as the figure's hand reached up to pull off the hood. Cora stood there, her lips and face pale despite the brisk air outside. It had done nothing to brighten her cheeks. Yesterday Pippin had thought Lily had seen a ghost. Now it looked as if Cora had. Oh God, were the Braxton Hicks contractions back? Or was she in labor? Pippin shot out of her chair, crossing the small restaurant in a few strides. She clasped Cora's shoulders. "Is it time?"

Cora's nostrils flared. Pippin could feel her body trembling under her hands, as if she were hooked to a vibrating machine that shook her from head to toe. Cora's gaze skittered this way and that, as if she were searching for something.

Pippin gave her cousin's shoulders a little shake. "Cora!"

Cora blinked. Brought her gaze to Pippin. "Lily's gone. She's gone again."

Pippin felt the earth shift on its axis. Cora's knees buckled, but Pippin kept her upright. Kept herself steady. The next second Jamie was beside them both, guiding Cora to their table, signaling to the waiter for another glass of water.

Pippin sat facing Cora. "What do you mean, she's gone?"

Cora put one hand on her belly. Her chin quivered as she spoke. "She's afraid. The baby's coming soon."

They all were. "Where'd she go?" Pippin demanded.

"Someone picked her up...took her..."

Pippin clasped Cora's hand. Squeezed. "What do you mean, took her? Who took her? Jed?"

"No. It wasn't Jed." A shudder coiled through her and her voice turned raspy. "His eyes..."

Pippin's stomach dropped. Hugh. *Aodh.*

"They were white. Clear. Transparent. I don't know how to describe them."

Jamie leaned forward. "Did Lily go willingly?"

Cora's eyes brimmed. Nodded.

Pippin couldn't speak. Couldn't fathom why Lily would have gone with Hugh. What could he want with her?

"Do you know where they went?" Jamie asked.

She choked back her tears. "She said she had a plan."

"A plan to..." Jamie prompted.

"To break the curse."

"Where?" Pippin asked. "Where did they go?"

The color drained from Cora's face and her voice became a distressed whisper. "To the marina."

CHAPTER 20

"*The bravest are surely those who have the clearest vision of what is before them, glory and danger alike, and yet notwithstanding, go out to meet it.*"
~Thucydides

OH GOD. To the marina. Panic rose in Pippin like a squall. If they really had gone to one of the marinas, then she knew what Lily was planning. She was ready and willing to dump everything and the kitchen sink into the ocean if it would save Cora from her fate.

Wenna's words came back to Pippin. *A person's destiny, Pippin, it is written.* But it wasn't.

It wasn't!

Pippin squeezed Cora's hand. "We'll find her."

Cora started to nod but stopped suddenly. Clutched her belly. Let out low moan.

Pippin froze, her fear from a moment ago back. "Are you okay?"

Cora closed her eyes and sucked in a breath through her

teeth. She slowly exhaled. Her eyelids fluttered open and she nodded. "It's okay. I'm okay." She pushed herself out of her chair. "Go. Please. Go find Lily. I need my sister."

Pippin looked at Jamie. He nodded. A silent communique. "We will," she said, and without another word, they tore out of the restaurant and down the street toward the parking lot near the bookshop where Jamie parked his car. They ran into the wind, the force of it slowing them down. Pippin felt as if she were trying to walk under water. Jamie grabbed her hand, pulling her forward.

They threw themselves into his car and he backed out of the parking spot. He slammed on the brakes and pounded his fist against the steering wheel. "Which marina?"

Pippin racked her brain. Hugh and Lily. Lily and Hugh. When did the man make contact with her cousin? How had he convinced her to go with him? How would they get onto the water to make whatever offering she was planning, because Pippin knew that *was* Lily's plan. And then it hit her. Jed. Jed had met Leo at the marina where their boats were moored. Jed had a boat. Lily had told Cora she'd been on his boat. "Devil's Cove Marina!"

The Outer Banks was home to a number of large marinas that housed fleets of charter vessels for inshore fishing, sound fishing, offshore fishing that took anglers twenty miles—and even farther—into the Atlantic. They offered wreck-diving trips and boat moorage.

Devil's Cove had only a handful of small marinas with the same services, but on a smaller scale. Leo had moored his boat at Devil's Cove Marina. He'd been friends with the dock master, had known everyone, and that was where he'd felt at home. That is where he'd met Jed Riordin, and that is where Jed's boat was probably still moored. So many boat owners left their keys on the boat. If Jed was one of them,

Lily may have seen where he stashed them. It was all they had to go on at that moment.

Jamie sped out of the parking lot, turning south on Main Street, passing the pier. What were Hugh and Lily planning? If they went out into the open water and tried to make an offering...the ocean...the curse...Lir..., it had almost taken her and Grey. It might take Lily, too. And Hugh. He was a descendant of Morrighan and Titus. Fated to be swallowed by the sea. Oh God, she thought her head might explode. "Hurry!" she shouted.

Jamie stepped on the gas. Her heart pounded in her chest, crackling like thunder. She worked to calm it as they flew past the random taco shop that had melt-in-your-mouth tortillas and the best crab tacos on the Eastern Seaboard. Past Marina Motel. Past surf shops. Past hole-in-the-wall restaurants.

They sped past Dolphin Marina, the biggest on-island marina with their small fleet of charter vessels. Finally, there was Devil's Cove Marina. The place was a ghost town in December. Boat owners used the cold months to do maintenance. Vessels had been lifted out of the water, dry-docked. In July and August, the place buzzed with people, but in December, it was as still as marsh water.

Jamie parked as close to the marina entrance as he could. The place was fifty years old. Half of it had been updated with new docks and pilings, wide berths that could fit two large boats each, and white dock boxes dotting the walkways. Boats were moored to the pier, tied to cleats mounted on the docks. White lighthouse shaped covers hid the electrical outlets. Homage to the Cape Hatteras and the other OBX lighthouses.

An old house with wide steps and a wraparound deck had been converted into the dock master's office. Salt water, wind, and hurricanes did plenty of damage to everything on the barrier islands, and the doddery building showed its age. She and Jamie bounded out of the car. Her eyes searched the marina, hoping against hope that she'd see Lily, but it was deserted.

The sound of someone else's tires squealing on the pavement cut through the wind. Pippin whirled around to see a truck careen into the parking lot. As it approached them, it veered to the right, slammed into park, and Grey jumped out. He spotted them. Raced to them.

"How did you—"

"Cora called me." He looked toward the marina and the no wake zone. "Any sign of them?"

"No," Pippin said.

They hurried from the parking lot to the dock. Pippin led the way to the older section of the marina, which showed its age with worn docks, narrower berths, and old pilings that sat low in the water. Leo had moored the fishing boat he'd named Cassandra here twenty years ago, before Bev and Mick, who owned the marina, had done the renovations.

The water rocked the moored boats. Pippin led the way to the slip her father had leased for so many years. If Jed still moored his boat at Devil's Cove Marina, it wasn't in this area; all the slips were occupied. She spun around, searching. Looking for any sign of people. Of life. Not a single person was in sight.

Grey grabbed ahold of Pippin's hand. "I hear a motor."

She listened, but only heard the lapping of the water. Grey cupped a hand around his ear and closed his eyes to focus on sound. Jamie and Pippin did the same. And then Grey jerked into motion again, barreling down the dock past the moored and dry-docked boats, heading in the direction of the rumbling motor and an area of the dock with a fuller view of the sound. He scanned the water. Pointed to flashing lights bobbing in the hazy distance. "There!"

The boat was too far away to see who was on board, but no one else was out boating in the cold, windy weather. It had to be Hugh and Lily.

Grey had turned and was stalking the dock, looking at the moored boats. He jumped on one of them, an old fishing boat, and searched around the captain's chair. A few seconds later, he leapt back onto the dock and moved two slips down to the next moored boat, this one a houseboat. Once again, he searched, and once again, he bounded back onto the dock.

Pippin watched him, a growing suspicion about what he was doing. "We can't take someone else's boat," she yelled as he disappeared into the cabin of the next boat.

"It's the only way we're going catch them," Jamie said.

Grey reappeared, holding his arm out, a keychain dangling from his fingers. "Let's go!"

He reached his arm out, grabbing Pippin's and propelled her from the edge of the dock onto the deck of the boat. The second Pippin's feet landed on the boat's deck, realization about what their plan, such as it was, hit her.

The near miss Pippin and Grey had had in Nags Head had been disastrous. She had thrown Titus's hilt into the water, only to watch it hurtle through the air back to the beach. The ocean water had churned into a frenzy, taking Grey under. It was a miracle they'd survived. The wind whipped around them, but Pippin didn't feel it. "Grey!" She yelled. Panicked. "You can't do this!"

"I have to, Peevie." He plunged the key into the ignition and cranked it, the motor sputtering to life. "She's with Hugh!"

The implication was clear. Hugh was a descendant. If the sea tried to swallow him, it could take Lily with it.

Jamie released the ropes from the cleats, then jumped onboard.

"Jamie can do it!" Pippin grabbed for the keys trying to wrench them from the ignition. Grey blocked her.

"I'm not experienced," Jamie shouted. "If we're going to stop them in time, he needs to drive the boat."

She opened her mouth to say that she would do it. She would drive the damn thing. Anything to get Grey away from the water. But the words wouldn't come out because Jamie was right. If they had any hope of stopping Lily and Hugh before something happened to them, Grey had to captain the boat.

CHAPTER 21

"Hazel's anxiety and the reason for it were soon known to all the rabbits and there was not one who did not realize what they were up against. There was nothing very startling in what he had said. He was simply the one—as a Chief Rabbit ought to be—through whom a strong feeling, latent throughout the warren, had come to the surface."
~Richard Adams, *Watership Down*

PIPPIN HEAVED the boat's seat cushions off, searching for life vests in the holds. She found them, snatching them out and throwing one to Jamie, slipping one on herself. She maneuvered her way to Grey. He was stone still, eyes forward, keeping the distant light in sight. He'd pushed the speed past the five mile an hour 'no wake zone' rule. A V-shaped wave angled out behind them, straining the ropes attached to the boats moored in their slips. Now, past the orange and white bobbing markers, he pushed the throttle forward, gaining speed, closing the distance between the two boats.

But Hugh and Lily were still far ahead of them, cruising

through the Intracoastal Waterway. Pippin shouted above the roar of the motor and the thundering inside her own head. "Do you think they're leaving the sounds?"

Grey answered without taking his eyes off the water. "Yes."

He pushed the throttle again. The motor drove the stern of the boat down and lifted the bow off the water. Jamie sat next to Pippin, stretching his arm over her shoulder, holding her. They both had their bodies turned to face forward. A thousand thoughts careened through her mind.

He touched her arm and she turned. His voice rose above the roar of the motor. "What do we do when we catch up to them?"

She'd had the same question. They weren't stunt people capable of leaping from one vessel to the other in a single bound. "Figure out how to get them to turn around, I guess," she said, but she didn't know how they were going to manage that.

They faced forward again. Pippin watched Grey. He was as comfortable in the captain's chair of this boat as he was in his workshop building something or gliding through a marsh on a kayak or holding a fishing pole. Her jaw clenched with the observation. He belonged on the water, whether or not she wanted it to be true.

"Coming up on them!" Grey yelled.

Pippin jumped up. "Lily!" She screamed at the top of her lungs but the wind whipped her voice away.

Grey beeped the horn as he steered their boat alongside Jed's, but far enough to avoid a collision. Finally, Lily spun around. Thank God she had on a lifejacket.

Hugh looked over, his clear eyes piercing her like lasers. Grey drew a finger across his neck.

Even from where she was, Pippin could see Hugh's jaw

tighten, but he nodded. At nearly the same time, they both lowered the throttle to idle. The pounding in Pippin's head stayed loud and clear.

Lily gripped the edge of Jed's boat, her voice raised above the wind and the two motors. "Did Cora send you?"

Pippin's gaze flicked to Grey's for a split second. He gave a single nod, telling her to take the lead. She turned to her cousin. "We can't be out here, Lily. None of us should be out here! We have to go back in."

Lily waved a finger between her and Hugh. "We have a plan. To break the curse." She held something tight in her fist. A thin leather cord hung down, swaying in the wind. Pippin stared. One of the Roman coins. Lily had gone to their safe deposit box and taken it out. What a mistake it had been to add her to the account. "If something happens to either of us and you need the coins, you'll be able to get them," she'd said to Lily. The idea that her cousin would take them out...wanted to hurl them into the ocean as an offering...it was ludicrous.

"Lily, it won't work!"

"It might!" she hollered. "It has to!"

"But it won't. They're Roman. Connected to *Titus,* but *not* to Dagda or Morrighan. Those coins won't break the curse. They mean nothing to the Tuatha dé Danann. To Dagda. We're *going* to save Cora—we will! But this..." She pointed to her clenched fist... "It won't work. We need to stick to our plan!" The boat lurched over a swell of seawater. She stumbled. Grabbed the edge of the boat.

"The wind's picking up," Grey yelled. Around them, the waves churned turbulently. Ominously. Grey's voice was calm but Pippin could see the concern carved into it. White-caps exploded violently all around them. For Grey...and for Hugh.

Fear for Grey—for them both...for them *all*—coiled inside her. "Come on, Lily. *We have to go!*"

Grey wasn't waiting. He kicked up the throttle.

Lily screamed. "I have to try! Cora—"

Their boat lurched on a wave, ripping the last word away. Lily stumbled. Hugh's arm shot out. He grabbed her arm, keeping her upright.

"Hugh," Pippin said. "The curse is on you, too. Being out here, it's too risky!"

The waves swelled. The water plowed against their boats, lifting them up, then dropping them fast, like a roller-coaster cresting the summit of its track, then suddenly falling, as if the bottom had dropped out. Pippin's stomach rocketed to her throat. The boat fell and they caught themselves. "Please! Lily!" she sobbed.

"We can't wait!" Jamie yelled.

The water swelled again, heaving the boats sideways. Time seemed to stop as a rogue wave slammed against Jed's boat, knocking Hugh and Lily off-balance. In a horrifying split second, they both went overboard. The howling wind buried Lily's and Pippin's screams.

Pippin rushed to the side of the boat as if she could catch Lily. Stop her from falling. "Nooo! Grey!"

"Take the wheel!" Grey yelled as he lunged across the boat. Jamie grabbed it, steadying the vessel. From the corner of her eye, she saw him searching the communication system. Grabbing the radio from the base station. Pressing a button and shouting into it, "Mayday, mayday!"

Pippin lost sight of Grey in the sea spray, but he reappeared a second later with a ring buoy, a length of rope attached to it. His hands flew as he wound the other end of the rope around one of the cleats on the upper edge of the boat's side. He looped his arm through the donut and the next second he hurled himself into the water. He swung his head this way and that, searching for Lily.

"There!" Pippin pointed to Grey's right where Lily rose and fell with the swell of the water. Grey swam in a one-handed crawl, towing the buoy. With every stroke, he inched closer, then was pulled back.

Lily cried for help. Over and over and over, her shrill voice was swept away on the wind.

"He's coming!" Pippin yelled. "Grey's coming!" Lily heli-coptered her arms to stay afloat. One hand was still clenched in a deathtrap around the coins. "Drop them, Lily! They don't matter!"

And then her head went under. Pippin stared. Couldn't breathe. She watched in horror, searching the spot for any sign of her cousin. "I don't see her!" she yelled to Grey. He swam with all the power he could muster. And then Lily reappeared, sputtering. Oh, thank God. She breathed again, and, finally, Grey reached her. He threw the ring over her head. Once she had slipped her arms through, he fought against the tumultuous waves, towing Lily toward the boat.

Jamie had moved it as close as he dared. "I can't see Hugh!" he hollered, putting the throttle back to idle.

Pippin couldn't take her eyes off Grey. Every second he stayed in the water he was a second closer to possible death. It was the same for Hugh, she knew, but she didn't dare look away from her brother.

It seemed to take a lifetime, but they finally made it to the boat. Jamie rushed to Pippin's side, both of them reaching down to grab Lily and the buoy. Grey held onto the rope. "Give me the ring!"

Lily bent over so Pippin could pry it off of her. She turned and threw it back into the water. Grey grabbed for it. Pippin and Jamie stretched for him, but instead of reaching for their arms, Grey flung himself back. "No! Grey! What are you doing?!"

Grey had looped his arm through the ring again and kicked his legs, propelling him to where Lily had been moments before. "Hu—! D—yo—e—hi?"

The cold and wind and waves ripped Grey's words away, but she knew what he was doing. He was searching for Hugh.

Jamie had stripped off his jacket and wrapped it around Lily, who had sunk to the floor, shivering from the biting cold of the Atlantic. Now he was back at the helm, scanning the water's surface, edging the throttle up to move closer to Grey. A few seconds later, he pointed at something bobbing in the water. A head. "There!"

Grey looked at Jamie. Followed his arm to where he pointed. Took off swimming that one-armed crawl. He moved slower than before, his energy depleted by the frigid water. Oh God, oh God, oh God. Panic flared through her. How long could he stay in the water before hypothermia set in?

She kept her attention on Grey, afraid to look away and lose sight of him.

"I can't see him!" Jamie yelled.

Lily crawled to the bench where Pippin perched on her knees. Clawed her way up and searched the water. Her lips were blue. Her skin pale. Her voice quivered as she spoke. "The curse..."

Another wave of panic surged through Pippin. Had the sea swallowed Hugh? Tension coiled inside her. Grey had to get out of the water and into the safety of the boat.

She yelled to him, but he kept swimming. Jamie brought the vessel around. If Hugh was still above water, he was somewhere in between the boat and Grey. Her eyes were blurry with fatigue, staring into the dark vastness of the ocean, searching for a bobbing head like a needle in a haystack.

Lily shrieked and pointed. "There! He's there! To your left, Grey. Go left!"

Grey turned his head and Pippin's stomach turned hollow with fear. His lips were bluer than Lily's, his face paler. She sobbed his name, willing him to hear her. To listen. To come back to the boat.

But he kept swimming. And then suddenly he was there, and Hugh was there, barely keeping his head up, the choppy water beating him down. Grey caught Hugh's arm. Helped him hold onto the ring. And then they kicked and crawled and kicked and crawled. Jamie edged closer and then Pippin and Lily and Jamie were pulling on the rope, hauling them out of the water, into the boat. They collapsed on the floor, waterlogged and beaten down. The second they were in, Jamie was back at the helm. Throwing up the throttle and leaving Jed's boat behind, they sped back to the marina and, hopefully, safety.

CHAPTER 22

ithout a family, man, alone in the world, trembles with the cold."
~Andre Maurois

IT TOOK a solid twenty-four hours for the disquiet in Pippin's soul to dissipate. Hugh was at the hospital in Nags Head. Lily had withdrawn to herself, looking broken. Her plan had failed. Cora lay on her side on one of the inn's couches, staring at the lights on the Christmas tree, her hand on her bump.

Grey and Pippin had avoided the subject of Ruby's pregnancy. Focusing on Cora's was urgent enough. They'd spent the last hour in The Burrow going through their father's books for what felt like the billionth time. They'd come up empty. Outside the window, the crow cawed, swooping in and out of view.

"What about the stones?" Grey asked. "Did you ask Jamie about them?"

With everything else that had been going on, she hadn't had a chance. "I'll do it right now," she said.

They descended the narrow staircase and pushed through the secret doorway into Pippin's bedroom where Cora had left the bed unmade and pieces of clothing draped over the back of a chair. She went straight to her closet. The old safe sat on a shelf, purchased well before the 2000s, plainly visible. They hadn't known of its existence until Grey had discovered it hidden behind sheetrock. It had taken a solid month of spinning the dial and trying different combinations of numbers before Pippin had discovered a clue. Leo had written a series of numbers and symbols on the flyleaf of a copy of *Treasure Island*. The number 73 was the first *aha*. Pippin and Grey were both seventy-three seconds apart. Eventually, they'd figured out the correct order of the numbers and had opened the safe. It had held—and still did—a collection of old photos of their family before Cassie had died. Now, it also held the three stones found in Edgar's boat and Leo's water-damaged journal.

She removed the drawstring bag. The guests were all out doing their holiday activities so she and Grey left the inn in Hazel's capable hands, and went to see Jamie. Pippin almost always preferred to walk or ride her bike. The weather was still on an upward swing. She rode in Grey's truck so she could walk back to the inn. But instead of stopping in front of the store to drop her off, he pulled into the parking lot. "I might as well hear what your boyfriend has to say."

Pippin could feel a flush creep up from her chest to her cheeks. "He's not my boyfriend."

"I know, you don't want to put a label on it," Grey said, managing to crack a grin despite their near death experience the day before. "I understand completely. It's easier that way."

"First of all, that's not it at all," Pippin said. "And second, what do you mean, it's easier that way? You got my friend pregnant. Are you putting a label on *that*, or is Ruby just another one of your commitment-phobic flings?"

He frowned, but threw his hands up. "I deserve that," he said, "but that's not how it is."

He did deserve it. One hundred percent. Having more than a casual one-night-stand with local waitresses or tourists was as far as Grey ever went. But then he surprised her. "I care about her, Peevie," he said, the glint in his stormy gray-green eyes communicating his sincerity.

"I'm glad to hear it," she said, unable to keep a sliver of skepticism out of her voice.

"Yeah, well you *sound* glad to hear it."

She looked at him. "Of course I am. I just...I don't want you to break Ruby's heart by making her a single mother," she said, her mind flashing to Grey. He might have lost his life then and there. "If she makes you happy, that's great. But Greevie, her being pregnant...? If we don't succeed in breaking the curse, then her baby...*your* baby...will carry it, too."

"You think I don't know that?" he snapped. "We weren't being careless. It wasn't supposed to happen. The takeaway here is that nothing is foolproof."

She didn't want to know the details. The end result was all that mattered. Right now, they had to wait for the Full Cold Moon just after the winter solstice in order to finish what they'd started. The whole thing felt too ambiguous... too disconnected from the Tuatha dé Danann—to actually work. It wasn't as if there was information out there on how to break an Irish curse from the ancient deities. All they had was myths and hope.

Grey threw the truck into park. They started toward the

bookshop, in stride together. "What about you and Jamie?" he asked.

"What about us?" Was there even an 'us'?

"Everyone sees the way you look at each other," Grey said. "And I know what you're going to say. That you can't have kids and can't risk your heart because of that. But love is love."

She cocked a brow at him. "Maybe it is, but I'm not willing to take that risk yet," she said. For her, becoming pregnant was a much greater risk than it was for Ruby.

"So you can't have kids," he said, completely avoiding talking about the fact that he was now going to have one. "But he already has his girls so there you go. Instant family."

Whoa. He was getting ahead of himself. She didn't move at lightning speed like he and Ruby had. "We've been on a few dates," she said. "Plus, like you said, nothing is foolproof."

"You don't have to go out on *formal dates* for something to develop into a relationship," Grey said, making air quotes.

She gave him a look. "As if you know so much about that."

"I do now," he said, "but we're not talking about me anymore." He threw up his hands again. "But it's your life. I'm just telling you how I see it."

Just as they reached The Open Door, the front door of the bookshop flew open, crashing against the wall. Pippin and Grey stood back to let a group of customers exit, their arms laden with heavy bags of books. Grey stepped in after they cleared the threshold and held the door for Pippin. She held the drawstring bag close, protective of it. Discovering anything belonging to her family was like a gift. Even a bunch of stones.

Miss Havisham let out a mournful squall from where

she lounged on one of the wall shelves, her sleep disrupted by the last minute shoppers and the banging of the door.

"Pippin, love!" Erin waved from the checkout counter, elbow deep in complementary gift wrapping. They used plain brown rustic looking paper and red and green raffia string. Erin tied sprigs of greenery that looked like it had been cut from the loblolly trees scattered around the island.

As they passed Miss Havisham, Pippin got a strong sense that the longhaired gray cat thought she owned the place. She eyed the royal feline, whose eyes were closed again. Was she really already asleep again, or just playing possum? The cat's nose twitched, but she didn't move. She was the queen of the bookshop, that's all that mattered.

Pippin glanced around, but there was no sign of Jamie. "He's upstairs with Cyrus," Erin said, anticipating the question with a wink. "He'll be back down in a jiffy." She finished wrapping the book she'd been working on and handed it to a silver-haired gentleman. "There you go, Jerry," she said, flashing him a bit of a coquettish smile. "Come back soon."

The man—Jerry—smiled back and gave a little flick of his brows. "Don't you worry, I will." He left, tossing a parting smile back at Erin before he let the door close behind him.

"He looks smitten," Pippin said.

A splash of red spread over Erin's cheeks. "I could do worse," she said.

"Erin! You're a catch! Don't you dare sell yourself short." Pippin glanced over her shoulder toward the door. "He is cute though. A silver fox."

The blush on Erin's face deepened. "I'm almost sixty," she said.

Grey leaned his elbow on the counter. "You can fall in love at any age and with anyone," he said.

Pippin turned to stare at him. First his new relationship

with Ruby, then his pep talk about her budding relationship with Jamie, and now this. "When did you become such a romantic?"

He shrugged. "It's true, isn't it? We can't let arbitrary rules stop us from living."

So this was about the curse and how it stifled him. When Hugh and Lily had headed out to sea, they had all reacted, dismissing the possible consequences. It was a miracle any of them had survived, especially Grey and Hugh. Now she worried that her brother would become emboldened after being on the sea twice and surviving. That he'd weigh the risk verses the reward, and would take his chances. Her skin turned to gooseflesh. She couldn't think about that. Couldn't be distracted by *what ifs*.

Erin saved her from having to react. She looked at the drawstring bag. "What do ya have there, love?"

Pippin set the bag down and worked the string until she could reach in and take out the smooth stones. She laid them on the counter.

Erin peered at them. "Stones?"

Pippin and Grey nodded. "We found them on our grandfather's boat," Grey said. "Thought your son might have a thought about them."

CHAPTER 23

The raven ravenous
Among corpses of men
Affliction and outcry
And war everlasting
Raging over Cúailgne
Death of sons
Death of kinsmen
Death! Death!

~Morrighan's Prophecy of the coming war (Táin Bó Cúailgne-The Cattle Raid of Cooley)

JAMIE and his grandfather had returned to the shop. Now they stood around the checkout counter, off to the side, with Noah manning the register.

"This is the strange thing. They were hidden away in a secret space on the boat Grey's refinishing," Pippin said, explaining the stones to them.

"Which also happens to be the boat your grandfather Edgar built," Cyrus said thoughtfully. He was a dapper gentlemen who favored grays and blacks and whites, collared three-quarter zip sweaters, and he kept his white hair neatly combed back. The twinkle in his eyes was ever-present and Pippin had come to care about him. Deeply.

"How'd you find it?" Erin asked, her Irish accent lilting her words. "The boat, I mean."

"Our father did, actually," Grey said. "He wrote about it in one of his old journals. I tracked it down."

Erin turned to Grey. "You are sure about its history?" Erin asked him.

"As sure as I can be. We found two old photographs. One of our grandfather standing in front of the same boat—The Blessed Siobhan. He named it after *his* grandmother, Siobhan O'Quinn. There was another photo of our great-great-grandparents, Artemis and Siobhan, on a huge rock platform in front of a stone cross."

Jamie's eyes narrowed. "How big of a cross?"

Pippin spread her arms wide. "Huge. Like, really huge."

Jamie and Erin looked at each other. "Tory Island?" Erin said quietly, and Jamie nodded.

"It could be the Tau Cross," he said.

"I'll bite," Grey said. "What's the Tau Cross?"

"It's a massive stone cross that dates back to the 12th century," Jamie said. "There are actually two. One is on Tory Island. The other one is in Kilnaboy in County Clare. People there think the crosses have magical, protective powers."

"Why would they think that?" Grey asked.

"Because there have been people who have tried to destroy them. It's impossible. They've been standing for centuries."

A giant cross. That image teased a memory somewhere in Pippin's mind, and then it came to her. Moira's notebook. There was a sketch of what looked like a stone cross on a huge platform. She hadn't connected it to the old photo of her great-great-grandparents. "What's so special about Tory Island and the Tau Cross?" she asked.

"A Cromwellian soldier tried to take the cross down," Erin said. "He used his sword but he couldn't do it. It was like the cross was invincible."

"Right. So the fishermen on Tory have always thought it would protect them. Most islanders are fishermen, or they work on the oil rigs in the North Atlantic. They pray to the Tau Cross before going out on their ships."

"It greets you as you come to the island, standing tall over the pier," Erin said. Her brogue thickened as she continued the tale.

"Okay, so the photo is of Artemis and Siobhan on Tory Island," Pippin said. A very pregnant Siobhan, along with Ruth and Trevor as toddlers.

Once again, Jamie and his mother looked at one another. Erin looked at the stones from Edgar's boat. "The cursing stones," Erin said.

There was something about the name of the island that tickled the edges of Pippin's brain. Jamie disappeared down the hallway, returning a minute later carrying his laptop open on one hand, typing with the other.

Pippin and Grey stared at them. "What are cursing stones?" Pippin asked.

"*The* Cursing Stones," Erin corrected. "They were hidden on the boat? Very peculiar, that." It was undeniably peculiar. "Three stones," Erin muttered again. "Three stones. May I?"

Pippin placed them in her outstretched hands. Each was twice the size of an egg, but flatter. Erin cradled them as if they were baby chicks.

"Tory," Erin muttered, and then she looked at Pippin. "It

means 'steep rocky heights'." She leaned against the counter. "It is an interesting place, to be sure. You can only get there by ferry. And if the seas are rough, in the winter, only by helicopter. You won't catch me flying in one of those beasts. Do you know Irish history?" she asked Pippin as she rearranged the stones in her hands.

"I've learned a lot about the Tuatha dé Danann. And Jamie's told me where he got his degrees, in Galway and Maynooth." She pictured a thousand shades of green painting the rolling hills and vales of County Kildare. She had Irish roots, but hadn't been to the country. Some day.

Erin O'Donnell was born and raised there. If her lilt didn't convey it, her storytelling did. "The Tuatha dé Danann. Yes, yes. But about Tory. There was a great battle there. With the Fomorians. Jamie can tell you the details better than I can. Jamie, love?"

Jamie looked up from his computer. "The Fomorians are supernatural and enemies of Tuatha dé Danann. History depicts them as monsters. Hostile and violent. They held Conand's Tower on the island as their fortress, but they were beaten down by the Nemedians. Short-lived, but important. The island was home to Balor, the Fomorian king."

"We Irish, we love our legends," Erin said. For a moment, she looked bemused. "Well, maybe not legends exactly, right? It all seems to be more real than we ever understood, doesn't it?"

It did. Erin had been there when they'd discovered Seamus O'Dulany's book. When they'd realized that Morrighan had birthed twins. According to Pippin's own history, Irish mythology was alive and kicking.

"There's a story about Tory. About a shipwreck in the 1880s," Erin said.

"1884," Jamie said. "The HMS Wasp. It was a Royal Navy ship."

The name rang a bell. It took a moment before Pippin could place why. Moira's notes. She'd written HMS Wasp. She'd put so many pieces of the puzzle together.

"Right. The story is that the islanders hadn't paid their rent. The ship came to deal with it. With them."

"What does that mean, to deal with them?" Pippin asked.

"Eviction," Jamie said.

Erin continued. "Some bailiffs were on the ship. And yes, they were sent to evict the people who were behind on payment. Which was actually the whole of the island. Well, the ship, it never did arrive. No one knows what for sure really happened, but most believe that the senior officers were asleep. The junior crewman, they were inexperienced. Instead of sailing around the island like they were supposed to do, they tried to maneuver between the island and the mainland. *And* they had shut down the boilers. No steam power meant they could only use their sails. And that meant they couldn't navigate through the rocky coast. You should see pictures of the place. The rocks jut out of the ocean like Stonehenge. It is a sight to behold. Rocks surround the island and in the middle of the night, the ship ran aground."

Pippin listened with rapt attention. There was no doubt where Jamie got his love of Irish history from. His mother was a fount of knowledge. "It sank?" Pippin asked, eager with interest.

"Oh yes," Erin said. "And fast, too. They say that within thirty minutes, only the mastheads could be seen above water. Just a handful of crewman managed to survive by climbing the rigging."

"What does this have to do with the stones?" Grey asked, nodding his head at Erin's hands.

"Ah, now this…this is interesting. It is about the famous *Cloch na Mallacht* at the north end of the island."

Those Irish words were so hard to pronounce. Pippin didn't even try to repeat what Erin had said. "What does that mean?"

Erin looked up at Jamie. He'd set his computer down on the checkout counter and leaned back, arms folded. His dark hair curled up at the ends. His button-up shirt, open with a t-shirt underneath and his wire-rimmed glasses, made him look like a professor. Which he'd actually been. That was something Pippin recently learned. This man. They were so completely opposite, but at the same time, perfectly matched.

He cleared his throat before launching into the next bit of the history lesson. "*Cloch na Mallacht* is a bullán—or ballaun. That's a large stone that has a depression in it. People thought the rainwater collected in a bullán had healing properties. That it was magical. And sometimes a bullán would hold smaller stones like those. St. Brigit's Stone in County Cavan, for example. Even now it has its curse stones." He nodded toward the three stones his mother still held. "As the story goes, there are two bulláns on Tory. One next to the lighthouse, and the other near the ruins of an old church. The Church of Seven, named for seven of the crew members from the wreck of the HMS Wasp who were buried there. Six were men. One was a woman. The seven deceased were laid to rest in a single grave. At daybreak, islanders found the body of a woman…a corpse…on top of the grave. The islanders were superstitious, to say the least."

Erin clucked her tongue agains the roof of her mouth

and took over the story. "Now, love," she said to Pippin. "This is Irish magic at work. They thought that she was thrown from the earth—from the grave—because she was not the wife of any of the men they'd buried. And not kin. As such, she refused to share their grave for eternity. The islanders dug her her own grave and buried her there, and there she stayed."

Grey stepped aside as a customer approached. Noah had stepped away from the counter to help a different customer so Erin passed the stones back to Pippin. She rang the customer up quickly, bagged her purchased books without offering to wrap them, and politely shooed her off to the door. Once they were alone again, she nodded at Jamie. "Go on, love."

Jamie pointed to Pippin's hands, now holding the three stones. "They're called the cursing stones. They date back to the New Stone Age—or the Neolithic period. They're connected to prehistoric art, similar to the cup-marked boulders found on Europe's Atlantic seaboard. That includes Ireland. There's a bullán—or ballaun—with a depression."

"Like a shallow bowl," Grey said.

"Yep. Exactly like a shallow bowl," Jamie said. "And smaller stones sit inside. Now Tory Island has a *King*." He made air quotes around the word. "He is unofficially elected by the people. Believe it or not, the tradition is still carried on today. Back to the shipwreck. People back then thought that the King of Tory used a cursing stone to make the HMS Wasp wreck."

Pippin moved the stones around in her hands. "So they have magic in them?"

"I guess it depends if you believe in magic," Jamie said. "Which I now do, by the way. You're living proof. So I'd say that, yes, if they're from Tory Island, they probably have magic in them."

Pippin thought back to the photo of Artemis and Siobhan in front of what was probably the Tau Cross. They had to have take the stones from the island. Passed them on to Trevor, and then to Edgar, just like the Roman coins had been passed on. She lifted her hands. "Specifically theses? They can be used to curse something?"

"Artemis and Siobhan must of thought so if they took them from Tory Island," Grey said, clearly coming to the same conclusion she had.

Noah was back behind the counter and a queue had formed. They waited while he rang up customers. Erin quickly gift wrapped a few of the purchases. After Noah wandered off to help another customer, they were alone again. The stones clacked as Pippin shuffled them. "How does it work?" she asked.

"That's what I was looking up," Jamie said, nodding to his closed laptop. "To curse someone, you perform the ritual of turning a small stone clockwise in the bullán."

Clockwise to curse. "What happens if you turn it counterclockwise?"

"It makes a blessing."

Pippin's thoughts turned and wove in her mind as she tried to piece together what this meant. Artemis and Siobhan had never figured out how to make the stones work. Nor had their daughter, Ruth, or their son, Trevor. Or Trevor's son, Edgar. So Edgar had hidden them away in the boat he built to keep them safe. Leo had tracked down the boat. Grey had bought it. And found the stones.

A charge went through her. Now it was up to them to figure out if they really had the power to break the curse, and if so, then how?

The shop was busy. Grey went to Devil's Brew to check on Ruby, and Erin went off to help a customer. Jamie walked her outside. He took her hand and pulled her close. "You're close, Pip," he said. "*We're* close."

They talked it through for a few more minutes, but the customers kept coming. "I better go," he said with a disappointed twist of his mouth. "I'd rather stay with you."

"I'd rather that, too," she said.

He dipped his head and kissed her. "The girls are with Miranda," he said. "I'll come over later?"

She was already counting the minutes. Grey was right. They didn't have to label it. And if they could break the curse, save Cora and her baby...save Grey's and Ruby's baby...then she and Jamie had a chance.

She turned to leave, but stopped, catching Jamie before he went back inside. "What do you know about Morrighan?"

He stopped and leaned against window frame. "She's a complicated figure. Some believed her to be a king maker and protector. Dagda is considered to be a great god. Kind and caring."

Which made it all the more puzzling that he cursed an entire bloodline. Everyone had a dark side, though. The question was what might push a person over the edge and into the abyss.

"She has several names. She was a shapeshifter and a prophet. Her name means great queen or phantom queen. Some believe she was also a triple goddess, but others disagree."

"A triple goddess?" Pippin asked.

"Maiden, mother, crone," he said. "The maiden is virginal. Innocent. The mother represents abundance and fertility. It's not about having children. It's more a metaphor for the growth and gaining of knowledge a woman experiences. And then there's the crone. She's seen as the hag and wise woman. She represents the dark of night. Death. If you connect it to the seasons, the maiden is early spring. Birth. The mother is spring and summer. And the crone is fall, leading to winter and the dying earth."

So Morrighan gave life, and ended life just like Dagda ended every life that had sprung from Titus's and Morrighan's lineage. Ultimately, though, it was *her* actions that wreaked havoc on every one of her descendants. She'd fallen in love with Titus and gotten pregnant with his children, setting in motion a chain of events and consequences that had lasted through two millennia.

CHAPTER 24

"*Divination is the quest to understand more about the past, present, and future. In other words, Tarot readings are an attempt to understand ourselves better and discover how we might live better in the future.*"
~Theresa Cheung

THE LIGHTS of the Christmas tree twinkled. If only death wasn't hanging over Cora so imminently, and if only the meaning of the stones wasn't so ambiguous, Pippin might have enjoyed the fact that it was Christmas Eve day. The guests had all checked out and the inn was closed for business through the New Year. Hazel was off until after the New Year. Without Lily and Cora, she would have been rattling around the old house like an aimless ghost with no one to haunt.

But she did have her cousins. Cora's bulging belly was a constant reminder of impending doom.

Lily sat on the couch leaning over the coffee table, tarot

cards laid out in front of her. She'd recovered from the boat incident, but had been unsettled ever since, doing reading after reading after reading with her tarot cards. Pippin knew she wanted the deck to reveal different cards than it kept giving her. Now Lily was determined to do a reading for her. "Ready?"

Initially, Pippin had been skeptical about whether Lily's readings could really reveal anything about the past or foretell the future, but she also had the gift of bibliomancy, just as she and Cora both did. Just like all the Lane women. Lily didn't shun her divination, but she preferred tarot over books.

"Ready." Pippin sat next to her. Lily gathered up the cards, shuffled them, and told Pippin to take the deck. To hold it for a moment. Lily didn't usually let other people touch her tarot deck, but she'd seen something in Pippin—an energy. And the reading had been interesting. It had focused on her past, present, and the future.

Now Lily took the deck back and blew on the edges. She fanned them out, compiled them into a stack again then knocked on the top of it with her fingertips. This cleansed it, Pippin recalled.

Just like she'd done then, she looked at Pippin and said, "Close your eyes and take some breaths." She did as she was told. "Visualize white light," Lily said. "Imagine it flowing from the crown of your head straight into the cards."

Pippin pictured the light like a glowing rope of satin curving from her mind to the cards. Lily handed her the deck. "Shuffle it," she said. Pippin did, then handed them back. Once again Lily fanned out the cards, then she held them up. "Do you remember?"

Pippin nodded. "I take three."

"Well, this time you take ten. One at a time. Use your left hand."

"So not the past, present, future reading, like before?"

"I want to do the Celtic Cross this time. It gives the past, present, and future, but it goes deeper than that. It gives a strong overview of your life as it is now. It hones in on fears, hopes, and the outcome of whatever you seek. First, set an intention," Lily said.

The process was similar to her bibliomancy ritual. Pippin closed her eyes and thought about what she wanted to know. What she wanted to happen. She needed guidance on how to free the Lane family, now and in the future, from Dagda's curse. What it boiled down to was freedom. Would she be successful in breaking the curse? Would she and the Lane family, now and forever, be free? That, more than anything, is what she needed. "Okay. I'm ready."

Lily held out the fanned cards. One by one, Pippin pulled out a card with her left hand, passing them to Lily. Lily arranged them in a specific order. The first she lay facedown in the center, with the second right on top, horizontally. The third was above and the fourth was below. She placed the fifth card to the left of center and the sixth to the right. Finally, the last cards were offset to the right of the cross Lily had formed, with the seventh card at the bottom and the tenth at the top.

One by one, Lily talked through them. The Chariot showed Pippin in her current situation. It was a time for determination. "You've been on a journey. And you've made a decision," Lily said. "Now you are ready to move forward and navigate through it."

The second card, laying across the first, symbolized something positive in Pippin's life. "The Lovers. On the card, two people stood as if in the Garden of Eden, the sun shining down, the angel Raphael blessing them. "The relationships in your life will greatly impact your future." Lily waggled her brows. "Jamie McAdams. He's the real deal. He offers true love, but here's the thing. You have to be willing to follow your heart."

"But the curse—" she started.

Lily held up one hand. "You can't worry about that when it comes to love. Your head will always talk you out of it. You have to be willing to take a risk."

Like Grey had with Ruby. Pippin had fumed over the risk they'd taken, but she'd had to let that go. She had to believe they could change the future.

Of course Cassie and Leo had believed that. So had Moira. So had every Lane who had come before.

The fourth card, The Queen of Pentacles, represented the reason behind Pippin's intention. "You are the benefactor of your family," Lily said. "This is amazing, Pippin. The Queen cares for the world around her. She works hard and is determined to achieve success. That's you and your determination to help all of us."

Gooseflesh rose on Pippin's skin, the truth of Lily's words like pinpricks. She was resolved to protect everyone. Giving up and hiding from her fate wasn't an option.

Lily moved on. The fifth card was the Magician, upside down. "This is the past. When this is upright, this card is about transformation. But this is reversed. That means that instead of being a positive card that symbolizes focusing on your power, it is negative. The magician becomes a trickster. What you see is not the truth."

"Does this represent Dagda as the trickster?" Pippin asked.

Lily lifted one shoulder in a shrug. "Could be. Instead of the good god, for our family he has been a horrible god."

The sixth card, labeled The Sun, showed a serene face on the sun rising over a stone wall, sunflowers sprouting up behind it. A smiling child carrying a flowing red flag sat on a horse.

"What?" Pippin asked. "Is it bad?"

Lily's eyes grew wide and her lips curved up. "Not bad at all. The fourth card represents the near future. When this card is upright, it signifies the end of a challenging time. It symbolizes success. All aspects of life will get better." She tapped the figure. "The fact that this is a child is significant. It may represent childhood, and the idea that after the success, anxiety and fear will be lifted. The innocence of childhood will be reclaimed. The child is on the horse, in the foreground. There is a way forward."

A way forward without the curse. The idea seemed impossible, but if Lily's tarot reading was correct, then it felt as if it might be within reach.

Lily turned the next card. "The Ace of Swords. This is *you*. It is a prediction of new beginnings. Of clear thinking and the sound decisions you're making." Lily squeezed Pippin's hand. "You're on the right track. Almost there."

God, she hoped so.

The eighth card was the Three of Cups. "This is the external things affecting you. Affecting us. The curse. See the way the three women holding up their cups are almost one? This may represent the three aspects of the goddess. The women themselves come from the tarot virtue cards. They are Strength, Justice, and Temperance. Here they are vitality, balance, and reunion."

Pippin studied the card and thought about the symbolism. She couldn't quite figure out how this represented her current environment

The next card represented Pippin's hopes or fears. It

showed a man holding three swords, with two others discarded and two other figures turned away. Five of Swords. It felt ominous. Did it mean she would lose the battle? That she would be defeated?

"Interesting," Lily said. "Your fear may be losing the battle with…whoever…or whatever. It shows the stress and the challenges you face, and the possibility of defeat. But see, he's still standing. He still holds three swords. That is a message of hope. All is not lost, so you need to tamp down the fears."

Lily paused before flipping over the tenth card. Her silver rings glinted, her ever-present bangle bracelets jangling. She tapped the first card. "This is it. The outcome."

Pippin had to remind herself that none of this was written in stone. No matter what people said, or what the cards or books like *Watership Down* told her, she could change whatever fate was predicted. Lily seemed to read her mind. "Remember, we have choices. Whatever this card reveals, think of it as knowledge that affects those choices."

"Knowledge is power."

They turned to see Cora waddling into the great room from the kitchen, belly first. Lily's gaze slipped to the basketball under her sister's shirt. A shadow of fear passed over her expression, there and gone in the blink of an eye. So much was at stake. She looked back at Pippin. Nodded. Then flipped over the last card.

A shudder coiled inside Pippin. Death.

Lily, though, squealed. "This is good, girls. This is really good."

Cora had maneuvered herself into one of the armchairs. "How is the Death card good?"

Pippin's question exactly. The card showed a grim reaper on horseback, death in various forms all around him.

But Lily was not deterred. "Because death means change. It doesn't have to mean a physical death. It can mean the end of a chapter or era. It brings endings, yes, but it also brings new beginnings. Really, it means transformation."

Pippin zeroed in on one thing Lily had said. It represented the end of an era. A new beginning. If they succeeded in ending the torment plaguing the Lane family, there would be deep transformation. They'd all turn the page to a new chapter and begin again without the burden their family had carried for centuries.

The tarot cards predicted success. Would her bibliomancy do the same? An hour later, Pippin sat cross-legged on the floor of her room with the paperback copy of *Watership Down*. She set the same intention as she had before Lily did the reading. Would she be successful in breaking the curse? Would she and the Lane family, now and forever, be free?

She placed the book on its spine, took a breath and let it fall open. The pages fluttered. Seemed to rearrange themselves until they finally decided where to land.

Pippin saw the lines darken instantly. They lifted from the page, quick and bold.

"To come to the end of a time of anxiety and fear! To feel the cloud that hung over us lift and disperse—the cloud that dulled the heart and made happiness no more than a memory! This at least is one joy that must have been known by almost every living creature."

THE WORDS PERMEATED every cell of her body, like water soaking through the skin. The dark cloud would lift. They would end the fear and anxiety they all lived with. At long last, they would be free. She exhaled. Stood. Once and for all, she was going to face down the demon threatening her family.

CHAPTER 25

Like icebergs, people normally expose only a small part of themselves, and generally just the part they wish to show."
~Nikki Yanofsky

PIPPIN'S HEAD spun from all the new information about Artemis and Siobhan, Tory Island, and the cursing stones, Lily's tarot reading, and from the promise her bibliomancy found in *Watership Down*. The end was in sight. If only she could see it.

She needed to get out. To talk through things with someone. Even though she had a community of people in her life now, Pippin felt at a loss. She couldn't rehash everything with Grey, and Jamie would be handling last minute shoppers. Plus, she needed a new perspective on things.

Cyrus McAdams. Jamie's grandfather. *That's* who she needed to talk with. The dapper old gentleman had been a confidant of Cassie's and Leo's. He had been one of the first people Cassie had trusted enough to tell about the curse on the Lane family. And he'd done his best to trace the family tree and to help her figure out how to protect herself and those she loved.

She walked to the bookshop. She was right. Both Jamie and Erin were up to their eyeballs in customers and gift wrapping. She slipped past with a wave, went up the stairs, and knocked on Cyrus's door. Like her mother, she trusted him to guide her. "Ah, Pippin, my dear," Cyrus said as he opened the door to her, his eyes sparkling with joy. "What a delightful surprise, and on Christmas Eve no less!"

He stepped back, ushering her into his flat. Black, white, and gray were the predominant colors. Like him, his living space was neat and sophisticated. He had a small artificial Christmas tree in one corner, but that was the only decoration. Somehow it worked, giving just enough holiday spirit to the minimalist space.

He situated her at the low backed couch with a glass of water and sat opposite her on one of the modern chairs. "This is not a social call, is it?" he said.

How he could read her mind, she didn't know. "No, it's not. I..." She trailed off for a moment to gather her thoughts. "I think we are on the brink of figuring this whole thing out," she said, jumping right in. Cyrus knew everything, from the romance between Titus and Morgan, or Morrighan, to Hugh guiding her to Seamus O'Dulany's book, *Dagda and the Curse of Morrighan*. Frustration tinged her voice. "I just...I don't know how it all fits together. I don't know what it all *means*."

She proceeded to fill him in on the conversation she'd just had with Grey, Erin, and Jamie, about Artemis and Siobhan on Tory Island, about the bullán and the cursing stones Edgar had hidden on the boat he'd built.

Cyrus sat completely still, his silvery hair catching the

light, his head tilted slightly. He listened intently to every word she said. "The stones can curse or bless," he said when she was done, whittling everything down to that one fact.

"Yes. But we don't know how it works. First, we don't have a bullán. And second, even if we did, the stones can make a curse or a blessing. There's nothing about breaking a curse. But Artemis and Siobhan must have hoped they could, right? Otherwise they wouldn't have taken them from Tory Island. And Edgar wouldn't have hidden them away for safekeeping."

God, her head hurt from trying to figure all of this out.

"I have been thinking about Seamus O'Dulany's book," Cyrus said.

"What about it?"

He rose and strode to the open shelves against one of the living room walls. He retrieved a single sheet of paper from atop a neat stack of books. "This passage," he said. "I asked Jamie to write it down for me."

He handed it to her. She'd read it so many times that the words came easily to her now.

'I pray that the unpretended descendants of she who called herself Morgan Dubhshláine and Titus of Roma, within the dark side of Clann na Morrigna, return to Dagda what he so seeks and was taken from him. Only then will the curse that the truest god did place upon the children of the betrayers, and the unfortunate that came after, be broken.'

"What about it?" she asked.

"I wonder," Cyrus said thoughtfully, "if we have been looking at this all wrong."

She looked at him, then at the paper, puzzled. "What do you mean?"

Cyrus sat back in the chair, interlacing his fingers, a serene smile on his face. "It says the descendants of Morgan Dubhshláine and Titus must return something to Dagda. Something that was taken from him."

"Right," Pippin said. "We think Titus took his cauldron, but that his ship went down in the Black Sea. We'll never find it. And even if we could find it, he's in a fairy mound in Ireland."

"Yes, yes, I recall our discussion and the conclusions that were made. But, my dear, I believe there is something else that was taken from Dagda...something much dearer to him than a cauldron."

She stared at Cyrus. "Like what? He had his treasures. The Stone of Destiny. The Invincible Spear. The Shining Sword. And the Cauldron."

"Yes, yes," Cyrus said again. "But those are material things. Items that were valuable, but they didn't speak to his heart, did they?"

Pippin tried to tease out his meaning. For a long moment, it eluded her, but slowly comprehension took hold and she understood what Cyrus was saying. "Oh my God, I think you're right. We have been looking at this all wrong."

She jumped up and gave him a kiss on the cheek. "Thank you, Cyrus. Thank you!" And then she ran out the door.

～

Later Pippin sat out on the back deck with Sailor. A standing heater and her peacoat kept her warm. She thought about Dagda. About his missing cauldron. About Titus's sword, and the coins, now safely back in the bank box.

Her thoughts, though, kept straying to Morrighan. Jamie had said her history was complex. He'd told her some basic facts about her, but Pippin wanted more. She roused Sailor and retreated to Hazel's old room. She took out her computer, propped herself up with pillows on her bed, and began the search. There was plenty about Morrighan. She read slowly. Carefully. The letters flipped and turned, but her brain eventually put them right and gradually, she made sense of the pages she landed on. There was nothing, however, to tell her if the goddess was vengeful. Or how she interfered in the lives of humans around her.

Morrighan. She was a shapeshifter. She'd become Morgan. Did that mean she stuck to names similar to hers? She opened up a new browser window and started a new search. There were various spellings and connected names. Morrighan. The Morrígan. Mórrígan. Morrígu. In modern Irish, the name was Mór-Ríoghain. Like Jamie said, it meant "great queen" or "phantom queen".

She started to type the word into the browser window again, this time looking at the auto-fills that popped up. One in particular caught her eye.

Morwenna.

It triggered something.

Changing tacks, she scrolled and clicked on the link. Morwenna was a 5th or 6th century daughter of a Welsh king. She ended up in Cornwall, but spent time in Ireland. They weren't one and the same, Morrighan and Morwenna. So what was the connection?

She kept reading and found an interesting tidbit. The name Morwenna meant *maiden*, the first of the three parts of the maiden/mother/crone cycle Jamie had told her about. She kept searching, digging deeper, and found a little used definition for the word. A noun, meaning *all knowing and powerful.*

Another idea knocked loose and threw her for a loop because it changed everything. By all accounts, Dagda was a good king. A caring god. Not the kind of god who would lay a curse at the feet of an entire family.

But Morrighan, who had easily betrayed Dagda...who had birthed twins...who was the death raven—she very well could be the kind of goddess to lay down such a curse.

She prophesied, foretelling of doom and death.

She took different forms. A she-wolf, a cow, a horse, a young woman, an old woman, a raven, or a...*crow.*

Pippin's heart stopped. A crow. She snapped her head to the side to look out the window, half expecting to see *her* crow...the one she had nicknamed Morgan...gliding around with its single tug of white feathers marking her. Hattie had told her there had been a crow when Cassie had been here on Devil's Cove. Hattie thought it was a harbinger of death, but Cassie had seen it as a protector.

The crow was symbolic, but was it more than that? Was it...could it be Morrighan herself, here to keep watch over her descendants?

But why?

Pippin's thoughts went back to the discovery of Seamus O'Dulay's book, *Dagda and the Curse of Morrighan.* They'd interpreted that to mean Dagda had done the curse. He'd been the one betrayed by his wife and had doomed her children born of Titus, but after her conversation with Cyrus, she saw it in a new light.

"The Curse of Morrighan" meant the curse *Morrighan* had placed.

She and Grey and Jamie had hypothesized that Titus had stolen Dagda's cauldron, and that Lir had taken Titus's ship down, the cauldron lost to the depths of the sea forever.

She dug deeper into the perspective she and Cyrus had taken. As Morgan Dubhshláine, Morrighan was betrayed. Dagda had lost the goddess he'd wed. His protector. What if Dagda wanted Morrighan herself returned to him? He was dead now, laid to rest in the Neolithic mounds at Brú na Bóinne on the banks of the River Boyne. The ancient mounds, older even than Stonehenge and the Great Pyramids, dated back to 3200 BCE, which Jamie had taught her meant Before Common Era. "The Gregorian calendar begins with year one, which is the Common Era. BCE is everything that took place before year one."

"Like AD and BC?" she'd asked.

"Exactly the same, but those are based in Christianity. AD for *Anno Domini,* which is Latin for in the year of the Lord, and BC for Before Christ. Now CE and BCE are more often used to eliminate the religious connotation."

Pippin pressed her fingertip to her temples, teasing out her thoughts. Dagda lay specifically at the mound called Newgrange, which symbolized his role as the king of the seasons and the ruler of day and night. He lay alone, for eternity. Unless his Morrighan was returned to him.

She went back through the tabs she had open on her laptop, clicking the X to close each one. Morrighan. BCE. The triple goddess.

Her finger hovered over the X on the page about Morwenna.

Was Morrighan really the crow who had taken up residence in the eaves of Sea Captain's Inn? It felt possible. But that was only one of her forms. She moved her mouse to the menu bar and the History tab. She reopened one of the pages about Morrighan. She took many forms. A she-wolf, a cow, a horse, a young woman, an old woman, a raven, a crow, she read again. She'd fixated on the crow, but now backtracked to another of Morrighan's shapes. That of an old woman.

The first thing that came to mind was the day Pippin, as a little girl, had been with her mother down on Main Street. They'd been at the pier, Cassie watching for Leo's fishing boat to return. Eventually they'd left the pier and headed home, cutting across the street at an angle between the bookshop and the library. Cassie refused to step foot in either.

But they'd passed an old woman who had dropped a book. Could that old woman have been Morrighan shifted into the crone?

Had she inserted herself into Pippin's life as a mother? As a maiden?

Camille. Camille Gallagher, wife of a Venatore. She had tried to find the ancient treasure the Venatores all searched for. In fact, Pippin hadn't seen hide nor hair of Camille in months. Her head spun. Could she have been Morrighan in the form of a mother?

Pippin scanned the page again, but this time her gaze shot to the open tab on Morwenna. It was the name that felt like an icepick to her brain. Morwenna the maiden. That word—maiden—took her back to the triple goddess. Morrighan the shapeshifter.

She grabbed her cell phone and dialed Grey, then Jamie. Finally, she hollered for her cousins.

CHAPTER 26

"... *His Emanation is Conwenna, she shines a triple form*
Over the north with pearly beams gorgeous & terrible..."
~William Blake

THEIR ARRIVALS WERE STAGGERED. Cora came in from Pippin's bedroom, walking slowly. She held her belly and stopped for a moment as she grimaced and breathed through the Braxton Hicks contractions rolling through her abdomen. Lily came downstairs, her bangles jangling. Grey arrived next, followed by Jamie and Erin and Cyrus. They gathered in the great room and she got right to it, explaining what Cyrus had worked out, and what she now believed to be absolutely correct. Cyrus nodded his agreement as she talked through it.

It felt like an explosion that, when the smoke cleared, revealed a long-buried hidden treasure. "So it is not Dagda's cauldron that needs to be returned to him. It's Morrighan. *Morrighan!*"

They all stared at her, processing. Jamie looked at his grandfather who had moved to a straight-backed chair near the sideboard. He was like a guardian angel, there to hold Pippin up. He hadn't told Jamie, or anyone else, their theory. He'd left that for her.

Grey paced. Ran his hand down his face. "Let me get this straight. You think that passage from Seamus's book means we need to return *Morrighan* to Dagda? That *she* is the thing that was stolen from him?"

"Yes," she said. She pulled out the paper Cyrus had given her with the passage from Seamus's book and read it aloud:

'I pray that the unpretended descendants of she who called herself Morgan Dubhshláine and Titus of Roma, within the dark side of Clann na Morrigna, return to Dagda what he so seeks and was taken from him. Only then will the curse that the truest god did place upon the children of the betrayers, and the unfortunate that came after, be broken.'

"RIGHT? DO YOU SEE?" she asked, barely containing the excitement bubbling inside her. "'Return to Dagda what he so seeks and what was taken from him.' The only thing that has emotional value—that he really cared about—is *Morrighan*. I mean, sure, the cauldron was a loss with its magic and everything, but his wife? That loss was worse than some material object."

"Indeed," Cyrus said. His voice was a mixture of authority and wisdom.

Cora stood with her back to the Christmas tree, hand on

the top of her belly. She looked at Cyrus and asked, "And just how are we supposed to do that, return Morrighan to Dagda? We have no idea where she is. What if she's buried in some other fairy mound somewhere?"

"Oh, but she is not. She is alive and well," he said, speaking as if he knew something none of the rest of them did.

"How do you know that?" Lily asked.

Cyrus angled his head slightly, the corners of his mouth rising just a little bit. "I have a theory," he said, but he waved his arm. "But carry on."

Jamie's head snapped up as if an invisible line had yanked it up. "Oh my God. I have an idea." He looked at Pippin. "Where are the cursing stones?"

"In my office," Pippin said. Her heartbeat had ratcheted up from the revelation about Morrighan, but now it threatened to beat right out of her chest from Jamie's urgency. Any idea he had would be a good one.

She hurried to her office to grab the drawstring bag from her desk, quickly sliding them out and placing them on the coffee table where they looked innocent and about as far from magical as something could get.

Jamie picked them up, handling them as gently as if they were disks of blown glass.

At that moment, a pounding sounded on the door, startling them all. Lily yelped, putting her hand to her chest. Cora jumped with a grimace, seeming to brace herself against the tightening in her belly.

For a second, time stopped. Pippin waited for Cora's cry. For her pronouncement that this was it, labor had started.

The distorted expression on Cora's face softened, though, and Pippin breathed again. She spun around as a click sounded and Hattie strolled in, unlit cigarette clamped between two fingers, a red and white striped beanie with a green pompom planted straight on top, pulled low on her head. She wore her puffy jacket, her candy cane striped legs poking out from beneath it. Dabba, looking like her twin, was on her heels. "Are we missing the party?" Hattie asked.

"An exciting moment, but not a party," Erin said in her lilting voice.

Hattie puckered her lips and looked around. "No food. No drink. I can see that."

Pippin looked at Dabba, then at Hattie. "Does she know?" she asked. After Grey's and Ruby's big pregnancy reveal, she was pretty sure Hattie had filled her sister in on everything related to the Lane curse.

"Every last bit," Hattie replied unapologetically.

Lily dropped her hand back to her side. "Playing devil's advocate here, but Dagda's dead and in that fairy mound in Ireland—"

Cora broke in, visibly swallowing the practice contraction that had just rolled through her. "Right. And we don't have a clue how to summon Morrighan. Or if it's even possible."

Pippin's pondering had led her to another pivot in her conclusions. Even Cyrus didn't know what she was about to say. It was now or never. She drew in a breath. "I don't think Dagda is the one who put the curse on Morrighan and Titus's descendants."

Hattie's face lit up. "This is *much* better than a holiday party, though I wouldn't mind a brandy eggnog."

Dabba reached in her giant tote bag and pulled out a bag of ready-made popcorn. Hattie snatched it from her, kicked off her red Crocs and planted herself in one of the chairs with aplomb. "This'll do."

Pippin gestured toward the couches and chairs. "Take a

seat, everyone," she said, plopping down on one side of a couch, tucking one leg under herself. She grabbed a chenille throw pillow and clutched it on her lap. Lily, Cora, and Erin took the couch opposite. Grey took the available armchair. Hattie spun hers around. She scooted over to make room for Dabba, who balanced on the edge. And Jamie perched on the arm of the couch next to Pippin. Cyrus stayed put where he was. Their expectation weighed heavily in the air.

Five pairs of eyes swiveled to look at Pippin. Grey spoke up first. "If Dagda didn't curse us, then who did?" Grey asked, eyes narrow, jaw tight. His stakes had been raised when Ruby got pregnant. It wasn't just his own life he needed to protect.

Pippin squeezed the pillow, thinking about where to start. She went back to Seamus O'Dulany's book. "Okay, listen to this again. Seamus wrote: *'I pray that the unpretended descendants of she who called herself Morgan Dubhshláine and Titus of Roma, within the dark side of Clann na Morrigna, return to Dagda what he so seeks and was taken from him. Only then will the curse that the truest god did place upon the children of the betrayers, and the unfortunate that came after, be broken'*," she recited."

"Right. His cauldron," Lily said, as if it was obvious.

"Except what if it's not the cauldron. We think Titus stole it, right? He betrayed Morgan Dubhshláine, leaving her pregnant and with an upset husband, who had also been betrayed. The woman—or triple goddess—he married had changed. She cheated on him."

"The gods all cheated," Jamie said. "Dagda had an affair with Boann, *and* got her pregnant."

"Okay, but no one ever claimed the ancient gods were rational," Cyrus said from his spot by the sideboard.

"Or maybe cheating and falling in love are two different things," Pippin said. "If Morgan Dubhshláine *loved* Titus, which we think she did based on the letter fragments we have, Dagda would feel more betrayed than normal because his wife actually *loved* someone else."

Jamie considered her, processing. He nodded. "I see where you're going with this. Titus stole Morrighan's love."

"Exactly!" Thank God someone was following her train of thought. Cyrus nodded soberly. "The Morrighan he married, loved him and only him. Until Titus came along."

Cora groaned. Sat back.

Lily torqued her body to face her. "Are you okay?"

Please not labor, Pippin thought for the umpteenth time. The Braxton Hicks came and went. Any minute they could actually be the real thing.

Cora blew out a breath. She pressed her fingers and thumb against her temples. In the background, Hattie and Dabba crunched their popcorn, riveted. "I'm okay," Cora said. "Go on, Pippin."

Pippin hesitated, watching Cora. When it seemed clear the moment had passed, she turned back to the group.

Grey spoke again. "That still points to Dagda. If Morrighan fell in love with Titus, that's still a betrayal. And when he found out Morrighan was pregnant with Titus's children? It makes sense that he cursed them...and us."

Cora sat with her eyes closed, her nostrils flared as she inhaled and exhaled, deep and slow. Pippin kept one eye on her as she nodded. "Yes. That's one possibility, but hear me out. Those pieces of a letter written from Morgan to Titus made the depth of her love very clear. But if Titus didn't feel the same, if he *left* her, knowing she was pregnant—*and* he stole Dagda's cauldron—well..."

She trailed off to let them think about that. Lily finished the thought. "She'd be a woman scorned."

Jamie stood. Walked to the sideboard and put a hand on his grandfather's shoulder for a moment. Then he walked back again, cupping his chin as he thought. He stopped short. "Shit. She cursed her own offspring because of Titus. Because *Titus* betrayed *her,*" he said.

Cora's eyes popped open. "She cursed her own children? And all her descendants? That's just evil."

"She has always been feared," Erin said. "Next to Dagda, she is the most powerful of the Tuatha dé Danann. Those deities thought nothing about the consequences of their actions. Dagda impregnated Boann, then cast a spell on her husband to basically stop time so he wouldn't notice the pregnancy. Even the good ones weren't honorable."

Grey was up now, pacing. "Okay, let's get back to the problem. You're saying we need to *find* Morrighan and return her to Dagda?" He shook his head. "How the hell are we supposed to do that?"

Pippin went back to her research from earlier. This was the second bomb she was going to drop. "Morrighan was known as a triple goddess. Maiden, mother, crone. She was also a shapeshifter. She was known to turn into a raven—"

"The Battle Raven," Jamie said.

At this, Cora and Lily looked at each other. Lily's eyes went wide. "Remember we said a raven always hung out at the little family cemetery. Like it was standing guard."

"Or just waiting for us to die," Cora said.

Pippin nodded and went on. "A raven...and a crow." They were all aware of the inn's resident crow, but only Hattie's eyes pinched. She stopped munching her popcorn and Pippin hurried on. "When I was researching Morrighan, I came across something else. Morrighan is also known as the triple goddess. She could become a mother. A crone. Or...a maiden."

And then she'd seen it. Morwenna, the maiden.

The name turned her veins to ice. It felt as if Morrighan had been toying with them all along. *Morrighan. Morwenna. Morwenna. Wenna.*

Wenna, who had told her about destiny. "*A person's destiny, Pippin, it is written.*"

Pippin had balked. Disagreed, but Wenna had held firm. "*Your future, it will unfold however it's meant to. You don't know what's going to happen, so how can you change it?*"

Wenna...

She came back to the moment. "For centuries, Morrighan has destroyed the Lane family—the descendants of Titus. She wrote herself out of the equation, her rage at his betrayal superseding everything else. Anything connected to Titus had to be punished. It's been her all along."

They stared at her, not quite comprehending. "What are you sayin'?" Hattie asked, her eyes pinched.

"I'm saying that Morrighan is the triple goddess. She's the maiden, the mother, and the crone. The crone, Hattie. *Wenna.*"

Hattie bolted out of her chair. "Are you sayin' that woman —my friend—who has been around here since the dawn of time, you're saying she is a flippin' evil goddess?" Pippin's silence was her answer. Hattie drove the filtered end of her cigarette between her lips. "Unbelievable."

And it was. Wenna, the old woman with a map of wrinkles on her face, but whose voice was clear and strong, and whose hands were those of a younger woman.

Wenna...

Morrighan taking the name of a saint in utter irony. Morrighan as the crone.

Cora's voice turned harsh. "*She* killed Moira," she said, as if a cog had slotted into place.

Olive's tale came back to Pippin. Had it been Morrighan in the form of a bird that had spooked Moira? Had Moira been getting too close to the truth? She didn't know for certain, but if she had to guess, she'd say that yes, Morrighan had caused the death of another Lane descendant...Moira.

Pippin looked pointedly at the stones on the coffee table. She shifted her gaze to each person in the room, pausing at each to emphasize the importance of what she was about to say.

"Morgan Dubhshláine. The crow outside. Morwenna. Wenna. It doesn't matter what form she takes, or what she's called. She is Morrighan, and she is the one who cursed us." She nodded to the stones. "And those are going to help us break that curse once and for all."

CHAPTER 27

ou can't go back and change the beginning, but you can start where you are and change the ending."
~C.S. Lewis

THE CLOCK TICKED TOWARD MIDNIGHT. Outside, hidden by the mist, the glow of the Cold Moon flickered. The time had come. They'd all set their watches to meet at 12 AM sharp in front of Sea Captain's Inn.

Pippin's mind wandered as she watched the second-hand trace its path on the clock's face. If the stones could bless or curse someone, could they also be used to *undo* a blessing or curse? Could a blessing counteract a curse? That was the first unknown.

And even if the stones theoretically worked, she still had the problem of not having Morrighan in front of her.

Then again, did she need to be? Was the HMS Wasp within sight of the King of Tory when he issued the curse? And surely the Irish people who pilgrimaged to bullán stones to bless or curse often did so without the recipients present.

All she'd needed was a bullán stone, the cursing stones Artemis had brought from Tory Island, and...and what? She held the piece of clay she'd mixed with ash sitting on the table. Looked at the interlocking curved lines, the Celtic symbol for Tuatha dé Danann, she'd engraved on it. It felt like a touchstone...like one piece of the puzzle.

Her mind wandered to Wenna again.

Bits and pieces of memories flashed in her mind. The crow soaring through the night when it almost snowed and then Wenna suddenly appearing out of nowhere. Wenna talking about the Dingle with the beehives and waves. Pippin had looked it up. The Dingle Peninsula was in County Kerry, Ireland.

Wenna had been in Hattie's house that night with Moira. Pippin's veins turned to ice. Wenna had *heard* Moira and Pippin talking as they left Hattie's that night. Moira had been getting too close to the truth.

The minute had clicked.

Hugh was the missing puzzle piece. He didn't have a disc of clay to smash under the crescent moon. He was barely alive, being treated in Nags Head. Would his absence matter? If they succeeded, would the curse be broken for them all, or would Hugh still carry it?

She might never know the answers to those questions.

Tick. Tick. Tick. The minute hand moved. 11:54. Tick. Tick. Tick.

Leo's journal sat in front of her. Without thinking or knowing why, she stood it on its spine and spoke aloud. "How can we break the curse?"

She let the sides drop. Her father's slanted handwriting

seemed to float on the pages. One line darkened. Lifted. A shadow beneath it.

Trap it in the blessing.

"A BLESSING," she said, and then, in a flash, she raced up to The Burrow. She scanned the shelves. She knew she'd seen a book about St. Patrick amongst her father's favorites. She ran her finger across the spines. Of course there were the JRR Tolkien's books. She skipped over those and found the section she was looking for. Books Irish history. The language. Poetry by Yeats. Volumes by Oscar Wilde. James Joyce. Bram Stoker. C.S. Lewis.

There. There it was! A book of Irish blessings. She grabbed it, checked the index, and flipped through the pages until she found it. St. Patrick's blessing.

I summon today
All these powers between me and those evils,
Against every cruel and merciless power
that may oppose my body and soul,
Against incantations of false prophets,
Against black laws of pagandom,
Against false laws of heretics,
Against craft of idolatry,
Against spells of witches and smiths and wizards,
Against every knowledge that corrupts man's body and
*   soul;*
...shield me today

Against poison, against burning,
Against drowning, against wounding,
So that there may come to me an abundance of reward.

TICK. Tick. Tick.

She tore the page from the book and raced back down the stairs. Grabbed her bag and ran to the front door. But she skidded to a stop from the anxious pull in her gut. She was missing something. She spun. Looked around. Hollered for Cora. For Lily.

Her gaze landed on her desk inside her office. It zeroed in on her father's water-damaged journal. She darted into her office and grabbed it, shoved the page and the journal into her bag, then raced outside.

THE MISTY AIR stirred in the waning light. It started slowly, gaining strength as it gusted in from the east. The street was littered with the blurry remnants of fall seen through the thickening marine layer. Crisp leaves circled on the ground before hurtling through the air, disappearing into the fog. Above, circling in and out of the mist, was a murder of crows. Icy fingers crept over Pippin's spine. One of those crows was not what it seemed. Her fear made her want to stop, but her determination propelled her forward. She couldn't stop.

Pippin threw her head back and yelled toward the sky. "I know who you are!"

The wind whipped her voice away. She walked on, heading for the sidewalk just past the walkway to Sea

Captain's Inn. "I figured it out!" she hollered. "I know who you are!"

One of the crows—the one with the tuft of white on the breast—spread its wings and plunged into a nosedive. For a split second, Pippin spooked. Thought the crow might smash right into her. At the last second, the crow juked left. Turned. Lifted again. Melted into the fog.

The figure appeared a moment later, still ten yards away. Barely visible, yet clearly there, a black smudge amidst the white of the heavy mist. Pippin walked forward, pushing through the mist, the current at her back propelling her forward. Her hair tangled as it parted on the back of her head, the strands criss-crossing in front of her face. She didn't bother brushing it away. She plowed on into the middle of the street.

And then she saw it happen. The crow vanished before her eyes and in its place was the old woman. She stood rooted to the ground, seemingly impervious to the force of the wind. It wouldn't have surprised Pippin to know Wenna —no, *not* Wenna—*Morrighan*—had somehow summoned the storm herself with some ancient Irish incantation. Her black cape flew out behind her. Her black dress glued itself to the front of her body, outlining her shape. Still, Morrighan didn't budge.

Step by step, Pippin drew closer. Her bag slung across her body felt heavy at her hip. She walked on, the fog like a tangible, thick barrier she had to force her way through. As she moved, the heavy mist seemed to swallow her, closing behind her and blocking her retreat. "I know who you are," she yelled again. "You're a Celtic goddess. One of the Tuatha dé Danann. You're *the* Morrighan. You're the goddess of war. Of fate. Of death."

Morrighan took a step back. One, single step, but it was

enough to verify that this old woman *was* the goddess of sovereignty. That she *was* creator of the curse that had tormented generation after generation of Lanes. And it was enough to show that she hadn't expected Pippin to know that.

Pippin half expected Morrighan to throw her head back and cackle in true Disney evil witch form, but she didn't. She leveled her gaze at Pippin, simply watching her as the wind continued to howl.

And then she tsk'd. "For centuries, the descendants of Titus have tried to learn the truth. More than two thousand years." She threw out her arms and lightening splintered across the sky. "So now you know, but as I told you, Pippin, you cannot change the future. It is written."

"Did you love him?"

The goddess of war balked.

"Titus? Dagda? Both? Neither?" Pippin pressed.

Morrighan wore a hooded cloak. She cocked her head, the fabric shadowing her face. "They both betrayed me."

The words from Mogan's letter to Titus crawled through her mind like ticker tape. In it, Morrighan had professed her love for Titus, saying that what they had transcended the obstacles they faced. The biggest obstacle was The Dadga himself. Morrighan was a king-maker. With her kiss, she had anointed Dagda. But she had been willing to give up her king for her Roman soldier.

"That was two thousand years ago," Pippin said, closer now. Above, in the darkening sky, the crows cawed and circled. Had they been called back by Morrighan, like Gandalf had summoned the Great Eagles to fight off the Orcs? Would they careen down as a collective to protect the Phantom Queen?

Pippin forced her attention to stay only on Morrighan.

She couldn't see them, but she was bolstered by the knowledge that the others—her people—were behind her, camouflaged in the mist. Morrighan was her oldest ancestor. Morrighan's blood coursed through her body. Through Grey. Through Hugh. Through Lily and Cora. It had coursed through Moira, and now through the baby Cora carried in her womb, and through the baby Grey and Ruby had created.

All this time Pippin had believed that Morgan Dubhshláine was inherently good. That Morrighan was watching over her. Cassie had seen the crow as a good omen, not a harbinger of death. How wrong they both had been.

Now it was up to Pippin to defeat this deity. Pippin, whose divination was centered around books and prophesy. How was she to be a match for the second most powerful diety in the Tuatha dé Danann? As Morgan Dubhshláine, she'd been a maiden. Giving birth to Aisling and Aoife made her a mother. And here she stood before Pippin as Wenna, in the crone manifestation of the maiden/mother/crone cycle.

But first and foremost, Morrighan was the goddess of battle and war. If a soldier laid eyes on her in battle, it was his death call. He would not walk away from the battle. Jamie's words rattled around in Pippin's mind. "She was known to be untrustworthy, clever, and sly. She was a shapeshifter, the crow being her favored form."

The crow. Morrighan had been watching her all along, but also Pippin's great-grandfather Trevor. Her grandparents, Edgar and Annabel. Aunt Rose. Cassie and Lacy. With a single flap of her wings, she could probably transport herself across the country. Hell, she'd probably flown alongside the ship Artemis and Siobhan had sailed on back in 1924 when they'd made the crossing from Ireland to America, carrying baby Moira and the stones that Pippin hoped would be the crow's downfall.

Pippin had thought she was watching *over* her, but no, Morrighan was just watching. Watching and waiting for the curse to rumble to life again with each new member of the Lane family. The wind howled and Morrighan's words shot out of her mouth like bullets from a pistol. "Two thousand years is but a blink in the lives of the gods. As long as Titus the betrayer lives on through his descendants, I will never rest."

"You will rest. You will go back to Dagda, where you belong. I'm...*we're*...going to send you there. We're going to return to him the wife he lost."

Morrighan threw her head back and gave a mirthless, cackling laugh. "To do that you need to break the curse, and that you cannot do. It is for all eternity."

Watch me, Pippin thought.

Without severing the connection between them, Pippin reached into her satchel. Her hand found the page she'd torn from the book of blessings. Next, she took out the flat, oval piece of clay she'd created in The Burrow. Behind her, Grey, Cora, and Lily moved forward, as stealthy as Miss Havisham moved through the bookshop. In her peripheral vision, she saw them fall in next to her, Grey on one side, her cousins on the other.

Jamie appeared next. He carried something heavy—a rock with a concave bowl he'd created. Their very own bullán. He set it down in front of Pippin, then stepped back.

Hattie, with Dabba by her side, materialized last. She'd gone home to get Rizzo, her trike, from her shed. Now she straddled it, feet firmly on the pedals, ready to race down the street if necessary. Not that she'd be able to catch

Morrighan if the goddess morphed into a crow, but she was prepared, nonetheless.

Dabba stood back, probably wishing for a bag of popcorn.

They all knew that if Morrighan wanted to vanish, she could do it in an instant, but she just watched them, amusement on her face.

And then Pippin reached in her satchel for the three cursing stones.

CHAPTER 28

When asked what skills the Morríghan would bring to battle, she replied, "What I shall follow I shall hunt."

    ~The Legend of The Morríghan

PIPPIN STARED AT MORRIGHAN. Before her eyes, the affable, warm woman she had known as Wenna morphed into someone cold and hard. The goddess grabbed ahold of the hood and slid it off. Fiery-red hair fell in loose waves around her fair complexion and shamrock eyes. The features on someone else would have been beguiling. On the Phantom Queen, they were disconcerting and intimidating. Her piercing gaze slid to the bullán Jamie had placed on the pavement and Grey with the three stones. Morrighan scoffed. "Rocks? How quaint."

She spoke now with a strong Irish lilt, any pretense of hiding it completely gone. Pippin cocked her head and curved her lips up into a sweet smile. "Isn't it though?"

"Are you planning on smashing me over the head with

it? You forget. I am standing before you now, but in the blink of an eye, I can be gone." She spread her arms wide, as if they were the wings of a bird.

"I'm aware. Very clever of you to hide in plain sight."

The island wind whipped Morrighan's cloak back, making it look as if she might take flight any second.

"Feel free to go," Pippin said. "We really don't need you here."

Dabba strode forward, her own red hair glimmering under the light of the misty street lamps, her Crocs thudding lightly on the road. Beside her, Hattie rotated her feet on the pedals of Rizzo, then rotated her wrist and hand in the air. "Fly away, evil bird."

Morrighan snarled a laugh. "Oh Hattie. You are so tiresome. Believe me when I say I won't miss you."

"Likewise," Hattie said. She rode to where Pippin stood, meeting her eyes for a beat. Hattie had done just what Pippin had asked her to do, which was to bring something Wenna had touched. She had no idea if that would even matter, but it seemed like a safe precaution.

Hattie had done one better. She slipped off her trike and crouched, releasing the tied red stem of a maraschino cherry into the bullán. "From your drink last night. I fished it out of the garbage," Hattie said with immense satisfaction, her smiling pink lips revealing smoke-yellowed teeth.

Morrighan watched with amusement. "How sweet. You really think you can do this, don't you?"

Hattie returned to Rizzo and rolled to the side of the road next to Dabba. Grey stepped closer to Pippin. "What makes you think we can't?"

Morrighan spat out a chuckle. "Oh Grey. I have watched you from the moment you were born. Incredible your mother survived your birth. I do not know how or why that happened. But no matter. She did lose in the end. Another of the betrayer's line snuffed out. You've been a fighter, though, I will give you that. You should have succumbed to the curse ten times over."

"The crescent moon," Lily said from the shadows.

Morrighan heard her. She peered up at the glowing slice of light shining through the patchy fog. She raised an amused brow when she looked back at them. "You're like children playing with magical spells. Do you have frog's legs and eye of newt?"

Pippin was done playing. The Lanes had spent centuries at the mercy of Morrighan. Cassie and her sister Lacy had both lost their lives to the curse. Leo was gone. Artemis and Siobhan. Trevor, Emily, and Ruth. Edgar and Annabel. Rose. Her own baby brother who died in birth with Cassie. And Moira.

They were all gone. They'd all had enough. "Enough!" she shouted. And then she threw down the clay disc. Instead of shattering into a thousand pieces, the talisman cracked like an old oil painting by one of the masters. Fine lines appeared, but it remained whole. Grey threw his down next to hers, then dug the heel of his boot into it, grinding the dried clay into mush.

Morrighan jerked. Hitched at the waist. Her fiery hair whipped around her face and she convulsed. The amused curve of her lips evaporated. Like a ghost, she raised her arm, pointing. "What...?"

Pippin ignored her. Lily threw her clay disc down. She bent down and pounded it with both fists until it crumbled.

Morrighan's body wrenched back as if a rope had looped around her, yanking her back.

As Cora threw hers down, the air around Morrighan turned fluid, as if it were a desert mirage, wavy and blurred.

She raised her black cloaked arms. Before their eyes, those arms morphed into black feathered wings. Her body changed form. Shrank. Disappeared. A loud cawing echoed in the night. And then a crow appeared. It soared above them, circling like an ominous vulture.

Cora gasped. Stumbled back. In her peripheral vision, Pippin saw Lily put her arm out to catch her sister.

The crow glided lower and lower. Its white tuft of feathers looked gray in the darkness. It made a wide swath through the fog then disappeared. Pippin scanned the area, searching for the glow of the crow's dark eyes. She couldn't see it. Not it...her.

Fear raked the back of her neck like talons. She forced herself to focus. Tried to still her trembling hands. She tried to flatten the page with the Irish blessing, but the crow careened toward her. Pippin lost her balance and was knocked off her feet. The page was ripped from her grasp with an invisible force. She reached for it, but the wind whipped into a frenzy. It spiraled through the air, out of reach. She scrabbled up. Grabbed for it, but it shot higher and higher until it disappeared beyond the Loblolly pine standing tall in Hattie's yard.

A shrieking caw cut through the air like a banshee. She knew it was impossible, but she swore she could hear the crow's wings flap. Hear them pulsing and angry. Then the caw again. A disturbance in the air. The bird appeared like a dark shadow. It let loose another harsh caw as it plummeted right at her. Grey yelled. Jamie called her name. His feet pounded the pavement as he ran toward her. Cora and Lily screeched. Yelled, "Run!" and "Watch out!"

But Pippin couldn't move fast enough. She ducked and threw her arms over her head. Her bag skidded across the road.

The crow—Morrighan—made a sharp upward turn and disappeared into the ether.

And then Pippin saw it. The journal, Leo's journal, the pages whipping to and fro in the wind. She lunged for it. Grabbed it. A flash of a memory shot into her mind. An old woman dropping a book in the street. Cassie crouching to pick it up. Dropping it as if it was made of fire. The foretelling of Leo's death. "It was you!" she yelled.

A caw sounded in the darkness as if to say, "Yes, it was me. It's always been me."

Pippin grabbed the journal and clambered upright. Her vision blurred with rage. Enough. Enough! She flipped the journal over, giving a cursory glance at the pavement-smudged pages, but then words blackened. Shuddered on the page. Lifted and glowed so she could read them.

She felt invisible forces on either side of her, holding her up. She stared at the page. At the poem that wavered there, bold above the white page. This...this was what she needed to read! The talismans they'd made had weakened Morrighan, but this...this poem, along with the cursing stones...*this* is what would break the curse.

She fell to her knees in front of the bullán. "The stones," she hissed.

Grey crouched next to her. Jamie, Cora, and Lily made a circle around the concave stone. Grey placed the small stones in the depression. Pippin's brain felt muddy, her thoughts loose. She tried to remember. Was she supposed to rotate the stones clockwise? Or the opposite? She couldn't get it wrong. She looked at Jamie. He read the question on her face. "Clockwise to curse. Counterclockwise to make a blessing."

She blew out a nervous breath.

From somewhere above, the crow screeched again, and

then it was shooting toward them like a bullet. A rogue thought hit her. This was what Moira had gone through, Morrighan hurtling toward her with a murder of crows alongside, knocking her from her precarious perch on the railing of the pier.

Pippin grabbed one of the stones. Grey took another, and Lily took the third. They kept them firmly rooted in the base of the bullán. "Turn counterclockwise."

They hesitated. "That's a blessing," Lily said with a hiss.

Her father's journal earlier had shown her. *Trap it in the blessing.* "I know. That's what we need. Counterclockwise."

She sensed them catching each other's eyes, felt theme questioning her. "I'm right!" She hoped. "We have to create a blessing to counteract the curse." She pointed to Leo's journal now open on the ground in front of her. "Leo said it here."

The crow came at them again like a stealth fighter appearing from the clouds. Cora ducked her head. Screeched. She fell backward, landing on her side with an audible thud. Her cheeks burned bright as she crawled to the bullán. "Hurry!"

"Counterclockwise," Pippin hollered above the screeching crows in the distance. "T*urn*, turn!"

Quickly, she met their gazes one by one. They each acknowledged her directive before dipping their heads against another attack from Morrighan. They had their hands on the stones at the ready. Pippin read—nearly shouted—the blessing from Leo's journal. The wind swept her voice away—carried, she hoped, straight to Morrighan and the Tuatha dé Danann.

At the river they meet,

The Dagda.
The Morrighan.

The king and
the king maker.
The chief
and the phantom queen.
The bearded man
and the crow.

Forever more.

Until a broken promise.
The fearful Morrighan bringing
betrayal and
darkness.

The coire ansic—
A stolen treasure.
Now forever empty,
of a man, his truest measure.

In the womb,
creations beget
of lies
and deception.

Her scars run
dark and deep
into the River Boyn.
Into the depths they seep.

From the ruins of a damaged heart

only the relics of a family will remain.
The schemes of a phantom goddess
destroying the future of his name.

The betrayed cursing the betrayer.

Hark! Rejoice!

For when the moon wanes crescent.
When the sea sighs at high tide.
When the stars blink bright
in the blanketed sky.
Listen for the crow.
For her cry in the night.

Turn once.
Turn twice.
Turn thrice.

IN THE NIGHT SKY ABOVE, the crow released a feral cry. Grey and Lily turned the stones counterclockwise, but Cora released hers. Let out a strangled, guttural cry. She clutched her belly. Fell back. Her face was contorted with pain. Pale in the mist and faint moonlight. She let out another pained scream. "It's coming! The baby's coming!"

Panic surged through Pippin. Oh God. They were out of time. They had to finish. "Keep going!" she shouted. She put her hand on the stone Cora had released. Read again from Leo's journal.

Turn once.
Turn twice.
Turn thrice.

Now, Battle Raven!
return to wence you came.

Now, Morrígu!
Back to your anointed king.

Now, Great Queen!
Lay with The Dagda
at Brú na Bóinne,

The king and
the king maker.
The chief
and the phantom queen.
The bearded man
and the crow.

Forever more.

A SHOCKWAVE of thunder clapped in the sky. A blaze of bright light sliced through the fog and darkness. The murder of crows overhead scattered, shooting out like shadows from the arcing flares of a firework.

Pippin waited. Murmured the words of Leo's poem aloud again. "Turn once. Turn Twice. Turn Thrice." Grey and Lily watched her. Followed her lead as she turned her stones counterclockwise again.

The horrendous wail of a banshee sounded. Pippin looked up and saw it. A single black crow stealing through the night. Then careening. Spinning like a Blue Angel, but out of control and streaking toward them—toward the descendants—like a heat-seeking missile.

They acted in concert, releasing the stones and stumbling away from the bullán. The crow hurtled down. Someone screamed. Ruby, Pippin realized. She stood, horrified, on the sidewalk. In her peripheral vision, Pippin caught sight of Hattie and Dabba scurrying backward, Rizzo on the ground, forgotten.

Grey grabbed Lily and yanked her further back. Cora let out another pained shriek and Grey moved again...hurled his body over hers, protecting her. Pippin scrambled back. Braced herself for the attack, curling her arms in front of her face, protecting her head. She felt the weight of someone's arms curve around her.

Jamie.

She turned her head, daring to peer under her arm. The crow—Morrighan, the phantom goddess—seemed to spin in slow motion, wings pulled in tight agains her body.

Five feet to the ground.

Four.

Three.

It let out a deafening shriek.

Two feet.

The crow's wings spread wide. Its talons shot out like the landing gear on an airplane, readying for impact.

Pippin held her breath.

One foot.

Another wail.

And then another clap of thunder. Another blaze of

lightning breaking the sky apart. An explosion of black feathers. A burst of sparks.

And then nothing. The crow was gone.

A single white feather wafted down, settling onto the open pages of Leo's journal, then, as if Leo himself was right there, an invisible force holding both covers, the book slammed closed, locking the feather away.

Pippin's breath came again, slowly at first, then ratcheting up to match her thundering heartbeat. And then the storm stopped in its tracks. The howling wind fell silent. The attack of thunder and lightning evaporated. In an instant, the night fell deafeningly quiet, broken only by the Cora's tortured cries. The baby was coming.

CHAPTER 29

Better to light one small candle than to curse the darkness.
~Chinese Proverb

PIPPIN CLIMBED INTO BED, but she knew she wouldn't be able to sleep. Sailor, already dreaming, curled up on her plush dog bed.

She'd tucked Moira's notebook in the drawer of her bedside table, but now she took it out and leafed through it, seeing the pen and ink sketches through fresh eyes. Moira had the pieces of the puzzle right here, she just hadn't been able to put them together. Guilt knifed through her again. If only she had listened to Moira's questions. If only she had invited her inside that night they'd all met at Hattie's. If only, if only, if only...

She found the drawing of the enormous stone cross called the Tau Cross. The drawing of Wenna. Moira had captured the map of wrinkles on the crone's face. She'd shadowed her face with the hood Wenna had often worn.

She fanned the pages, stopping at the sketch of a woman from behind, hair dancing in the wind. She stared at to sea, her long dress blowing. Moira had captured the movement. Pippin started to turn the page, but something in the fine lines of the drawing caught her eye. A picture within a picture. She studied the woman's hair, tracing the lines with her eyes to make out the shape.

A crow. It was drawn carefully into the woman's hair, each thin ink line deliberate. The woman and the crow; two sides of the same coin.

A chill crept over Pippin's skin. Moira had known. On some level, she had known Wenna was more than she seemed.

BY THE NEXT MORNING, Pippin felt light, the weight of two-thousand years lifted from her shoulders.

The cursing stones. Those blessed cursing stones, which Artemis and Siobhan had taken them from Tory Island and Edgar had protected in the hopes that they would help free himself and his family from Morrighan's curse.

And Leo. Her determined father had written the poem that had harnessed the power of a blessing. It was like a ballad—the unfinished story of Dagda and Morrighan, only now they'd returned the phantom queen to *Brú na Bóinne* to rest with the king.

Cora had given birth...and lived. That wasn't a guarantee that they'd succeeded in breaking the curse. Cassie had survived birthing her and Grey, after all, only to die six years later. But Cora's survival felt like a good sign.

Morrighan was gone. Vanquished. The experience had been otherworldly, like trapping a genie in a bottle. They'd trapped a single feather from Morrighan, the crow, in Leo's journal, caught between the pages where he had written his poem.

"You should burn it," Ruby had said, but Grey had shaken his head. "We can't. Not until we know for sure it worked."

Destroying anything of Leo's felt like betrayal. Grey felt the same. Their connection to their parents was gossamer thin; they had to hold on to everything they possibly could that would keep them tethered to one another.

Pippin was afraid to ever open the journal again. It felt like a magical tome that had to be kept shut at all costs. Letting the genie out of the bottle could unleash havoc. She'd wrapped it up in brown paper, scrawling DO NOT OPEN on it and placed it in the safe in her bedroom.

Now, leaning against one of the armchairs with Sailor at her side, she gazed at the Christmas tree's twinkling lights and let her thoughts zoom in on the problem at hand. They needed to know for sure the curse was, indeed, broken.

But how?

A chill tiptoed through her. That was the big question, wasn't it? She needed a steaming cup of coffee to chase away the goosebumps. She stood, scratching Sailor's head so she'd stay put, and started for the kitchen.

She stopped short in the archway to the kitchen. There, on the quartz counter, was her father's copy of *Watership Down*. Of course! The answer hit her. Her bibliomancy! *That* would be the test. For whatever reason, intentional or not, Morrighan had gifted the Lane women with the magical divination. If Pippin no longer had the gift of bibliomancy, then that would *prove* the cursing stones and Leo's poem had worked.

She grabbed the book and sat at the long family table

made of reclaimed wood. She felt her heartbeat in her temples. This moment. It felt monumental. She wished Grey was here by her side. At the same time, she was glad she was alone. The relief she would feel proving they had succeeded was tinted bittersweet. Since coming back to Devil's Cove, she had come to trust her insight when she practiced bibliomancy. Success in breaking the curse meant the loss of the divination.

Her chest thundered from the weight of what this book was about to tell her.

She placed the spine of *Watership Down* on the kitchen table, holding it steady with her hands on the front and back covers. She closed her eyes. Took a deep breath. Asked her question. "Is the curse against the Lane women and men broken?"

She released the covers and let the book fall open. The pages fanned out and then settled. She drew in another inhalation as she opened her eyes. Instantly, her eyes pricked with tears. A wave of emotion crashed through her. Most of the words on the page faded and blurred before her eyes. One passage darkened. Lifted.

She still had magic in her.

They had failed.

She blinked away the frustration and anger. Bit back the scream lodged in the back of her throat. She forced her eyes to focus and read what the book had to tell her.

"I have learned that with creatures one loves, suffering is not the only thing for which one may pity them. A rabbit who does not know when a gift has made him safe is poorer than a slug, even though he may think otherwise himself."

SHE READ and reread the words, trying to make sense of them as they related to her. To Grey. To Lily. To Cora. To her new baby boy. Trying to assign meaning to the passage that could help her understand. *A rabbit who does not know when a gift has made him safe is poorer...*

"When a gift has made him safe...safe..." she murmured. "We should feel it. We should feel different. Or just know." Which she already did. She felt light. She felt the weight of the curse lifted from her. She had felt the vice constantly wound around her heart loosen. She knew in her gut that they *had* succeeded.

But how, then, was she still able to see what the books had to tell her?

If anyone might have an idea, it would be Jamie. She called him.

He answered the phone with a bright, "Merry Christmas, Pip!"

Just hearing his voice and Heidi's and Mathilda's laughter in the background lifted her mood. "Merry Christmas," she said.

"The girls are excited to come over. Is ten minutes too soon?"

Something Grey said floated into her head. Jamie was a package deal. It was him and his girls. If things with Jamie grew into something solid, she would have them all. "Ten minutes is perfect."

Jamie must have sensed something in her tone. "Are you okay?"

"It feels unbelievable," she said.

"I can imagine. It does to me, too, and my family hasn't been living with it for two millennia."

"But Jamie, what if…" she started, but trailed off, and then she finished. "My bibliomancy. I thought that if I tried it and it no longer worked, well, then, we succeeded. Right? But it *does* work." She told him about the quote revealed on the pages of *Watership Down*. "I think it's saying we *are* safe. We have to just accept it."

He was quiet for a moment, only the sound of Heidi and Mathilda chattering in the background. "That makes sense," he said.

"But if the divination is connected to the curse—"

"You don't know that for sure," he interjected. "Seamus O'Dulany didn't say anything about bibliomancy one way or another."

All along they'd thought Dagda had cursed the Lane family. Revenge for his wife's infidelity. But he was known for his kindness. For being a caring deity. "Could Dagda have done it somehow? Given us bibliomancy as a blessing to counteract Morrighan's curse? To eventually help us stop it?"

"That may be something we can never prove, but at this point, I'd say anything is possible."

They hung up and Pippin wandered back to the great room to gaze at the Christmas tree lights. Lily danced lightly down the stairs. "It's beautiful," she said. "A lovely tree. A perfect Christmas."

"It is."

"I talked to Cora. She and the baby are doing great," Lily said. She squeezed Pippin's hand. "We did it! *You* did it. You did it, Pippin."

"Not alone. The generations before laid all the groundwork. Seamus O'Dulany. Artemis. Siobhan. Edgar. And my dad."

"That poem is beautiful."

It was locked away, never to see the light of day again. She couldn't remember the words, only the sentiment—that Morrighan needed to go back to *Brú na Bóinne,* back to Dagda. Even with her thin veil of worry, she still felt light. Free.

A knock on the door brought her out of her thoughts. Heidi and Matilda burst in, energy instantly filling the house. Jamie ushered in Erin and Cyrus, closing the door behind them.

As Pippin watched those around her revel in the joy and hope of the holiday season, she thought of the quote again. She wasn't going to be a rabbit who didn't know when the gift had made him safe. She *was* safe. Grey was safe. Lily and Cora and the babies—the one born, and the one yet to be—were safe.

It was over.

The End, *for now...*

I hope you enjoyed this installment of The Book Magic Mysteries. Reviews help other readers discover great books. They really do matter! If you are inclined to leave a review, I'd appreciate it. You can do so HERE.

And join my newsletter for updates, character profiles, recipes, and more!

RECIPES FROM DEVIL'S BREW
AND SEA CAPTAIN'S INN

Hattie's Harvey Wallbanger

Ingredients:

- 3 ounces Blue Shark Vodka
- 4 ounces fresh Orange juice
- ¾ ounce Galliano®
- Orange wedge (garnish)
- Maraschino cherry (garnish)

Put Vodka, orange juice, and Galliano in a shaker with ice. Poor into glass of your choice. Garnish with an orange wedge and a Maraschino cherry. Enjoy!

Ruby's Gluten-Free Cranberry Orange Muffins

Ingredients

- 1 ¾ cups 1:1 gluten free flour such as King Arthur or Pamela's
- 1 tablespoon baking powder
- ½ teaspoon salt
- 1 1/2 cups fresh or frozen cranberries
- ½ cup granulated sugar
- ¼ cup brown sugar
- 3 eggs
- ½ cup full fat plain yogurt
- 1/2 cup (1 stick butter), melted
- 2 teaspoons orange zest
- 2-3 tablespoons orange juice

Streusel Topping

- ½ cup brown sugar
- ¼ cup 1:1 gluten free flour such as King Arthur or Pamela's
- ⅓ cup butter, cold and chopped into small pieces
- ½ tsp ground cinnamon
- dash nutmeg

Instructions

1. In a mixing bowl, blend together flour, baking powder, and salt. Set aside.

2. Finely chop the cranberries. Set aside.

3. In a large bowl, whisk together the sugar, brown sugar, eggs, yogurt, butter, orange juice and orange zest until smooth.

4. Add the dry ingredients to the wet ingredients. Stir until just blended. Do not over mix.

5. Gently fold in the chopped cranberries.

6. With gluten free baking, it is important to allow the batter to hydrate. Cover the mixing bowl with press and seal or plastic wrap and allow to rest for 1 hour or overnight.

Streusel Topping

1. In a small bowl, mix together brown sugar, flour, and cinnamon.

2. Incorporate the diced butter until you have a crumbly texture.

When You're Ready to Bake

1. Preheat the oven to 400 F.

2. Place baking cups into a standard muffin pan. Fill each cup, dividing the batter equally.

3. Top with streusel.

4. Bake for 18-22 minutes. Inserted toothpick should come out clean.

5. Allow to cool in the pan for 10 minutes before removing from pan.

LETTER TO READERS

Dear Readers,

The Book Magic mystery series is such a joy to write. With each book, I discover more Irish history to love and connect with, more complexity in the various characters in the stories, and more ways to love books.

Like all mythology, the history and stories of the Tuatha dé Danann abound in potential storylines, replete with twists and turns, betrayals and deceptions. The liberties I've taken with the relationship between Morrighan and Dagda, are mine alone. While the core of their stories is based on the accepted mythological elements, like Dagda's treasures and Morrighan's many names, her shapeshifting, connection to the raven and crow, and her power of prophesy, Morrighan's love for Titus and her betrayal of Dagda is my own creation.

If you picked up this book without having read the others in the series, I encourage you to go back to the beginning to experience the full breadth of the story and the curse.

Thank you for reading!

Melissa

AN EXCERPT FROM MURDER ON RUM RUNNER'S LANE

Laurel Point. It was a spit of a town nestled between a forest of evergreens and the vast Pacific Ocean, a place stuck in time. Quaint, most people said, but to Cassandra Lane in had become stifling.

Laurel Point wasn't precisely home for Cassie. She'd grown up on the outskirts—on Cape Misery.

Being stuck on the cape was isolating. On top of that, she was burdened with a fate from which she wanted—no, needed—to escape.

She couldn't wait to get away from the everything Cape Misery represented.

She couldn't wait to get away from the *magic*.

From the moment they could verbalize, and possibly even before, Cassandra and Lacy Lane had known they were different from other people. For starters, they had no mother and no father. Oh, of course, they'd *come* from a union between two people, but Edgar had died in a tragic fishing accident in 1969. Later that same year, when Cassie was just three years old, Annabel died giving birth to Lacy.

The weight of responsibility for their mother's death lay

heavy on Lacy, though Cassie never blamed her. The fact was, Annabel and Edgar had fallen victim to the Lane family curse: the men were taken by the sea and the women lost their lives during childbirth.

It simply was the way things were. The sisters' fate was written. They had vowed from the beginning never fall in love and to never, ever—under any circumstance, get pregnant.

The Lane sisters didn't live in an ordinary house in an ordinary town. Instead, they lived in the lighthouse on Cape Misery. Edgar and Annabel, in the decade before they'd died, had taken over the family's lighthouse, turning it into the bookstore it now was.

"How many kids can say they live in a lighthouse?" Cassie asked her sister at least once a year, trying to make it sound more exciting than it was. "Not many," Lacy always answered with a smile. She didn't seem to mind the isolation. She immersed herself in the volumes shelved in Books by Bequest, happy as a pirate with a jug of Jamaican rum.

Cassie didn't want her classmates to whisper about her behind her back, but they did it anyway. The girls came from a family of bibliomancers, and while the townspeople visited Aunt Rose for guidance in the way one might see a therapist, the town's kids made fun of what they didn't understand.

"Witch!" some hollered.

"Unnatural!" others said, mimicking what their parents said in the privacy of their own homes.

Cassie and Lacy had each other. That had to be enough.

When Edgar and Annabel both died, the girls' eccentric Aunt Rose took over their upbringing. Rose was the only mother the girls had ever known. She was their rock, even if her presence in their lives was more an ever-shifting tidal pool than a sturdy, unyielding lighthouse.

As she grew up, Cassie's favorite spot in the world was the bench at the top of the hill near her parents' graves. When she sat on the bench, the Lane family graveyard was to her left. To her right and down the hill was the white stone tower that was the lighthouse, with its arched wooden door, red reflectors, and black iron accents at the windows. The blue expanse of the Pacific Ocean lay beyond, its white-caps churning wildly, its secrets buried, never to be revealed.

The small cemetery was dotted with gravestones made from slate or sandstone. Each of the tablet stones was placed vertically at the head of its particular plot, a few tilted one way or the other, but most upright, standing sentry to the souls of the people buried beneath. Cassie supposed it was because of this little graveyard that she'd come to love the earth so much. The flowers that bordered the picket fence around the space. The flowers she and Aunt Rose planted alongside each headstone every spring while Lacy holed up inside Books by Bequest, reading every ancient tome she could get her hands on.

This was the core difference between her and Lacy. Lacy loved the family's gift of bibliomancy. She loved books, the stories they told, the secrets they held, and the future they predicted, while Cassie preferred life outside and the way flowers in the spring gave the promise of a new tomorrow and how the falling leaves in autumn meant a cleansing of the soul and a time to reflect and rebuild. She *wished* she could read the books in the store, but the truth was, she didn't trust the messages the books gave, and she didn't want to glimpse the future. Lately she'd begun to wonder if Lacy trusted them, either. So many times, Cassie had seen Lacy absorbed in her divination, gleaning messages about the past, or predictions about the future, only to see frustration take hold as Lacy slammed closed the book that had been open in her lap, or on the table before her, or on the pillow of her bed.

Cassie had eventually become convinced that the Lane women's divination was actually another part of the curse that plagued her family. Teaching them how to use their gift of bibliomancy had been Aunt Rose's greatest joy when the sisters were younger, but now she furrowed her brows at Lacy when the books didn't tell her what she wanted to hear, and at Cassie when she refused to even pick up a book. "I don't want to know," Cassie would say, and Aunt Rose would nod as if she understood, but deep down, Cassie knew she didn't. Aunt Rose wondered how a person could deny such a big part of herself, and though she worried about Lacy getting lost in it, she also worried that Cassie having nothing to do with it would end badly.

Because, Aunt Rose always told the girls, you can't run from who and what you are.

But that was exactly what Cassie was going to do. The first opportunity she had, she was getting away from Cape Misery. Away from Oregon. Putting her past behind her.

Leaving Lacy, Aunt Rose, Annabel and Edgar, and the lighthouse wouldn't be easy, but it was essential, because no book was going to tell Cassie what her future held. This place that tried to hem her in with its coastal fog, its isolating cape, its stone-walled lighthouse—this place would not contain her.

She was going to make her own destiny.

Keep Reading!

ACKNOWLEDGMENTS

Taking a book from inception to publication is a mammoth endeavor. Thank you to everyone who had a part in making this book the best it could be, which includes my copy editor, Sarah Simonec, my awesome proofreaders, Barbara Marquart, Susan Slovinsky, and Cecelia Conneely, my mom, Marilyn Bourbon, for her early read and for her request that there be a pronunciation chart for all those challenging Irish names and words, and to the very special people who are part of my ARC team. Your ongoing support is so appreciated.

And a special thank you to Deborah Holt from Alabama for bidding on and winning the auction item to have her name in this book. The character of Dabba lives on in Hattie's novella, *A Pickled of a Murder*, and in future Foxy Lady Mysteries.

ABOUT THE AUTHOR

Melissa Bourbon is the national bestselling author of more than 30 mystery books, including the Pippin Lane Hawthorne (Book Magic) novels, the Lola Cruz PI series, the Harlow Cassidy (Magical Dressmaking) Mystery series, the Bread Shop Mysteries, written as Winnie Archer.

She is a former middle school English teacher who gave up the classroom in order to live in her imagination full time. Melissa, a California native who has lived in Texas and Colorado, now calls the southeast home.

A former secondary English/Language Arts teacher and Creative Writing teacher with Southern Methodist University's CAPE program and the Osher Lifelong Learning Institution with North Carolina State University, she has applied her love of teaching to the creation of WriterSpark Academy, an online school for aspiring and new writers seeking to hone their craft.

When she is not writing or igniting her WriterSpark through teaching, she hikes, practices yoga, cooks, and cuddles with her precious rescue pups, Bean, the pug, Dobby, the chug, and Pippin, the pint-sized super mutt. With her five kids scattered throughout the country, she and her husband are enjoying the empty nest.Learn more about Melissa at her website, www.melissabourbon.com, on Facebook @MelissaBourbon/Winnie ArcherBooks, on Instagram and TikTok @bookishly_cozy, and learn about about WriterSpark at www.writersparkacademy.com.

VISIT Melissa's website at http://www.melissabourbon.com

JOIN her online book club at https://www.facebook.com/groups/BookWarriors/

JOIN her book review club at https://facebook.com/melissaanddianesreviewclub

ALSO BY MELISSA BOURBON

<u>Book Magic Mysteries</u>

The Secret on Rum Runner's Lane

Murder in Devil's Cove

Murder at Sea Captain's Inn

Murder Through an Open Door

Murder and an Irish Curse

<u>Lola Cruz, PI Novels</u>

Living the Vida Lola

Hasta la Vista, Lola!

Bare-Naked Lola

What Lola Wants

Drop Dead, Lola

<u>Harlow Cassidy (Magical Dressmaking) Mysteries</u>

Pleating for Mercy

A Fitting End

Deadly Patterns

A Custom-Fit Crime

A Killing Notion

A Seamless Murder

<u>Bread Shop Mysteries,</u> *written as Winnie Archer*

Kneaded to Death

Crust No One

The Walking Bread

Flour in the Attic

Dough or Die

Death Gone a-Rye

A Murder Yule Regret

Bread Over Troubled Water

Mystery/Suspense

Silent Obsession

Silent Echoes

Deadly Legends Boxed Set

Paranormal Romance

Storiebook Charm

9 780999 786618 6